THE
DEVIL
YOU
KNOW

ALSO BY P. J. TRACY

THE DETECTIVE MARGARET NOLAN SERIES

Desolation Canyon
Deep into the Dark

THE MONKEEWRENCH SERIES

Ice Cold Heart
The Guilty Dead
Nothing Stays Buried
The Sixth Idea
Off the Grid
Shoot to Thrill
Snow Blind
Dead Run
Live Bait
Monkeewrench

The Return of the Magi

THE
DEVIL
YOU
KNOW

P. J. TRACY

MINOTAUR BOOKS
NEW YORK

First published in the United States by Minotaur Books, an imprint of St. Martin's Publishing Group

THE DEVIL YOU KNOW. Copyright © 2022 by Traci Lambrecht. All rights reserved. Printed in the United States of America. For information, address St. Martin's Publishing Group, 120 Broadway, New York, NY 10271.

www.minotaurbooks.com

Designed by Devan Norman

Library of Congress Cataloging-in-Publication Data

Names: Tracy, P. J., author.
Title: The devil you know / P.J. Tracy.
Description: First Edition. | New York : Minotaur Books, 2023. |
    Series: The Detective Margaret Nolan series ; 3
Identifiers: LCCN 2022044326 | ISBN 9781250859945 (hardcover) |
    ISBN 9781250859952 (ebook)
Subjects: LCGFT: Novels.
Classification: LCC PS3620.R33 D48 2023 | DDC 813/.6—dc23/
    eng/20220926
LC record available at https://lccn.loc.gov/2022044326

Our books may be purchased in bulk for promotional, educational, or business use. Please contact your local bookseller or the Macmillan Corporate and Premium Sales Department at 1-800-221-7945, extension 5442, or by email at MacmillanSpecialMarkets@macmillan.com.

First Edition: 2023

10 9 8 7 6 5 4 3 2 1

To PJ,
who continues to take me on the best joy rides.

The golden apple devoured has seeds.

—Bette Davis

THE
DEVIL
YOU
KNOW

Chapter One

THE OCEAN WAS SINGING IN THE hushed, undulating tones of low tide on this still, damp night. Nature's beguiling lullaby swelled and ebbed in Kira Tanner's body, transfixing her as power- fully as the mist-furred brilliance of the sickle moon hanging in a starless sky. Its cool light frosted the water and spread a spangled path to the horizon, beckoning her imagination to walk it. What was beyond that bedazzled point? Someplace magical, she decided. Even more magical than this.

Santa Barbara was very different from LA—mellower, happier, and absent of the menacing, jagged edge of a huge city—that's why she loved it here. It was cold on the empty autumn beach, and the wet sand numbed her feet, but the discomfort was offset by the ethereal world that enveloped her, along with the warming, delicious embrace of local wine and good weed.

She selected a spot by a vaulting outcrop of rock, laid her poncho on the sand, and settled into lotus position. Her eyes never veered from that wobbling, moonlit passageway, and she would stay here as long as she could tolerate the seeping chill—it was much too beauti- ful and peaceful to go back inside just yet.

She was a million miles away from the squalid, broken-down tract house in dusty Oklahoma, where her lowlife father sat on his fat, drunk ass all day. For all she knew, he was in jail again, or maybe even dead, but she didn't care. Kira Tanner was meant for much bigger things, and she would do whatever it took to get there.

When her teeth finally began to chatter, she reluctantly plodded to the sloping path that led up to the house. *Trudging slowly over wet sand*—old song lyrics from a time before she'd been born popped into her mind and made her giggle for some reason. As she climbed through the beachside garden, she wistfully trailed her fingers along the oleander, rosemary, and delicate tendrils of jasmine. Everything was so perfect, so serene. She never wanted to leave, but of course she had to. She didn't belong here as much as this place didn't belong to her. But she still had the rest of the night to pretend it did. And one day, a dreamscape like this might be hers. That's why she was here. With a smile, she patted the pocket of her jeans, comforted by the tiny bulge of extra insurance there. You always had to have a plan B.

As Kira approached the steps that led to the broad deck, she heard the faint, droning rhythm of the house music she'd selected, muted by stone and timber. And above that, other sounds that were sharper; sounds that were wrong: the crack and hiss of shattering glass, the shriek of wood, a muted pop. Then urgent footsteps, getting closer.

Life had taught her to shirk at strange, erratic noises, so instinct propelled her into the shelter of fragrant greenery. She trembled there with a forgotten prayer on her lips as she listened to her frenzied heart trying to escape the captivity of her chest.

The footsteps eventually receded, silence reclaimed the night, and time passed—she had no idea how much—and she finally emerged from her coward's nest. The music was still pulsing into the night, but that was all she heard. Her legs felt like concrete pillars as she mounted the stairs, her ears and eyes straining for more sounds and any movement that didn't belong. She tentatively pulled open the big glass door and stepped into the house, pausing breathlessly in the violet shadows of the living room. *If you hold your breath, the monsters can't find you . . .*

Everything was just as she'd left it—there were no signs that anything had happened here. Maybe nothing *had* happened here, she was just paranoid from the last bowl she'd smoked. Hearing things, imagining things. Her highs could sometimes go in that direction. But it would be stupid to ignore the chilling, warning tingle that seized her spine, so she crept down the hall to the bedroom, where she'd left her tote bag. Inside it was a gun.

She saw the shards of a wineglass first, glittering on the floor; then the upended lamp and the looted drawers, hanging from their tracks. Clothing spilled from them like mocking, colorful tongues. And finally, the naked man, facedown on the bed. She didn't need to check his pulse to know he was dead. The blood and the two holes in the back of his skull told the story.

Acid and a scream rose up her throat in unison, but she swallowed them before either could break free from her mouth. Horror and terror vied for dominance—until now, she hadn't realized there was a difference between the two—then self-preservation usurped them both. Choking on sobs, she dropped to the floor and groped for her Louis Vuitton knockoff. She'd left it next to the bed, but it was gone now.

She wasn't supposed to be here. She *couldn't* be here, not with a dead man. But now someone knew she had been. Beseeching the murderous invader and thief to take what he wanted from her tote and dump the rest in a place it would never be found, she ran for her life, leaving her ruined dreams and the ruined body behind. There was nothing she could do for him now. And nothing he could do for her.

Kira hadn't expected the malevolent shadow waiting outside the front door, hadn't expected the blow to her head or her violent descent into blackness. She couldn't see, but she could hear ragged breathing;

feel cold steel pressed against her lips. In her last moments, her mind retreated to the beach and found peace in the gentle tug of the tide and the enchanted, sparkling path the moon had laid for her on dark water. She was going to find out what was on the other side of the horizon after all.

Chapter Two

January 10, 1864
Lancaster, Pennsylvania

Dear Brother—

I write again with news of your nephew Peter, as I know you have always had the greatest affection for him and are deeply concerned for his welfare. He has recovered well from the amputation and other physical injuries sustained, which is undeniably God's miracle. However, it aggrieves me to report that the disturbing episodes I have described in my earlier correspondence have persisted, if not escalated. Brother, when I look into my dear boy's eyes, I do not see him. I see only terror and pain—that of a trapped and badly wounded animal.

It is with profound regret that I tell you it has recently become necessary to tether him to prevent harm to himself or the younger children. He is currently in confinement in the attic room in accordance with Doctor Herman Groezinger's recommendation. I know you have never been overly impressed with

Herman since our childhood, but he has been devoted to Peter's
care since his return from Gettysburg.

It is the doctor's opinion that the violence experienced in battle
has bedeviled his mind and very soul. I believe this is a progres-
sive philosophy, and Doctor Groezinger has been employing the
latest treatments and elixirs, including hypodermic injections of
a soporific, which has a blessed, calming effect.

We are all praying that God will heal him and bring him
back to us. I ask that you keep him in your prayers as well. Our
regards to Livinia and the children.

Very fondly,
Henry Harold Easton, Esq.

Sam Easton couldn't take his eyes off the beautiful, florid script
a distant relation had painstakingly transcribed over a hundred and
fifty years ago. His contemporary mind perceived it as a work of art.
Elegant handwriting, like critical thinking, manners, and so many
other civilities, had virtually disappeared since this had been written. The only thing that hadn't disappeared was war, which made
him wonder if brutality wasn't the sole, immutable characteristic of
the human race.

He finally placed the letter on the dining room table beside his snif-
ter of after-dinner brandy and glanced up at his mother. There was a
melancholy in her lovely, dark eyes he hadn't seen in a long time.
"PTSD. Before there was a name for it."

Vivian Easton nodded. "They called it soldier's fatigue back then.
Perhaps the greatest understatement in the history of the English
language."

"I'm assuming the soporific was morphine."

"The Civil War spawned the first opioid crisis. It's painful to read,
I know."

Sam's gaze traveled the impressive Pasadena home where he'd spent most of his life before the Army. Before marrying Yuki. It was stuffed with generations' worth of priceless heirlooms from his mother's side. He'd never guessed it held treasure of a darker kind, from another branch of his family tree. "Where did you find this, Mom?"

"I finally started going through your father's desk and found a musty box of family military ephemera. I assume from your grandpa Dean after he passed."

There was poignancy in that simple statement. Jack Easton's damaged heart had left her a widow years ago, but she hadn't been able to bring herself to touch his desk in all that time. "This is extraordinary. Why didn't he share?"

"He would have, if he'd known about it."

Sam frowned. "That sounds mysterious."

Her eyes danced, warm and wistful. "Not at all. Your father kept a list of all the things he was going to do when he retired. I imagine going through this file was one of them. It would have driven him mad with distraction, and I'm sure he was aware of that."

Sam chuckled sadly at the truth of what she'd just said. Jack Easton had been a man of sharp and singular focus and had always known the limitations of his attention. He wished his father had realized there was no guarantee you'd be around for gratifications delayed, things left undone. "Are there any other letters about Peter?"

"This is the only one I found. The rest of the correspondence is from more modern wars; all equally heartbreaking. Is there ever truly victory in war?"

It was a complicated question, and fortunately, a rhetorical one. You could dissect the history of warfare and never come up with an incontrovertible answer. "Did Dad ever try to find any relatives out east?"

"He wasn't interested in genealogy. But maybe you are." She slid a thick file across the polished walnut. "This is yours. It's a part of you."

Sam took a last look at the letter that belonged in an archive or a museum—one day, he would make sure it got there—then slipped it back in the file. Five minutes ago, Peter Easton hadn't existed; now he flowed through Sam's veins. The connection had been immediate and powerful, and transcended time and space.

He *knew* him. He *was* him. He also knew that things probably hadn't ended well for Peter. For the first time in a long while, he felt truly lucky because he wasn't tied up in an attic. A hundred and fifty years ago, he would have been.

Chapter Three

DETECTIVE MARGARET NOLAN DETESTED GOLF. UN-der the duress of psychotherapy or torture—a fine line between the two, in her opinion—she may have been inveigled into blaming her father. He'd forced lessons on her as a child and spent too much of his free time playing a silly game when he could have been having high tea with her dolls. But the real truth was, she sucked, and being pathologically competitive, she was also a pathologically poor loser.

Golf was a head game, and her head space was currently very negative. So far, her performance today had been cringe-worthy, and would haunt her for the rest of her life. On her deathbed, she would think about how badly she'd screwed up at Braemar Country Club's first annual father-daughter charity tournament, humiliated herself and her family in front of hundreds of people. It didn't matter that the atmosphere was as boisterous as an Irish pub on St. Patrick's Day—she would remember the burning shame of failure, even if nobody else did.

In the spirit of Thermopylae, she approached the sixth tee like a mortal enemy, determined to compensate for her deficiencies with sheer mettle. Everybody liked a good fight, especially when the underdog went out in a blaze of hopeless, deranged glory.

Daddy—Colonel York Nolan, U.S. Army retired—spoke to her quietly as she brandished her weapon for battle. Presumably to be encouraging. There was no cutting discord or secreted agonies out here on the emerald greens of Braemar, or anywhere else in the family cloisters. Not anymore. Those had been buried months ago in the most dangerous, convoluted way imaginable.

"You're choking the club to death, Margaret. Relax, and loosen your stance. You're not throwing a hand grenade."

Apparently, some fellow club members in the gallery heard him, because there were lots of laughs. Military humor, ha-ha. While they were distracted by their jollity, she wound up, let it rip, and watched the irrelevant white ball sail into the morning sky. It briefly became a tiny cotton ball cloud in a clear field of azure before descending like a meteorite. Her fate was in the golf gods' hands now, and those sadistic hands would probably deposit that dimpled little bastard in a sand trap or a water hazard. Then she would pull out her gun and blast the damn thing all the way to the hole . . .

The cheers from down-green dumbfounded her. Her father gave her an approving pat on the shoulder; her reticent mother let out a startlingly resonant, "You can do it, Margaret!" and Sam Easton—formerly a murder suspect and more recently an accidental LAPD asset, family friend, and eleventh-hour coach—gave her an encouraging smile and thumbs-up. Maybe she would be able to finish twenty over par instead of thirty.

She and Daddy didn't get the trophy, but they did achieve a respectable third-place showing and made some money for Mattel Children's Hospital. Even Nolan's brutally exacting standards allowed for subdued celebration in the form of fried food and a dirty martini in the club's lounge. After celebratory toasts and woolly exposition on the highs and lows of play, courtesy of the colonel, her mother offered salvation by dragging him away to glad-hand friends.

Which left her alone at the table with Sam—potentially a shrewdly considered maneuver. From Emily and York Nolan's perspective, the match was perfect, it just had to be nurtured. Naïve wishes of well-meaning parents who had selected a future son-in-law to suit their needs instead of a mate who would suit hers. Or his. She and Sam had a lot in common, as killers who'd almost died together twice, and that was a bond that couldn't be broken. But violence had nothing to do with romantic love for either of them. And hopefully nobody else, although that was a sadly optimistic outlook.

Sam's angry, disfiguring scars split his face evenly between handsome and the horrors of a roadside bomb, but she no longer registered them any more than she would a mole or birthmark. They were evident, but not defining. As was his PTSD—something he would battle for the rest of his life to one degree or another. She'd come to know him as intelligent, brave, and selfless; a man whose inherent character could supersede the black, daily struggles that were the consequences of war. She was glad he'd made it home from Afghanistan even though her brother, Max, hadn't. There was gratitude in the mix, too, because he'd brought her grieving father back to life a little.

"You were fairly spectacular out there, Maggie." He lifted his beer with a gratified smile. "Congratulations."

She clinked his bottle with her glass. "Congratulations to you, Coach. You did the impossible and spared me lifelong embarrassment as a family punch line. My father is a great golfer, but a horrible instructor. Too used to giving orders."

"I can't take any credit. Bagger Vance did the job for me."

Nolan snickered. "It was a good movie. But I still never saw 'the field.'"

"Sure you did. You played the game you were born to play, and that's all any of us can do." Sam's smile wilted as he picked at French fries languishing in a greasy, paper-lined basket. "This is a little uncomfortable."

"Don't worry about sparing my feelings. I was anticipating that you would dump me, but I'm never playing golf again, so I won't need a coach anymore." When Sam didn't respond to her levity, didn't even rediscover his smile or meet her eyes, she was bewildered. "What's wrong?"

He sighed, releasing a ballast of troubled air. "I saw pictures of your father and Max in the Hall of Fame gallery this morning, and they hit me. I don't want you to think your father is trying to replace him, because he's not. I don't want you to think I'm trying to replace him, either."

Maggie's life was not heavily populated by forthright people, and Sam's honesty startled her. Unfortunately, it was founded in guilt, the most senseless and seductive emotion there was. "Don't be an idiot, Sam. You make Daddy happy. He has a fellow war hero as a golf buddy and you've both been to battle together in a way, up in Death Valley. You're a friend, not a replacement. Don't ever apologize for making a difference in somebody's life."

"He makes me happy, too."

"I know that. You've both lost a lot and you share that. You understand each other." She huffed with deflective, faux exasperation. "God knows nobody else can. I thought you and your shrink were making inroads with your survivor's guilt." It had been a harsh thing to say and she instantly regretted it, but an attenuated version of his smile returned. It seemed more honest and heartfelt than its predecessor.

"We are, but healing takes time. How are you doing, Maggie?"

It was a good question, one that came from a caring place, but it irritated her. First, it acknowledged her vulnerability; second, she didn't have a definitive answer. If you weren't a sociopath, you couldn't just kill without psychological repercussions, even if the killing had been in the line of duty to save your own life and the lives of others. Likewise, you couldn't dismiss near-death by a weapon of mass destruction or witness a self-immolation without losing pieces of your mind and soul. These were all living, breathing nightmares that slashed deep wounds that might never heal. And she shared every one of them with Sam, who had a million more nightmares of his own just like them, and worse. How was he still walking and talking? How did the world get so fucked up?

It always has been. Nothing new under the sun.

"I'm finding my way."

He nodded in empathy, then focused on the bar, his favorite feature in any dining establishment. The long bank of mirrors multiplied the bottles there, creating a mirage of infinite booze. "I didn't look in a mirror for two years after I got back from Afghanistan."

"What happened when you finally did?"

He shrugged. "Not much, which surprised me. Turned out avoiding my reflection was more terrifying than confronting it. That wasn't meant to be a metaphor for what you're going through, by the way. It's just that mirrors have a Pavlovian effect on me now, and compel me to salivate egocentric non sequiturs."

Nolan couldn't resist a chortle, but there was wisdom in his words, and she wasn't entirely certain it hadn't been an oblique outreach. She felt the shadows of the past descend on them both, displacing the air in the room. The lone olive at the bottom of her glass stared at her with a brooding pimento eye, rousing a truly disturbing thought: Sam was a facsimile of her brother, and her parents were trying to pair her with him, something she hadn't comprehended before. They obviously didn't see it that way, they only saw commonalities and connections, but there was too much Freudian weirdness circulating in the smothering ether. Time to change the subject.

"Have you given any more consideration to LAPD's offer?"

Sam twirled his beer bottle, trying to divine existential answers from the sudsy remainders at the bottom. "I'm in the process of considering it. Where I'm at now, it beats electrical engineering. I'm not ready to sit at a desk. But I'm also not a cop. I never will be."

"You don't have to be. It's a consulting position with SWAT, and you wouldn't be the only veteran there. Keep thinking about it. That's all I'm going to say."

"Heard. Who is that elderly coquette hanging on your father's arm?"

Grateful for the distraction, Nolan's eyes traveled the lively crowd and landed on May Strohm-Whitney, dressed for the day in a pink-and-green-plaid golf ensemble almost as obnoxious as the diamonds burdening her frail neck, wrists, and pendulous earlobes. Good for her. You can't take it with you, so enjoy the hell out of it while you're still breathing.

"She's a real estate heiress and a five-time widow. Delightful and harmless. Unless you consider the questionable circumstances of her much younger husbands' deaths."

"Wow. Who says country clubs are boring?"

"If humans have anything to do with it, it's never boring." She watched Sam's expression transform from bemused to tentative recognition.

"Is that May Strohm-Whitney?"

Nolan couldn't wait to hear this story. What an excellent detour from things more onerous. "You didn't date her, did you?"

He grinned. "I was eighteen when I met her, so she didn't ask."

"Restraint has never been her strong suit when it comes to younger men."

His grin expanded. "It would have been an unforgiveable breach of boundaries. My mother used to golf with her when she was living in Pasadena with one of her husbands."

"Pasadena was husband number three." Nolan knew this great big world was actually small, and it seemed to be compressing daily, from a juicy steak into a bouillon cube. At least relative to Sam. "Your mother must be quite a golfer. May was an LPGA champion in the sixties and she never played with anybody below that level."

"Vivian Easton is a golf goddess. If she hadn't been a devoted military wife, I think she would have turned pro."

"It's never too late."

"She's enjoying life too much these days to take anything that seriously. If the colonel ever wants to golf Valley Hunt Club, he should look her up."

"He would love that."

Sam glanced at her phone, which had suddenly come to life, buzzing and jittering on the table. "You probably need to take that, Detective."

Nolan glanced at the caller ID and stuffed it in her handbag with contrived urgency, along with a little self-admonishment for her insincerity. She felt craven for quitting a pleasurable situation when there wasn't a dead body waiting for her, but things were too heavy here, in a lot of ways she wasn't eager to examine. "I do. I'm sorry, Sam."

"Don't be, and good luck." He finished the dregs of his beer and stood. "I have to scoot myself, before the black widow finally seduces me and kills me. You were fantastic today, Maggie. Congratulations."

"I had a great coach."

"If I don't take that job with LAPD, maybe I can score a position here as a golf pro."

"You would have my full endorsement, and the colonel's, too, for whatever that's worth."

"It's worth a lot."

Nolan watched him walk away, thinking that a day that had started with a dingy haze of anxiety had actually transfigured into something quite fair. And the emotional weather promised to improve before the inexorable slide back into homicide and heartbreak and plaguing thoughts of blood spilled.

Chapter Four

SOMETHING WAS MISSING. SOMETHING HAD ALWAYS been missing.

Chronic discontent was Daphna Love's illness and it lorded over her. It was a monomania, an indefatigable feature of her personality, and the most influential in her repertoire of behavior. The primary manifestation was a nebulous sense of hopelessness, loneliness, and despair that always smoldered and sometimes flared. It wasn't depression, but a consequence of neurotic protective organization. At least that's how Freud would have diagnosed it. To her, it was elemental, and as painful as it was ironic—the psychological albatross of over-driven strivings had resulted in tremendous achievement that would never be enough.

The single thing that subdued the psychic ache was voyeurism, but not the sexual variety. She simply watched average, everyday people, imagining their behavior held clues that would help her understand her own affliction. After all, she'd once been an average, everyday person herself. She studied them tirelessly behind large sunglasses and wondered if they were really content, really complete. Her subjects always appeared to be, even in private moments, when they weren't aware of scrutiny. She was very careful with her surveillance, because when people knew they were being observed, they always tried to look happy and carefree—she understood that better than anybody.

My life is absolutely perfect, can't you see by my smile? By the way, did you realize there's only one letter difference between life and lie? No, you probably didn't.

This is what happened when you were empty inside. You obsessed over it and looked for the signs in everybody else; speculated about their lives, as if they shared your loneliness. As if they could be a soul mate, because you were so very desperate to find one.

At the moment, she was following the progress of a young mother who was circling the park with an expensive stroller occupied by a rosy-cheeked child. It wasn't just the stroller that was expensive—everything about the entire ensemble was undeniably posh: the child's jaunty sun hat and matching jumper; the mother's perfect golden hair and the stylish fitness clothing she wore; the grape-sized diamond on her left ring finger. She undoubtedly drove a German car and lived around here—Santa Monica or Pacific Palisades. Maybe Brentwood. A west side mommy. Was the child a girl or boy? She couldn't tell, and the gender-neutral clothing didn't yield any clues.

There were lots of giggles, lots of heartwarming, Instagram cuteness. But when the woman wasn't in the throes of baby lust, she was walking with purpose, her very thin, toned legs covering impressive distance with each stride. There was mission behind her gait, probably to get that last quarter-ounce of baby fat off, even though she was slender and fit.

Maybe that was this woman's emptiness. She was afraid that in spite of all her efforts, she still hadn't been able to fully restore herself to pre-childbirth glory. Her body looked perfect to Daphna, but maybe this woman's mirror told her something different. Maybe this woman's husband did, too.

Did he drape a tanned, muscular arm over her hip in bed at night, place a hand on her stomach, and chuckle about the loose, jiggly flesh there? Was he oblivious or just uncaring that the hideous imperfection of her body was the result of his sperm? Did he tell her about his colleague's wife, who'd just had a very successful tummy tuck after baby number three?

Boy, does she look phenomenal in a bikini, babe. He showed me some pictures from their vacation in Saint Kitts last month. I got the surgeon's number, he's a magician. Love you, sweetie, sleep tight.

It was an implicit threat: pull yourself together or else I'll have to start shopping around for someone who isn't loose and jiggly. What a bastard. Daphna realized this poor woman wasn't happy and complete at all, she was miserable, and no wonder. The beautiful young mother wanted to be outraged, but she was too afraid. There might be some other troubles, too, probably financial. You never knew who really had money and who was just pretending in Los Angeles. Most people here were just clawing for one more month on the lifeboat.

Don't ever rely on a man for anything. They'll use you, throw you away, and leave you begging for pennies. There's always a newer model on the showroom floor, and your father traded up like they all do. You're the only good thing that came out of my deal. Make yourself a better one.

According to her bitter mother, life was just a deal—a negotiation, an exchange of goods and services that had nothing to do with emotional fulfillment. That catechism was part of her emptiness, but it wasn't all of it. She touched her hard, flat stomach, unscathed by the indignity of pregnancy, and wondered how she would look now if she hadn't pursued life like it was a deal; if she had told Seth the truth. Probably loose, jiggly, and unemployable. That was never going to happen to her.

Temporarily sated by her analysis of this tragic, fearful woman's life, Daphna wandered back to her own German car and her own perfect lie.

Chapter Five

WHILE SETH LEHMAN WAS ON HIS hands and knees looking for his pants, his phone squawked a TMZ breaking news alert.
He harbored a fierce hatred for the app, but it was an occupational
necessity. They always knew before you did if a client had seriously
fucked up, and Saturday mornings were the most dangerous—even
worse than Sunday mornings. He knew from experience that after
an interminable week of work and reluctant sobriety, people most
often lost their judgment on Friday nights. The odds were fifty-fifty
that it was his only rainmaker who had done it this time, so it was
worth suspending his clothing search to confirm.

He perched pantsless on the edge of Amber's Pratesi-dressed
bed and called it up. The bold, black headline possessed astonishing
metaphysical properties, like the power to rearrange his anatomy: his
heart was beating in his stomach, which was now in the vicinity of
his throat, and his balls had apparently departed from his body alto-
gether, because he couldn't feel them. A monsoon of sour sweat burst
from places he didn't even know had pores. His life was unequivocally ending, but there was no bright, loving light at the end of this
tunnel.

He also experienced a surreal dilation of time. It stretched like seaside taffy and hung indefinitely, confirming the theory of relativity: when your future was moving toward obliteration at the speed of light, time slowed. This temporal anomaly wasn't a bad thing under the circumstances, but his brain ultimately resolved it just in time for Amber's disembodied, treble voice to punctuate the nihilistic bass line of his thoughts. In his current frame of mind, she sounded like an incessantly screeching crow, trying to articulate in avian language that coffee was ready, "or do you want an espresso instead, baby?"

Baby. A throw-away term of endearment, but a decisive upgrade from last week's "sweetie," which Amber used on everyone, from lovers to complete strangers. Had things really gotten so serious between them?

"Seth! Why aren't you answering me?" The crow had entered the room, her arms/wings batting the air with distressed, indignant urgency.

Seth looked at her and looked through her. She had become as insubstantial as air. It was possible his subconscious was trying to tell him something. "I have to go. Where are my pants?"

Her soft, suede-blue eyes turned arctic and blood started dripping from the shreds of his flesh hanging from her pickax beak. "Don't you dare be an asshole."

"I'm not being an asshole, Amber! I have a work emergency. Something you wouldn't understand."

"Fucking asshole!" The crow flew out of the room on an injured wing . . .

When the real, flesh-and-blood Amber walked into the bedroom, he realized he'd been having what he labeled a stress chimera. She was no longer transparent, no longer a squawking bird with a gory bill, but a swan of a dream girl: firm, slinky ballerina's body and translucent skin that glowed with the ephemeral light of youth; an

Odette incarnate, the vision Tchaikovsky must have conjured while composing his famous ballet.

She'd definitely inspired a minor Saudi prince five years ago when she'd danced for him. Now she was mother to royalty. The pregnancy had ended her career, but in recompense, it had also conferred a generous scholarship for her efforts. The House of Saud's boundless credit line was secure with the nanny in the guesthouse. He'd never met young Asad, and hopefully that day would never come. To him, all children were just quiescent pupa on the cusp of shedding their chrysalis to become wicked little tyrants.

"Seth, are you okay? Are you sick? You look terrible." She leaned over him and touched his forehead, her blond, citrus-scented curls tickling his face. "You're burning up, baby."

"I just need my pants, then everything will be fine."

Amber thought that was hysterically funny until she didn't. All of his stress chimeras were rooted in latent truths—projections of what negative events would result from a precipitating incident. He'd known that leaving after sex and before morning coffee on a Saturday was the deadliest sin of all, no matter how compelling the reason. He'd also known he would be punished for it.

He ducked, but the furious roundhouse still glanced his jaw. Thank god she hit like a girl, otherwise he would have been slurping meals through a straw for the immediate future. For most of his sexually active life, he'd believed that sleeping with women was a panacea to any problem, but he was beginning to think it *was* the problem.

An hour later, after a lengthy appeasement with Amber that Neville Chamberlain would have admired, Seth was fully clothed and pacing manic circles in his Beverly Hills office, his feet abusing the fluffy lambskin rug that hadn't been his idea. Neither had the soul-crushing color on the walls, absurdly named Tuscan Fig.

His window looked out on Robertson Boulevard and it was important to keep his voice low and calm so it didn't shatter the glass. Without that thin, transparent barrier, he'd be tempted to jump out. "Fuck, Evan. This is bad."

"It's *total* bullshit, bro! Somebody *deepfaked* that video! You think I'd do something that fucking *warped*? She's just a kid! I puked my guts out when I saw it. The feds are going to find the sick motherfucker who did this and bury him *alive*."

Evan Hobbes had a grating habit of verbally italicizing when he was agitated, usually over perceived slights and injustices—but this one time, Seth felt his client's hysteria was fully justified. Deepfakes were truly evil and the technology was getting more sophisticated by the minute. "The feds are involved?"

"Of course they're involved, it's child pornography! Whoever did this is going to *fry*."

Seth's vision blurred as he gazed on a ruinous horizon. "Who do you have on legal?"

"Guy Johns. He's going to give a presser later. We have to stand up to this bullshit right away. I had to shut down all my socials, you wouldn't believe the hate and rage out there. And I didn't do it!"

"I'm sorry, Evan . . ."

"*You* need to do some crisis management on *your* end, too. Guy will be in touch with Becca and work out a *plan*."

Seth knew that Becca's plan would be to shit-can Evan—something that would be hard to argue—but he was the only contender in his stable of nags at the moment, and he wasn't ready to euthanize him yet. He couldn't afford to. Then again, maybe he couldn't afford not to. No way to know how the situation would play out at this point. Besides, the final decision wouldn't be in his hands, it would be in Becca's. His life in Becca's hands—a truly horrifying, emasculating thought. "I'm glad you scored Guy Johns."

Evan scoffed indignantly. "Of *course* I did. He's the only lawyer in LA that matters when a celebrity is getting railroaded. He was all *over* it."

"That's good. Really good." Seth yanked down the knot in his Hermès tie that was now a slimy, malignant vine strangling him. It was the tie that had maxed-out his Barneys credit card last week. He thought about his Wilshire Corridor penthouse, his Tesla Roadster, and his art collection. Evan Hobbes had made those things possible, but Evan had inked his last significant deal two years ago, and the commission money was long gone. So was the money he'd borrowed from his sister.

And now Evan was a toxic liability. If irrefutable proof of his innocence didn't surface soon, Disney wouldn't stand by him. He would never be in front of a camera again unless it was at a courthouse, and Seth Lehman would be homeless, licking empty dog food cans on Skid Row.

He wondered if Amber would commiserate with how unfairly life was treating him and feel inspired to give him a loan. He would have to up his fealty game if that was going to happen: rub her deformed ballerina feet upon request, even though they revolted him (Tchaikovsky hadn't thought about that), and never skip postcoital morning coffee again. He might even have to meet Asad and pretend to adore him. Kiss his royal, preschool ass like everybody else probably did. Play stupid, little-kid games with him, like pin the tail on the infidel. Dignity, like love, was a commodity and the value fluctuated with the market. There was never stasis in supply and demand.

"Seth, are you even *listening* to me? I *need* you right now," Evan puled.

Want, want, want, need, need, need. His dark ruminations sizzled away like water sprinkled on a hot pan. "I'm strategizing."

"Great. It's all about optics and messaging now. We have to get in front of this. *I'm* the one who's been *victimized*."

Seth was suddenly exhausted and violently nauseated, and not from the hangover that originated with Amber's inexhaustible supply of Grand Cru champagnes. "Let me get to work on this, Evan. I'll be in touch. Stay cool."

He hung up and yanked out his AirPods. He had a single moment of peace before his phone blew up. He ignored everything but the summons to Becca's office at 2 p.m. sharp, only because she wouldn't be ignored.

Chapter Six

SAM'S THOUGHTS WERE ON MARGARET NOLAN as he pulled Grandpa Dean's Shelby Mustang into the garage. He knew her better through his recent friendship with the colonel than any of the horrific events he'd recently experienced with her, and that bothered him. Circumstances kept bringing them together, yet it hadn't made them confidantes, or even friends. There was definitely trust, loyalty, and mutual admiration between them, but they hadn't forged a battle-buddy relationship through all the violent drama they shared.

He supposed it wasn't surprising—they'd both effectively armored themselves in tough shells that dislocated them from the world, and consequently each other. Their reasons were different, but the result was the same. And for some reason, that was a disappointment. Maybe he was hoping for a breakthrough that would herald new personal advancement in his struggle with PTSD—an opportunity Peter Easton never had.

The tragic story was now a permanent resident in Sam's mind, and would forever be a mournful, reproving shadow; a tenebrous ghost constantly reminding him of the relativity of good fortune. And maybe that wasn't such a bad thing.

He checked his phone, which had been beeping an alert for the last twenty minutes of his trip home. Being a good and responsible citizen, he hadn't been tempted to look at it before he was stationary. Nothing was that important, and he didn't want to start killing people here. He'd done enough of that overseas.

It was a punctuation-free text from Melody:

hope mn kicked golf ass band practice tonight CU tmrw

Melody Traeger was the only person who'd breached the battlements since his return from war. It hadn't been a deliberate or sexually motivated decision, but a situational one, and probably lifesaving all the way around. They'd both been damaged, solitary creatures when they'd met at Pearl Club, where she was a drink-slinger and he was a barback. They'd come together like two cohesive substances, beading together on the surface of encumbered talent and dead-end jobs.

Their days at the Pearl were over, and the erratic, shifting sands of their private pain had stabilized, but her reentry into the LA music scene was another thing that troubled him. Their status as best friends informed his decision to always support her, steer her if she asked for guidance, but keep interference to a minimum. But the protective, judgmental part of his conscience gnawed at him, along with lurid, wholly unjustified flash-frames of a needle in her arm. It was too soon in her recovery to go back to the life that had sucked her into a black hole, wasn't it? Didn't he have an obligation to broach the topic?

No, he didn't. She was a savvy, tough, intelligent woman. She hadn't just survived the worst, she'd pulled herself up and out on her own, and she'd flourished. In some ways, Melody was more stable than he was. Their friendship was based on trust and he wasn't going to screw that up with misguided delusions of knighthood. They needed each other, which was why she sometimes spent nights on his sofa instead of going home to her own lovely apartment. Even lone wolves enjoyed honest, effortless companionship and a good drunk occasionally.

It suddenly occurred to him that she always escaped like a wraith long before he stirred. Probably to avoid a lecture she sensed might be in the offing with infallible feminine intuition. He was a million miles away from considering a relationship with anybody, but his association with two complicated women was scrambling him anyhow. His weakness, not theirs.

Everything seemed to be bothering him lately, from the trash collection he'd missed last week, to forgetting to water Yuki's persimmon tree during a drought. If your mind was right, you didn't forget to water your dead wife's prized botanical possession, where he had spread her ashes. That was a failure and a betrayal. All of this angst was a sure sign that he needed to establish a stable routine in a new life, which meant getting a real job. Forge ahead, leave the past behind. Adapt or die on this new battlefield.

A gig with LAPD was seductive and repellent at the same time. He could make himself useful, but he wasn't anxious to reprise his role of warrior, even on a smaller, domestic scale in a consulting position.

You already have. It's your drug of choice, his nasty, inner voice chided him.

Then there was the standing offer from Andy Greer, his former commanding officer, now officially running for Congress. Sam knew he could make a difference there, too, and he believed in Andy's platform and vision for reforming Veterans Affairs. But both positions felt like regression, pulling him straight back to Afghanistan. A place where he'd lost so many friends, parts of his soul and sanity, and very nearly his life. A place that had been delivered right back into terror's jaws with a shiny bow on top, after so much blood and treasure lost, like some cruel joke.

He thought he'd boxed up that time and place and put it on a mental shelf, accepting that it would always be with him, but knowing that it no longer circumscribed his present or future anymore. Was that just a big lie he told himself because he wanted to believe it so badly? If it was, he was a damn good liar, because he'd even convinced Dr. Frolich, his devoted shrink who'd talked him off the ledge of suicide a few times.

He emerged sluggishly from the car, feeling battered and dispirited. He saw a stack of unopened Amazon boxes on the workbench—a new water filter for the refrigerator, a new trickle charger for the Mustang. The rest were mysterious results of the evil click-and-buy. Tomorrow, he'd open up those boxes and remember what he'd forgotten.

He did a cursory inspection of his cherished inheritance and decided the Shelby couldn't just be dusted off after the drive to Braemar Country Club and back. But he wasn't in the mood for washing and polishing at the moment, just like he wasn't in the mood for opening up boxes.

Feeling guilty about that and a lot of other things, he let himself into the house that twisted his heart, because Yuki still inhabited it in so many ways. Every object he lived with now fell into two categories: before her death, and after. The classification was entirely unconscious most of the time, but still exhausting.

He went to the kitchen and poured the remainders of Detective Remy Beaudreau's gift of bourbon into a lowball—the glass was a "before" item, the bourbon an "after"—and sank into his sofa; another "before." He imagined he could still see the indentation of Yuki's tiny butt on her side, closest to the end table that held the TV remote. She had always wielded it like a cute, totalitarian sorceress with a magic wand that dispelled all sporting events.

He closed his eyes and wished he had the gift of napping. Wished he could sleep a full eight hours when the time came. Nightmares were almost a thing of the past, mainly because they'd been replaced by insomnia. He didn't do prescriptions anymore, but the melatonin did little to soothe his restive mind. The bourbon didn't help anymore, either. There were a lot of things he needed to sort out, and a clear head was where he needed to start—unfortunately, that was one thing he couldn't order from Amazon.

Chapter Seven

MAGGIE NOLAN CAREFULLY CONSIDERED THE ARRAY of choices at Bristol Farms's meat counter. She supposed it didn't matter much what she bought, since nothing was priced below a million dollars a pound. How could anything she chose be bad? She decided on rib eyes and upped the ante with some coveted spiny lobster, just in season. You couldn't go wrong with surf and turf.

The checkout lines were long, and she had the misfortune of selecting the one that stuck her behind one of LA's most aggravating denizens: an agent yammering at full voice into his phone. It was impossible to ignore, and she quickly discovered he was coddling a high-maintenance client, telling him imminent doom wasn't going to happen on his watch.

The handsome *primo uomo* in the beautifully cut and tailored suit was oblivious to the dirty looks directed his way, or the spectacle he was making. B-movie clichés of all kinds were a routine occurrence in LA, but if you didn't live here, you'd be very skeptical about the truth of their commonplace existence.

As Nolan weighed the consequences of telling this tool to take it back to the office versus a discreet kidney punch, he signed off, turned to look at her, and gave her a disingenuous smile of apology. She was nobody, nothing to him, and it showed.

"Sorry. Dealing with a crisis."

"Aren't we all?" She iced him with a glacial look. She'd been told many times her granite-gray eyes were spooky and intimidating, but from his look of replete ennui, they didn't affect him at all.

His eyes were a flat, deep blue counterpoint to hers, but they suddenly sparked in interest. It was disturbing, like watching a doll come to life.

"Hey, you're a cop, right? A homicide detective."

She nodded. "Have you killed anyone recently?"

He barked out an abrupt laugh that sounded borderline manic. "Yeah, yeah, Margaret Nolan! You were on the Monster of Miracle Mile case and that crazy shit up in Death Valley a couple months ago. You got tons of screen time, more than some of my clients. You have a sense of humor, too."

"I do, but that was sarcasm."

"Hardly a difference." He blithely produced a card out of thin air and shoved it in her hand. "Seth Lehman. Both of those cases are made for the screen. Call me sometime if you want to do a deal. I could get you one in a heartbeat."

A rapacious hustler, selling bullshit just like the street cons she encountered. The only things that distinguished him from the pimps and pushers were higher education, legal product, and nicer clothes. "I don't capitalize on victims or tragedy."

He shrugged, looking slightly bewildered by the mention of something as antiquated as ethics. "A unique point of view. But people change their minds. If you do, call me."

Was he really this soulless? "Trust me, I won't change my mind. You're up." She nodded at the angry checkout clerk who was gesticulating furiously for him to keep the line moving. He planted a deli salad and a bottle of kombucha on the conveyer. "No time for a power lunch at the Palm today?"

He flashed a blazing white smile. "You cut deep, I like that. I could be wrong, but it feels a little flirty. Nice meeting you, Detective Nolan. I'll wait to hear from you."

Letting some air out of his overinflated ego vis-à-vis a kidney punch became even more tantalizing, but she wasn't going to lose her job over Seth Lehman, and she wasn't going to let his arrogant, infuriating bombast ruin her day. Karma would take its pound of flesh eventually. It always did. The universe believed in justice, too.

Chapter Eight

REBECCA WODEHOUSE—FAIRLY HOT IF YOU didn't know her, a gruesome succubus if you did—was not related to P. G., although she intimated it at parties when she was drunk, which was frequently. She was a privileged Brit who'd inherited Wodehouse International Talent from her slothful, titled father. It had always been a snobby boutique agency that usually ended up with cast-offs from one of the Big Four, and that wouldn't change with her at the helm.

Despite her tornadic bluster and unfocused ruthlessness, Becca possessed the flaccid imagination of someone insulated by peerage and money, although Seth had his suspicions that the money was running out. Her single contribution to the firm had been revamping WIT's website so it was effectively contentless, with only a single, swaggering paragraph on the home page.

Having an empty website projects power and exclusivity. If you're worth a damn, you're already on our radar. Don't call us, we'll call you.

But she wasn't fooling anybody and Seth didn't believe she actually cared. He tapped record on his phone, adjusted his tie, and smoothed his jacket before he entered her office. Unfortunately, there wasn't anything he could do about the fetid smell of fear emanating from him. She would sense it immediately and attack the maimed antelope.

Disembowel it. What was left of the hide would take an esteemed place among the other dead pelts that defined her personal design style.

"Don't say a word," she hissed. "Just sit down."

He sank into an unyielding Gaudi chair and placed his phone on the edge of her desk. It was SOP for all meetings to have your phone silenced but always in line of sight, ready to intercept triumph or tragedy the moment it beckoned. Recording the proceedings was expressly verboten, but in the three years he'd been here, all the agents did it without ever arousing suspicion. Further evidence of her indolence and arrogance. Indogance? Arrolence? The OED needed to include a new term or two in their next edition for Becca and people like her.

She still wasn't speaking, and he dutifully obeyed her command of silence. Becca had a volcanic temper and had to be handled delicately. He knew she loved him in her own dysfunctional, predatory way, but borderline personality disorder was a bitch, and not to be trifled with.

"Our handsome Disney star is a fucking pervert pedophile," she finally said.

"The only pervert is the demonic asshole who deepfaked this vile bullshit. You know it's not real."

She conceded with a dispassionate shrug. "Maybe so, but it's guilty until proven innocent these days."

"Did you talk to Guy Johns yet?"

"I just got off the phone with him. He'll save Evan's life, but not his career—the damage is already done. There are thousands of fans out there who don't know what a deepfake is. They are shocked and disgusted by what they saw, regardless of reality. Those hideous images of their wholesome idol have scarred their brains permanently. He's already been convicted in the court of social media, and that comes with a death sentence." She clucked her tongue, but it wasn't a sympathetic sound. "Do you know why I hired you, Seth?"

"Great talent and better sex?" The confident, disarming smile that usually put her in a viciously amorous state of mind seemed to have the opposite effect today. Her odd, violet eyes blazed with the heat of a thousand collapsed stars and her bony hands, terminating in bizarrely pointy, metallic-polished nails were twitching. She was seriously pissed off, and not for the first time, he wondered if she might tear him apart one day just for fun. As a Krav Maga brown belt, it was well within her capability. That's why he always recorded their private conversations, even the ones that occurred in more intimate environs. If he ended up prematurely dead, he wanted to leave a trail that would make it easy for a homicide detective like Margaret Nolan to secure a nice cell for her up in Chowchilla.

"No, because your lovely sister Essie is married to David Baum. How could I go wrong with a fellow whose brother-in-law is a studio exec?"

"You can't. I brought you Evan."

"As it turns out, he wasn't such a good value." She tapped a claw against her magenta lips. It wasn't hard to imagine a venom-dripping sliver of snake's tongue darting in and out. Amber was a crow/swan, Becca was a snake. There was often an element of zoomorphism in his thoughts about women. Some would decry it as misogynistic, but he considered it complimentary. All animals, even reptiles, were far more noble than any human being he'd ever encountered.

"You haven't signed anybody in almost a year, and you've just lost your biggest earner, who was aging out anyhow."

"Don't let your cynicism discount Evan yet."

She let out a snort. She had transformed from snake to Komodo dragon, which made more sense with the nails. "Are you totally delusional, or just in denial? He's a corpse now. Unfortunately, not literally—that would spare some ongoing unpleasantness, and possibly WIT's image."

Seth's jaw ratcheted down in disbelief. "That's a horrible thing to say, even for you."

"Jettison him. Today."

"Evan is the victim of a hoax that's a few hours old! You can't just turn your back on—"

"I can, and you will. Or haven't you read the morality clause in his contract?"

"This is totally different! Deepfakes are *not* evidence of—"

"Still harm to the agency, Seth. Buy him a few drinks, smooth the path to his ignominy, but get rid of that stain. Once you do that, you're going to be quite weightless, my dear, so go to your sister's Malibu party tonight and get us a new deal."

Us? Yeah, right. Becca always meant "I, me, mine," whatever pronoun she used. "Is that a threat?"

"It's reality. I'm not operating a charity, so shake your money-maker tonight."

Seth was momentarily stunned. He hadn't been expecting her to blow liquid nitrogen up his ass by threatening to fire him. Fortunately, his innate cunning was always at the ready when he needed it most. It was a primary corollary of intelligence, but he visualized it as a sort of guardian angel. "If you jump ship on Evan before the studio does—*if* they do—and he's vindicated, you'll never sign another client again."

She breathed fire, but didn't say anything. Seth believed he'd actually made her think—something she seemed to avoid. "Give Evan the weekend then, and talk to your brother-in-law tonight, see if you can get a read on what Disney's going to do."

No fucking way, Becca, figure it out for yourself. "David's out of town."

"I assume he has a phone." She folded her hands with a smile—mocking and malicious. "In the meantime, tell me about the A-listers you've been successfully courting. I imagine there are several."

Her jeering tone was intolerable, and he couldn't restrain himself. "Daphna Love is supposed to be at the party and word is she's unhappy with her representation. She wants to get out of action films and do something more meaningful."

"That's a joke, right?"

"No."

Becca's expression curdled with derision. "You really are delusional. Love got twelve million for her last movie. I doubt she's going to ditch CAA and sign with an agent soon to be famous for representing a sexual predator."

Seth would kill himself before he told her that he and Daphna had a history. That was sacrosanct. She hadn't returned his calls because she'd never gotten the messages from her prick manager. At least that's the mantra he repeated to himself every day. "It's your agency, I'm just the hired help."

She lifted her chin imperiously. "I admire your ambition, but set the bar a little lower."

The rage came in through a secret back door Seth always struggled to keep locked—once it entered, he couldn't control it. "I did that when I started working here, Becca, because that's exactly what you do. You're the queen of low bars."

No alarm in her savage expression, not even an infinitesimal ruffle—just heated scorn, which infuriated him even more. "Clearly, Seth. You're a perfect case in point. Nobody else would have you."

Jesus, he'd set himself up. The rage had set him up. It made him do and say incomprehensibly stupid things, and he would keep doing it until his ire ran out of oxygen. "WIT's a corpse, too, it always has been. Rip up my contract, I'm done."

"No, you're not, and you know it. You can't afford the lawsuit."

"I'll be able to afford anything when I get Daphna Love." *How the fuck are you going to do that?*

"How the fuck are you going to do that?" Becca reflected his insecurity back at him like a demented mirror. "You're just not that talented. Not in bed, and not in your job." She flapped a hand dismissively, the gesture of someone swatting an irksome pest. "Get out of here. And stop screwing my assistant."

He wasn't screwing Lily, he never had, but she'd given him some wicked ammunition.

"Well, Becca, you kind of forced my hand on that one. You're just not that talented. Not in bed, and not in your job." Damn, that was good. A scalpel incision that would keep her up tonight. He didn't wait for a reaction or a rejoinder, just stalked out of the office, slamming his fist into the wall like a juvenile reprobate. It left a sizable pock in the drywall and a smear of blood—a marked improvement on Tuscan Fig. The pain was immediate and intense, but it receded as he jubilantly envisioned the various ways he might kill Becca and dispatch her earthly remains. He'd read enough scripts to nourish his imagination with a banquet of possibilities.

Murder would be easy, but the aftermath was the hard part, and always the downfall of the antagonist. But he would be smarter than a fictional killer. He might get some blood on him, but it wasn't anything a shower wouldn't fix. The clothes were a different story. He wasn't going to be a dumbass and throw them in a dumpster, so he'd have to incinerate them, but he'd rather go to prison than burn anything in his closet. A trip to Target or Ross to get something cheap was first on the punch list.

The thought of the beautiful, chilly Margaret Nolan pursuing him as a suspect was electrifying, but he would be too clever for her, and she'd never get that far. It was a shame. What was she in the spectrum of the animal kingdom? Something strong and athletic. Majestic, even. A horse, or maybe a puma. Yes, a puma. He loved big cats.

Did everybody in LA find solace in homicidal thoughts? Of course they did. You couldn't preserve your sanity without them.

Chapter Nine

NOLAN'S SLUMBERING MIND REGISTERED A DISTANT crash. Even from the depths of sleep, she reached for her gun. When she couldn't find it, she lurched up in darkness so complete, her eyes ached as they searched for a source of light. Dead to the world one second, crisis-ready the next, no coffee required. Cop-wiring. This was Los Angeles and you had to anticipate bad things happening at any moment and be prepared for it, even when you were partially unconscious.

Homicide detectives were intimately acquainted with nightmares, because horrible fragments of past cases inevitably slithered in when you were most vulnerable, but she was certain this hadn't been a nocturnal phantasm. Nightmares didn't grind your guts with percussive impact and they didn't cause wooden blinds to sway and rattle against windows. But earthquakes did.

Her flailing arm couldn't find the gun or the phone or the lamp on her nightstand; couldn't even find the nightstand, and that panicked her most. And then emergent clarity swept away the mist of the netherworld that bridged sleep and alertness.

You don't have wooden blinds. This isn't your bedroom. And you're naked.

The hours following the golf tournament began to reassemble as her light-starved eyes devoured the scant photons of a faint, ambient glow in an arched doorway.

Golf, a martini, Bristol Farms, rib eyes, spiny lobster, more martinis by the pool . . .

A ghostly, backlit silhouette manifested in the doorway—a slender, powerful shadow, also naked. Remy Beaudreau, her enigmatic colleague and now her occasional lover, which hadn't dispelled any of his mystique. She still wasn't used to waking up in somebody else's bed.

Nolan pushed herself up against the marshmallow-soft pillows that had recently cradled their heads. "I hope it's not the Big One, because I don't want to get out of bed."

"I don't want you to."

"What time is it?"

"Four."

Nolan heard him cover the distance from the doorway to the bed in softly thumping footfalls, then felt him sinking down next to her. He smelled faintly of chlorine. They hadn't gotten around to showering after the pool. There had been more pressing matters.

"It's not the Big One, I checked. Just tremors from a shallow three-point-six in Orange County, according to the U.S. Geographical Survey. I thought a semi crashed into the side of the house, so I was going to go out and shoot whoever interrupted our night."

She smiled in the dark, knowing Remy wouldn't see it. "When buildings get jostled, they complain. It's unnerving unless you've lived through it before."

"So, my family's Bel Air mansion was crying out in pain."

Nolan let out a mirthful snort. "I don't think it felt a thing. This can't be the first tremor you've ever felt."

"No, but it's the first one I've ever heard. I'm not a native, Maggie. Big thumps in the night and the ground moving and grinding beneath me is very disturbing." He whispered that into her ear, lighting up an intricate web of neural pathways with a shiver-inducing combination of heat and ice.

Nolan clamped down a lascivious verbal parry: how she hoped her moving and grinding beneath him hadn't been so disturbing. Jesus, she had to get her mind out of the gutter. But then Remy pulled her down and his hands began roaming her face, her neck, her arms, and the gutter was where she wanted to be most.

"How do you get used to this, Maggie?"

"It's not difficult," she murmured.

Remy's fingers traced a delicate path along her collarbone. "I don't mean this, I mean earthquakes."

"Oh. You have tornadoes and hurricanes in Louisiana, how do you get used to that?"

"You don't. But you always know they're coming. Predictability in natural disasters is reassuring."

"That's an excellent point." The house suddenly shuddered and protested loudly again, glass shattered somewhere outside, and a few car alarms started wailing, which had a chilling effect on the foreplay. Remy went rigid, and she wasn't particularly relaxed either. USGS could roll out statistics in real-time, but even they couldn't entirely predict something as capricious as Mother Nature when she was letting off steam.

"It's just an aftershock," she assured him, not remotely confident in her authority to discuss the effects of shifting tectonic plates. For all the years she'd lived in Los Angeles, she was shamefully ignorant about fault lines and Richter scale magnitudes and the difference between shallow quakes and deep ones. Complacency of any kind was always dangerous. "But we should find our clothes, just in case. Any idea where they might be?"

"Somewhere between the pool and here. But I don't think anybody would judge us too harshly if it was necessary for us to evacuate naked to avoid being swallowed up by a crater."

Nolan didn't want to put on her clothes, either. Didn't want this night to end, because it might be the last for a while. He was taking a two-week leave and flying to New Orleans at noon. Hope for reconnection with estranged family could be far more seductive than any new inamorata.

She harbored no maudlin expectations of enduring love between them, which was probably an unachievable state of grace anyhow. Theirs was a fledgling relationship, or maybe just a fleeting liaison, rooted in physical, professional, and intellectual compatibility with no architecture supporting it. And there might never be. But they had yet to exhaust the magnetism they affected on one another, and lust surpassed architecture any day. And if they did get swallowed up by a crater, dying in bed with Remy wouldn't be the worst way to go.

Her phone disagreed with muted ringing that was coming from somewhere nearby. She eventually found it tangled in the sheets at the foot of the bed. She had no recollection of the logistics that had made such a thing possible. She had to stop drinking martinis.

The one steadfast truth about earthquakes, no matter their size or depth, was that they shifted the terra firma and dislodged things. This one had disturbed an unstable Malibu cliff, depositing a lode of rocks on the Pacific Coast Highway. A body had come along for the ride.

Chapter Ten

HER PARTNER BEAT HER TO THE scene, which was a mess. A towering jumble of rocks blocked the northbound lane of PCH and a half-dozen squads were parked helter-skelter, shooting pulses of red and blue into the early-morning darkness. Patrols were standing in as flagmen and women, directing meager 5 a.m. Sunday traffic with mixed results. A news helicopter was trolling the coast, its lights smearing the inky, still Pacific, thumping rotors disturbing an otherwise peaceful predawn morning in Malibu.

Al Crawford was balanced on the top of the miniature summit like a well-fed, middle-aged mountain goat, shining his flashlight down at what she assumed was the body.

"Hey, Mags," he called from his lofty perch. "Thought you would have gotten here before me, coming from Bel Air."

She scowled and decided it was time to finally confront the ceaseless innuendoes with a riposte of her own. Al knew about her entanglement with Remy, had known even before she'd acknowledged it herself, but her senseless evasions had only fueled the needling. She deserved it, she supposed. He was not only a mentor, but a good friend, and a part of both those jobs was to challenge you when you were being ridiculously cagey. "I would have been, but I couldn't find my clothes."

Al let out a great, relieved gust of a laugh. "Good for you."

Equilibrium was restored. There would be no more badgering in her future, just like that. A life lesson about the benefits of honesty. "Any tremors in the Valley?"

"No. Bel Air?"

"Just a couple. Somebody lost some glass."

"A building in Westwood lost some windows, too, but that's all I've heard about. Just remember we're all living on borrowed time, Mags. Carpe diem."

"You have a uniquely sanguine way of expressing fatalism."

"I'm standing over a dead body and I'm still alive. I'll take any victory I can get. By the way, congrats on the golf tournament."

"Thanks, but we came in third. Isn't that an also-ran?"

"No, it's third place."

Al was always more sensible and less critical than she was. One of the reasons she loved and respected him.

"Be careful getting up here. It's a scree field."

It was exactly like a scree field, and the occasional loose rock made the ascent perilous. She was grateful for Al's advice on her first day in Homicide Special Section to always keep a murder suit and sensible shoes in her trunk, just in case. The sexy dress and strappy sandals she'd worn to Remy's would have been suicide, literally and professionally.

When she reached the top of the pile, he took her hand and they steadied each other on a boulder that seemed somewhat stable. At least for the time being. "How the hell did you get up here with loafers?"

"I crawled most of the way. Take a look and see why Malibu dropped this like a hot coal." Al shined his Maglite on a body broken by a fall on a large rock. The heartthrob face of Evan Hobbes was as unmistakable in death as it had been in life, even though it was now bloody and damaged. A beloved star who had become a reviled demon on social media seconds after a video of dubious origin hit the web. HSS was the squad that cleaned up high-profile messes like this.

"I don't see any obvious signs of homicide. No gunshots or knife wounds, anyhow."

"No, but he's too messed up to tell for sure, not until he gets on the table."

Nolan scrunched up her nose and sniffed. "I don't smell decomposition, but I do smell booze."

Crawford grunted assent and shifted his feet for better purchase. "Exactly. See these pieces of broken glass? From a champagne bottle."

"How do you know?"

He redirected his flash to illuminate a large shard with a partial label so recognizable, even an underpaid homicide cop would know it. "I wouldn't mind that being my last supper." He pointed up the cliff to a sprawling house where multiple lights still glowed. "I saw a feature on that modest little weekend shack in the *Times*'s Sunday magazine a few weeks ago."

Nolan had seen the spread, too. It was a storied property and the new owners had just completed a comprehensive renovation sanctioned by the authoritarian bureaucrats at the National Register of Historic Places. "That's David Baum's place. The Disney exec."

"There you go. Hobbes's big boss. I'm thinking they were having a party and our disgraced friend was there drowning his sorrows with some Dom. He wandered a little too far, lost his footing, and took a tumble. Probably accidentally, but maybe intentionally. He had a serious image problem, and image is everything for a guy like Hobbes. In an impaired frame of mind, walking off a cliff might have seemed like a solution to a bad dilemma."

Another depressing Hollywood tragedy? It was plausible. So was accident or homicide. "Must have gotten hung up in the rocks until the quake shook him loose. Have you checked him yet?"

"I was waiting for you."

"Give me some of your candle power." Nolan slipped on gloves and began the most unpleasant of a homicide detective's tasks: frisking a corpse. Rigor mortis was setting in, but he was still somewhat pliable, which made the job easier. In the inner pocket of his suede jacket she found a wallet, a cracked-up iPhone, and a capped, wooden cylinder that contained a partially smoked joint. She passed them to Al, and while he examined the treasures more thoroughly, she trained the mini-Mag over his body for a closer look. "His neck and jaw are broken."

"Along with most of his other bones. That surprises you?"

"No. But the bruises on his neck do. I don't think they have anything to do with the rock tumbler he went through."

Al crouched down next to her. "I'm sure there are a lot of people who wanted to throttle him once that video came out, fake or not. Doesn't necessarily read murder."

"If somebody witnessed an altercation at a party, it might. Alcohol plus high emotions equal lack of impulse control. It's a place to start."

He fanned open Hobbes's wallet and pulled out a business card. "Here's another place to start. Special Agent Darcy Moore. Cyber-crimes."

Chapter Eleven

WHEN CRIME SCENE ARRIVED, NOLAN STUCK around long enough for a cursory briefing, then stole away to her car. Al had gallantly offered to handle the walk-through, which had good potential to break the limbs of the living.

Darcy Moore answered on the second ring with a crushed gravel voice. She sounded wide awake.

"This is Detective Margaret Nolan, LAPD Homicide . . ."

"No shit? You killed us with that whole Krasnoport thing, it was a huge pain in the ass. But worth a month of sleepless nights. One of my greatest achievements to date, if I do say so myself."

Nolan searched her mind and couldn't conjure Darcy Moore as a player in her last case. "I apologize, but do I know you?"

"Hell, no. We're all trolls in a basement in Cybercrimes, not suitable for public viewing. We do all the hard work and the FBI brass gets all the glory."

"Thank you for that. You did an amazing job."

"What can I do for you this morning, Detective Nolan? Something a little less Byzantine, I hope."

Darcy Moore was refreshingly un-fed-like—computer people came with long leashes—and Nolan liked her already. "We're at Evan

Hobbes's scene in Malibu, and we found your card in his wallet. I assume it has something to do with the video that went viral yesterday."

"Yeah." She heard the brisk sound of shuffling papers, along with an exasperated sigh. "He's a homicide?"

"We don't know yet. It could be accident or suicide, but there are signs of violence before his death."

"I'm sorry to hear that. He seemed like a genuinely nice guy when he came in yesterday. Damn, there's an endless supply of scumbags, why don't they ever get murdered?"

Scumbags got murdered all the time, but that wasn't Cybercrimes' milieu, so Nolan reserved comment. "So, Evan Hobbes wasn't a scumbag?"

"At least not that I can find. He was absolutely a victim of a deepfake. A convincing, sophisticated one, for sure, but that's not him in the video. But the deepest tragedy in all this is the girl. She's real, and being molested by someone who's real. Have you seen it?"

Nolan swallowed the acid creeping up her throat. "No."

"That's good. Keep it that way, unless you're in the market for new nightmares. It was taken down almost immediately, but it's still floating around. Right now, we're trying to trace the source and hopefully send some kiddie porn peddling asses straight to Hell."

"When you find these . . . monsters, do you ever find the victims?"

"Sometimes we get lucky. But the sad truth is, the victims could be from anywhere or any time in the cesspool of child pornography on the dark web, which makes it almost impossible to track them down."

"What do you mean from any time?"

"The film of the girl may have been shot last week, or fifteen years ago. If the deepfaker just pulled it randomly off the dark web for his little project and has no direct connection to who originally posted it, we might never know."

Nolan's stomach lurched. Darcy Moore had seen this before, would see it again, and how did she live with it? She didn't ask any more questions, because she didn't want to hear the answers. "The deepfake is malicious. Personal. If Hobbes was murdered, we might be looking for the same guy."

"Agreed."

"What can you tell me about your meeting with Hobbes, Agent Moore?"

"Call me Darcy. Once this broke, he came right in with his lawyer. Guy Johns. I don't have to tell you who he is."

"No." Nolan scrawled a note on the pad she kept fastened to her dashboard.

"Hobbes was understandably very bent out of shape, mood fluctuating between enraged and despondent, but I wouldn't say suicidally despondent. He's an actor, I'll give you that, but I don't think he was acting. He couldn't comprehend why somebody would do this to him."

"He didn't have any ideas?"

"Not one. Of course, if he was concealing criminal activity on his part, he'd whitewash it. This might not have been a specific beef with Hobbes, either. People don't need reasons to commit crimes anymore, especially in the cyber world. It's empowerment and entertainment for socially impaired, dickless losers and psychos. Hobbes was fully cooperative, let us take a mirror of his computer hard drive and phone. None of that shit was on either, and no artifacts to indicate he'd wiped them."

"Any chance he had another device he didn't tell you about?"

"Ooh, you detectives are so suspicious. I like that. But it's highly unlikely. Hobbes gave us the key to his digital kingdom, and that kingdom wasn't very sophisticated. Everything is synched now, whether you know it or not. We have access to anything with a chip he ever touched in the past five years, including his shower. He uses a lot of water."

"That's a little scary."

"No, it's very scary. People have no idea how vulnerable they are."

Nolan felt vulnerable just talking to her, like there was some evil Big Brother laser on the other end of the line, homing in on her digital soul with intention to gut it.

"Look, there's always a chance he had another rig that he kept off the grid that might tell us a different story about the guy, but his user patterns and the software he was running cast severe doubts on his competency to do that. And his emails and texts don't support it, either—we've been through every one he sent and received for the past year. You're not sold on accidental death, Detective?"

Nolan heard Darcy Moore slurp something—coffee? Red Bull and vodka? "We haven't eliminated it. I appreciate your time, Agent Moore."

"Darcy."

"Darcy. Please keep us in the loop."

"Absolutely. I'm very into intra-agency cooperation, unlike some of the other pricks who work in Westwood."

Nolan was now officially a fan girl and had to stifle a laugh. "I hope this call isn't being recorded for quality and training purposes."

Moore was less inhibited and let out a crunchy guffaw. "It might be, but I really don't give a shit. I hope somebody is listening to me. Cybercrimes is on the front lines of the scariest war in history and they're trying to run it on budgetary fumes. I'm good at what I do, and if I get pink-slipped for trash-talking, I'll go corporate. The pay would be a hell of a lot better, but I happen to like serving my country. Give me your private number and I'll be in touch as soon as I know anything."

Chapter Twelve

SETH TURNED OFF HIS PHONE AND threw it on the floor next to the bed. Amber had been calling and texting him with increasingly vehemence, but in his current state of euphoria, he wouldn't be able to lie convincingly, not even by text. In the swiftly approaching morning, he would think of some credible explanation for not showing up, like he'd had too much to drink and stayed at Essie and David's. They would cover for him.

There was always the chance that she would drive over here and start whaling on his door, or use her key and somehow miraculously bust through the dead bolt, but he didn't think so—too humiliating, too reminiscent of the chaotic upbringing she'd fled. Not that Amber mattered anymore in the sphere of his life, but there was no reason to make an enemy of such a volatile woman. Disentanglement would have to be executed with caution.

He rolled onto his side and looked at Daphna Love's breathtaking profile: a fine, aquiline nose with delicate nostrils that flared with each breath she took; generous lips that moved almost imperceptibly as she slept; carved cheekbones and polished waves of chestnut hair that flowed over her pillow like caramel. A muse that inspired the florid, internal narration of a romance novel, not animal comparisons. His earlier thoughts of Amber's beauty seemed outlandish to him now. Daphna was the true apotheosis of earthly perfection—no, heavenly perfection—and now she was his lover again. And his client. Dreams did come true.

Rot in hell, Becca.

The angel stirred, rolled to face him, and opened sidereal green eyes that contained the cosmos. At least his cosmos. "I had a dream there was an earthquake, Seth."

He stroked her cheek. How could skin feel like silk and velvet at the same time? "There were some tremors, but it's over now."

"Good. Tremors scare me. Were you watching me sleep?"

"I've always watched over you. At least I tried to."

She sighed contentedly and gave him a faint, sleepy smile. "I know that now. I never got any of your messages, Seth. If I had, I would have called you back."

He knew it was even odds she was lying. Or acting. Come to think of it, how would he know the difference? *Was* there a difference? But he still felt a suffusion of unalloyed joy plump every cell in his body. "I'm really glad you came over."

"Me, too. Seth, I think I'm having a nervous breakdown."

"No, you're not, you're just under a lot of stress. You're working too hard, doing things you don't love, and getting used by people who don't care about you." A mirror image of his own life. Talk about synchronicity. "Don't worry, Daph, I'm going to change that. I'm going to get you everything you want and deserve, and more. Nobody will fight for you like I will." He marveled at the infinitesimal crease that appeared on her brow. Apparently, even Botox had its limitations.

"What is Becca going to do when you quit?"

"Go batshit crazy. Maybe kill me—"

"Seth, don't say that!"

"I'm sorry. Don't worry about Becca." He kissed her shoulder. "It's early, go back to sleep. I'll make you pancakes when you wake up."

"That's nice, but I'm gluten free."

Of course she was. It was a socially acceptable epidemic. "Then I'll make you a smoothie."

"I hate smoothies. They're like drinking puke."

She'd just ruined his morning routine forever, and a little of his joy trickled away. Fortunately, there was enough that he wasn't significantly impacted by the slight deficit. "Then whatever you want. What's your perfect breakfast?"

"Caviar. But only caviar from Petrossian. Real beluga is banned here because they're basically extinct, but their Special Reserve Kaluga Huso hybrid is close. If they don't have that, I can live with osetra, but only if it's absolutely necessary. But definitely not sevruga. That just tastes cheap."

Seth did some quick calculations. A trip to Petrossian would cost him a minimum of five hundred bucks, and his mind scrambled to think of a card that wasn't maxed out. Maybe his Discover. He hadn't used that in a while. Amber had an account at Petrossian, and that was tempting. It was extremely doubtful she had any awareness of her profligate expenditures since she didn't pay her own bills, but he probably shouldn't risk it. "I'll be there when they open."

Daphna rewarded him with another smile, this one luminous instead of faint and sleepy. She tucked into a vulnerable little ball and rested her head on his chest. "Thanks for being here for me, Seth. I don't feel so empty anymore. Last night changed everything."

With great difficulty, he contained his elation. Last night *had* changed everything. "I'm so happy for you, Daph." *So happy for me.*

"In this business, you're never alone, but always lonely. I've never known who I could trust. But I can trust you. I should have realized that a long time ago." She placed a hand on his cheek. "You were smart to get off this gerbil wheel and go to college."

Subtext: you're lucky you never made it as an actor. Talk about a backhanded compliment. But he didn't mind. She probably hadn't meant it like that anyhow. "I never really wanted to be an actor. I just went to the workshops because I was thirteen and stupid-blind in love with you."

She looked up with a tentative, wondering expression. "Is that true?"

No matter how much success you acquired, the insecurity that drove you there still inhabited the deepest part of your psyche—consequently, ego strokes never lost their allure. "One hundred percent." Well, maybe 30 percent. He really had hoped to become an actor. At least do some commercials for the residuals. "You didn't know I existed. It broke my heart."

She pushed him away playfully. "I did too know you existed, otherwise I wouldn't have slept with you on my sixteenth birthday."

"You were drunk and high."

"I wasn't drunk or high the second time I slept with you. And look at us now." She let out a soft, musical giggle. "If you hadn't been pissing in the trees last night, you never would have found me crying my eyes out, and we might have never reconnected."

"Long bathroom lines and my bursting bladder brought us together again. It was destined to be."

"You're silly." She sobered suddenly. "This is a mistake, Seth."

"No! No, it's not." He modulated the panic in his voice. "We're looking forward, not back, remember? And I love you, Daphna, I always have. How could that be a mistake?"

She sighed, and it sounded like a cross between a hum and a purr. It was her tortured stage sigh, made famous in her first blockbuster action film, *The Devil's Ward*. "Because love is an illusion. An artifice constructed by the human mind to conceal the bestial reality that life is nothing more than the beginning of death. And love always ends in tragedy."

Fucking hell, that was the blackest thing he'd ever heard, and ironic for somebody with her stage name. Had she been immersing herself in depressing poetry, Russian literature, and nineteenth-century nihilistic philosophy? She'd always been smart, but was she that smart? "You're wrong, Daphna."

Her eyes widened in delight and she burst out in plangent laughter. "That's from a script I'm reading! You can't take me seriously."

Seth felt a little bruised, and frankly, embarrassed that she'd set him up so handily. The pouty, passive-aggressive child that still lived inside him thought about skipping the caviar and making her a smoothie and pancakes instead.

"Oh, Seth, you're hurt. I'm sorry. I told you I'm having a nervous breakdown, I'm not myself. Hold me."

Peevishness instantly forgotten, he held her tight, her thin body spooned against his. There was scarcely a bone in her skeleton he couldn't feel jabbing into his flesh, and it made him feel even more protective. How sad that she had to keep her beautiful body so underfed to meet the rigorous requirements of her merciless vocation. But he could never mention it, just like he could never suggest to a zaftig woman that she should shed a few pounds.

After a few minutes, he learned that even angels snored. While she slept heavily, he extricated himself from the blissful, skeletal embrace and left a message and a text with Evan, then emailed him a draft of the press release he planned to distribute to media later that day. Then he texted Becca a terse missive, informing her that he was coming in on Monday morning to clean out his desk and that he was looking forward to the lawsuit. Onward and upward. Pleased to meet you, Seth Lehman 2.0.

He powered off his phone again, took one of Daphna's Klonopins, and snuggled back into the warm, dreamy nest of snarled sheets and protruding bones.

Chapter Thirteen

THE SUN WAS UP AND THE one-lane traffic on PCH was backed up as far as the eye could see. Tractor trailers loaded with earth-moving equipment were idling nearby, waiting for an all-clear. Phones hung out of open car windows—a rockslide *and* a death, double the fun! And just wait until they heard who the victim was! A fleet of media helicopters was buzzing the scene like wasps at an outdoor wine tasting, and Nolan could feel zoom lenses scrutinizing the scene and maybe the pores in her face. The checkpoints were keeping the terrestrial media out, but airspace was fair game.

Dr. Otto Weil, Los Angeles County Department of Coroner, was not a young man, and his stout body didn't project athleticism by any standard, but he was surprisingly agile. As he effortlessly followed Evan Hobbes's bagged body down the recently formed Mount Malibu, Nolan imagined him as a young boy, frolicking in the Alps . . . no, she couldn't imagine him frolicking at all. Ever. But he seemed weirdly jolly. Of course, her assessment was undoubtedly skewed by caffeine deprivation and the emergent headache that was beginning to tap paradiddles in her brain.

"Steady, girls and boys, don't drop my body!" Weil crowed to his corpse Sherpas like a Teutonic coxswain. "Tyler, I thought you were a climber!"

Nolan saw a lot of eye-rolls, but they all knew it was a boon to work with the esteemed Dr. Weil, so they kept their mouths shut. They'd complain about him later, at some bar's happy hour. Where did you go to drink after shuttling around human remains all day? She wanted to know so she could avoid it.

As the body was loaded safely into the wagon without mishap, Weil nodded his approval, then turned his attention to them.

"A body in such terrible shape, so many ways he could have died. This will be challenging."

It really wouldn't be, not for Weil, but he'd always been modest. "What do you think about the bruises on his neck?"

He shrugged, and somehow made her feel like an idiot in the process. "Very unlikely a result of the fall. Or falls, as it were. Once I examine him, I'll be able to tell you everything about them, but they may not reveal whether or not he was murdered. But you already knew that, Detective Nolan. You have a feeling that this is a homicide and not an accident?"

The same question Darcy had asked. *Did* she have a feeling? "It could be both."

Weil cast an introspective glance at the deep blue Pacific, his feathery hair as white as the breakers. "Manslaughter. Yes, that could be. We all have some work to do. Good luck to you both."

"Thanks. Same to you, Doc," Crawford said.

After Weil left, he gave her a gentle bump with his elbow. "The bruises were a good call, Mags."

"You're both right, they don't prove anything. I don't want this to be a homicide, so why am I trying to make it one?"

"You're not, you just care. No stone unturned and all that. And it might be your gut, too. You've always had good instincts."

"What does your gut tell you?"

"That this probably isn't going to be quick and easy." He looked up at the Baum house. Its white, multifaceted façade was now sparkling in the morning sun. "Next stop."

Nolan nodded at Roscoe Miles, who was running Criminalistics' Field Investigation Unit today. It was colloquially known as Crime Scene, because it sounded cooler than FIU. Television had forever changed the argot of death.

Ross looked pale and a little shaky on his feet as he approached in his whites. She knew it wasn't from the sight of a dead body—he'd probably seen thousands of them. "You want to tell him we're not finished, or should I?"

"He kind of looks like shit, so you break the news, he likes you better. I think he might have a crush on you."

She rolled her eyes like a grounded teenager. "He's gay."

"So? Crushes have no boundaries. Hey, Ross, are you okay?"

"No. I hate heights. I hate rock climbing."

One mystery solved. "Anything good?" Nolan asked hopefully.

"Doubtful, but don't let my cynicism ruin your Sunday."

"It's already ruined," Crawford carped.

Ross nodded. "Heard."

Heard. Exactly what Sam Easton had said to her when she'd pressed him about a position with LAPD.

You're thinking about him too much.

Heard.

She gestured to the Baum house. "Ross, we think that's where he went down. If we're right, that's the primary scene."

He let out a long-suffering sigh. "You want us to stand by."

"Yeah, but don't let that ruin your day." She smiled. "It's a beautiful October morning in Malibu."

He smiled back grudgingly. "There is that."

Chapter Fourteen

NOLAN DIDN'T UNDERSTAND THE LOGIC BEHIND a mink sofa throw in Malibu—too après ski—but the way Essie Baum was quietly wringing the poor pelts into a second death, maybe it was a security blanket she carried with her everywhere, in case calamity struck.

She was shaking her head as tears streamed unabated down her pale cheeks, and her hands trembled—genuine grief. Angry, purple shadows cupped her eyes and her hair was a tawny, disarrayed nest, but not from the ravages of anguish. Those were tells of a long night of SoCal partying, which had certainly made the early wake-up call of gutting news even more excruciating. But in spite of being diminished by multiple circumstances, Essie Baum was still a classic beauty.

A beautiful woman in a beautiful house. The *Times* photo spread hadn't done it justice. The design was classic California coastal, with demure strokes of blue and sand tones in a predominantly beachy-white palette. Even the mink throw was pearl-colored in observance of the overall vision. There were lots of naturalistic, primitive touches in the interior landscape, like variations on driftwood, petrified sea critters, and chic sculptures that gave the illusion of floating stones.

And plenty of art on the walls, the most curious being a huge canvas of an empty-eyed Gorgon with seaweed hair. Medusa looked hungover, too.

But the jaw-dropping vista of the ocean beyond glass doors eclipsed everything. Nothing but sky and sea and manicured grass that appeared to end at the water line, creating the illusion that you could dive straight into the ocean from the edge of the lawn. You would never guess the busy PCH snaked two hundred feet below this cliff-dwelling aerie.

It was too damn bad there weren't security cameras covering the area, but there was no way to access the house from this vantage point unless you scaled that cliff. The Baums had no reason to worry about a rear land invasion by paparazzi or thieves. Or would it be a front land invasion?

"Ms. Baum, I know this is a very difficult time, but can you tell us a little about your relationship with Mr. Hobbes?"

She nodded and sniffled in misery as she collected herself. "My husband, David, and I have known Evan forever, since very early in his career. He was family. He didn't have one of his own."

"Thank you for letting us know. You're the proper person to notify, then."

"Yes. He was a son to us." Her voice broke.

Nolan estimated that Essie Baum was midthirties, roughly the same age as Evan Hobbes. Not exactly a son, but the sentiment was clearly authentic. "And you mentioned he arrived at the party around nine?"

"Yes, about then."

"With anybody?"

"No, he came alone. I happened to be outside when he arrived, making sure things were running smoothly with security and the valets. David usually handles that, but he's out of town, so I felt it was best to be proactive. There can be issues with party crashers. And paparazzi. They're ruthless."

Nolan didn't have to micromanage parking or security at her min-iscule Woodland Hills rental, or deal with paparazzi or party crash-ers. Rich people had a lot of problems. "Was he in a relationship?"

"No. He was focusing on himself and his work. He told me that relationships had become too distracting."

Didn't she know it. "How was Mr. Hobbes's mood? Anything about his behavior that struck you as out of sorts?"

She seemed nonplussed by the question. "He was upset, of course, because of that hideous video, and I know his heart was broken, but he was being brave." Her face darkened, then flashed with surpris-ingly viciousness. "Nobody believed it was real. We all told him so last night. And there was no question in any of our minds that he would be exonerated." The waterworks started again. "Goddamned predators on social media, all they want to do is ruin lives."

An echo of Darcy Moore's assessment. Nolan found the pack of unopened tissues she always kept in her suit pocket for occasions like this, and passed them over. "When was the last time you saw him?"

Essie Baum blotted her eyes and considered carefully. "I guess it must have been around eleven, because I'd just sent the caterers and servers home. He came into the kitchen to thank me. He was very drunk by then—who wouldn't be under those circumstances? I told him I was taking his keys from the valet and offered him a bedroom for the night, but he said he'd take an Uber home. He liked his cham-pagne. He especially liked it last night."

So much so, he'd taken a bottle with him over the edge of the cliff. Tripped, pushed, or jumped? They were all still strong contenders in Nolan's mind.

"Where did he go after he talked to you?" Crawford asked.

She gave him an astonished look. "There were over a hundred people at the party. When you host parties of that size, all you ever see is a blur of bodies. In and out."

Nolan could only imagine. It was an introvert's worst nightmare, and she fell into that category. "Did you notice or hear of any confrontations Mr. Hobbes had while he was at the party?"

"No. Evan was a gentle soul and everybody here loved him. Drunk, yes. Belligerent, no. Why?"

"We noted some bruises on his neck that his fall wouldn't necessarily account for. We need to discount the possibility of a homicide." Crawford got to the heart of the matter, to Essie Baum's abject horror.

"Nobody would kill Evan! He didn't have an enemy in the world. It had to be an accident."

"Whoever posted that video is definitely an enemy," Nolan pointed out.

"Yes, you're right. But that person was *not* at my party."

"Did you notice any bruises on his neck when you saw him?"

"None at all."

Nolan mentally noted a confrontation after 11 p.m. What had happened after a drunken stumble into the kitchen to thank his hostess? Or maybe the bruises had been sustained in the fall, but Weil didn't think so, and neither did she. "Did you notice if Mr. Hobbes was spending time with anybody in particular?"

"No, but my brother, Seth—he's Evan's agent—told me he was shadowing him, forcing water on him. Trying to wrangle him, as he put it." Her face crumpled anew and a fresh river of mascara broke the dam. "This is going to destroy him, too."

Seth. Nolan felt her scalp prickle. "We'll be in touch with him. What's his last name?"

"Lehman."

Oh, God. A six degrees of separation nightmare. How could that jackass be related to this lovely woman?

Essie started to exhibit signs of an impending panic attack: hand-wringing, shortness of breath, wild eyes. "I need Seth to come over,

I'm all alone, and I just . . . I can't be alone right now." Her voice gradually descended the decibel scale all the way down to mute.

Perfect. They wouldn't have to bother hunting him down. "Yes, please call him, Ms. Baum. We'll speak with him here, but as you know, please keep this in the immediate family until LAPD issues a formal statement, and tell him to do the same." In other words, tell your prick, loudmouth brother to shut the hell up. He was the only one she didn't trust to bury his head in the sand like all good Hollywood families did at the sniff of scandal.

The gratitude in Essie Baum's shadowed, swollen eyes was pitiful, and Nolan absorbed some of her pain like a sin eater, glutting on misfortune, as if she could do the impossible and take some away. She always did that at notifications, probably to her great detriment. Even Crawford seemed a little slushy.

"Of course, Detective Nolan. I'm grateful to both of you for your discretion in handling this. A Disney spokesperson will release a statement when it's appropriate, along with Evan's agency." She straightened with purpose, anxious for escape from the omnipresent reminder that a friend—or rather, a family member—had died on her property, on her watch. "If that's all, I'd like to call Seth and David now."

"Just a few more questions first."

Her spine sagged as she resumed kneading the fur on her lap like a prematurely weaned kitten. "I don't know what else I can tell you, Detectives."

"What time did the party end?"

"I closed the gates at two thirty, after the cleaning people left. The last of the guests were gone by one thirty."

Nolan was amazed by the complicated logistics of throwing a large party. Lots of moving parts an average person like her couldn't imagine, unless you'd walked down the aisle, which she hadn't. And wouldn't, now that she knew what a pain in the ass it would be. "When will your husband be home? We'll need to speak with him, too."

A flash of irritability beneath Essie Baum's grief? Why wouldn't there be? She'd been left holding the bag of a gigantic party that had ended in a family tragedy, and she didn't have a shoulder to cry on.

"He's supposed to come home Tuesday or Wednesday, but when he hears about Evan, he'll come back right away."

"Please let us know when he does."

"I will." She stared out at the lawn and the ocean, then shook her head despondently. "Poor Evan. He can't even defend himself now. Complete strangers do the cruelest things these days. An obsessive fan, somebody who hated his last film, who knows? Public figures are vulnerable to all the crazies in the world now. The internet is destroying people and society."

Crawford leaned forward and rested his hands on his knees. "We'll need your guest list, ma'am," he said gently. "And the names of the companies that staffed the party, and any individuals you employed personally. Household workers, caterers, valets, security. They often see things nobody else does."

She looked confused. "If somebody had seen him fall, they would have called the police."

"In case we do find evidence of foul play."

She seemed very uncomfortable about the possibility of her high-profile guests getting harassed by the cops. "Yes. I can provide that information."

"Thank you. Detective Crawford and I will take a look outside now, if you'd like to make your calls and print out that list."

She didn't just straighten, she popped out of her seat like an amphetamine junkie jack-in-the-box. "Yes, I'll do that. Thank you."

Nolan watched in sympathy as she hurried away and disappeared down a hallway like a frantic ghost. It was always depressing to see the emotional aftermath of somebody who'd lost an important person in their life, homicide or not. It also reminded you of your own grief and stirred up the pain all over again. Death resonated with survivors until they followed their dearly departed into the grave. She hoped Essie Baum's husband and brother would step up for her, but she had her doubts.

She and Al adjourned to a flagstone patio corralled by pink and white roses and followed a stone path to the pool area. The property was pristine—any party detritus had been cleared by the industrious, nocturnal cleaning staff, who all undoubtedly had families they never saw on weekends. "I had an encounter with Seth Lehman yesterday," she said quietly.

Crawford's eyes expanded in disbelief. "That's totally bizarre. Where?"

"Bristol Farms. I was behind him in the checkout line. He was on his phone, reassuring a client that his career wasn't going to crater. I'm thinking that client may have been Hobbes."

"What was the encounter?" He crooked his fingers in air quotes on the final word of his query. "Not sexual, I hope."

Nolan allowed herself a soft snort, grateful for the opportunity to open the pressure valve a little. "Does wanting to neuter him with a rusty knife count as sexual?"

Crawford smiled back. "Depends on your psychiatric profile."

"He's an arrogant prick."

"Took him down a few notches, did you?"

"Tried, but that doesn't faze guys like him. I really want to kick the shit out of him, Al."

"I won't get in your way."

Chapter Fifteen

"I'M SORRY, SIR, BUT THIS CARD has been declined, too."

The Discover card he hadn't used in months? Goddammit. Seth gave the prissy, minimum-wage counterman an imperious, *do you know who I am?* smile. He wasn't impressed, as if he *knew* he had more money in his checking account. "Just charge it to Amber Harrison's account, then."

After the declined cards, the clerk's demeanor had shifted from unctuous to suspicious. Like this skinny little fuckwad was going to hit a panic button and call in the cops. Like Seth Lehman, dressed snout to tail in Cucinelli, was some dirtbag looking to pull off a scam. Who scammed for caviar?

"I'll have to check with Ms. Harrison, sir."

"Please don't. It's an anniversary surprise."

He flashed a smug smile and looked over Seth's shoulder. "I think the surprise is already ruined."

He jerked his head around and saw Amber stalking from the restaurant into the boutique on python stilettoes, confused hurt and malicious intent in her eyes. Too late for a duck-and-run. What the fuck was she doing here in the morning? She never got up before noon on Sundays. "Amber! Hi!"

Her rage was a tangible thing, and not restrained by the standards of socially acceptable behavior. She smacked him in the chest and started yelling in front of the startled clientele and amused clerk. "I've been calling you all night, where the fuck have you been?"

Every pair of eyes in the place was boring holes into him, waiting for his response and the next scene in this cinema verité. He tried to take her arm, but she shook him off.

"TELL ME."

"Take it easy, Amber, I'm sorry," he said in a low voice, hoping to set a new, calmer tone. "You know I was at Essie and David's, and I had too much to drink . . ."

"Then why didn't you call an Uber?! Why didn't you call me? I was waiting for you, you asshole!"

"Should have called," some reedy-voiced puke in the ad hoc audience commented.

Playing the drunk card wasn't good enough for Amber, and the other hyenas in the pack were turning against him. Time to improv. "It's more complicated than that," he whispered with grave sincerity. "There's the thing with Evan, and I had to keep an eye on him. Then a family situation kind of blew up. I sat up with Essie all night. I couldn't leave her."

She went from Def Con Four to Def Con Two, but she was still *very* pissed. It was in her posture, in her face, and hovering above her like a dark, malefic halo. "You should have at least texted me."

"Should have texted," the asshole reprised his commentary.

"I should have, Amber, I meant to, but it was really intense. Nothing was more important than being there for Essie. I was afraid for her . . . afraid she might . . . it was a bad night."

Her anger deflated a little further, but she wasn't ready to let go yet, because this was still all about her. Amber was a spoiled brat with a robust sense of entitlement, created by the toxic stew of a marginally successful career as a dancer and a windfall of Saudi oil money. "I'm sorry," she said stiffly. "So why are you here?"

"Essie said she wanted some caviar, that it was the only thing that would make her feel better. And I wanted to get some for you, too, as an apology."

Her pout had always seemed cute to him, but this morning, she looked like a lamprey, one of the most grotesque creatures on God's earth. He offered his hands in faux penance and she took them. Excellent.

"I really am sorry about your sister. Is it David? Everybody knows he's such a pussy hound."

Seth knew it was true, which enraged him, but he tried not to think about it too much. They had a miserable marriage of convenience, but Amber didn't need to know about that, or about Essie's multiple affairs with other prominent Hollywood wives sick of their pig husbands. Or her out-of-control kleptomania—a cry for help if there ever was one. Thank God the lawyers had buried that unpleasant incident at Neiman Marcus. There was only so much humiliation a person could take.

"I'll tell you about it later, Amber, but I have to get back there. Please don't say anything to anybody. I don't want Essie to have to deal with more rumors. She's not in a good place." He didn't have to manufacture tears—they filled his eyes easily, because Essie truly broke his heart.

Amber's lamprey mouth turned down into a moue of compassion that made her look somewhat cute again. She patted his arm sympathetically. "I'm sorry for blowing up, Seth, I was just hurt."

"I'm sorry, too, baby." He kissed her cheek, redolent with Clé de Peau moisturizer. "I'll make it up to you, I promise. Why are *you* here? It's early."

She tossed her blond mane toward a formidable phalanx of Amber clones he hadn't noticed before, glowering at him from the passage between Petrossian's restaurant and the boutique, ready to attack. "Caviar and champagne with my girls to ease my broken heart. I was up all night, waiting to hear from you. Do you want to meet them?"

Hell, no. "I can't now, Amber, I really have to get back to Essie." His gaze jittered back to the angry girl posse. "Tell them not to kill me on the way out, okay?"

She giggled and waved her arm at them, like a posh La Eme crime boss calling off assassins. They receded back into the restaurant, but they didn't turn their Balenciaga-clad backs as they did. *Eyes on you, fucker. One wrong move, you're done.* It was chilling.

Amber had the upper hand and was benevolent about it. She gestured to his uncompleted purchases. "Put that on my account. A gift to Essie from me. She deserves it."

Kissing up to the connected family at the perfect time. Amber and her insatiable ego—almost a sentient being itself—wanted desperately to be a famous actress. "That's so nice, thank you. She'll really appreciate it."

She batted her dense, fake lashes and the effect was comical, like humping tarantulas. Probably not her intention. "Will I see you tonight?"

"I'm not sure, Amber. Things are in flux right now, but I'll try. I'll be sure to let you know either way." He leaned in for a full mouth kiss and she responded. The formerly hostile audience in the boutique started clapping. All the world was a stage.

Seth was so distracted by his good fortune and the beautiful woman waiting at home for him, he never noticed Amber's Aston Martin tailing him.

Chapter Sixteen

THE BAUMS' YARD WAS LARGE, THE turf still spongy from the overnight soaking in the marine layer. The cliff's edge was almost entirely obscured by a coastal garden of grasses, gumdrop-shaped myrtle shrubs, and giant blue agaves, their saw-toothed leaves as hard as dried shark skin. Nolan had always considered them living exemplars of the prehistoric world.

The garden provided a natural barrier against accidents, unless you were drunk and stoned and sitting on the carved teak bench that faced the ocean. Its location was roughly in line with where they'd found the body, but the rockslide made it almost impossible to calculate trajectory with any accuracy.

Her mind framed an image of Evan Hobbes sitting on that bench last night, guzzling champagne and staring at the unknowable Pacific while he pondered his damaged image. Decided life wasn't worth it anymore? Stumbled and lost his footing? Fought with somebody and ended up the ultimate loser?

The quake had taken a jagged bite out of part of the cliff. She wondered if the diminished footage would affect property value. Probably. It was Malibu, after all, where inches mattered. She looked back toward the house, then at Al, who was crouched in an awkward, yogi-esque posture, scanning the ground.

"There are no landscaping lights out here, no cameras, and it's a good distance from where the party action was, Al. Easy to wander out here in the dark and disappear."

He looked up at her. "Right. Which Hobbes did."

"Don't get so close to the edge, it doesn't look stable."

He stood abruptly and backed away. "Good advice. We'll let Ross handle it since he loves heights so much."

"You're mean."

"I just want everybody to suffer equally. Find anything closer to the house?"

"Not on the first pass. You?"

"No litter, no signs of where he might have gone over, no drag marks or blood, if you want to go that route."

"I don't."

"Of course, the quake could have taken that down. But it didn't take this." Crawford gestured to a patch of intermittently flattened grass and dented sod near the drop to PCH. "A lot of footprints, and pretty close to the edge." He started walking back and forth on the squishy ground.

"You're clearly demonstrating something. Show pony? Tortured artist? How to destroy a possible crime scene?"

"I'm demonstrating that a pacing person doesn't leave marks that deep."

Nolan looked up at the cloudless sky, considering. "The sun has been up for a while, drying out the lawn."

"It's not that dry."

"A struggle?"

"When you're in a physical confrontation, you use your feet as leverage." He shambled along the edge of the garden, eyes on the ground.

"Maybe your Bristol Farms babysitter can shed some light. He might be the last person who saw him alive."

"Fantastic. Can we frame him?"

Al snuffled the way he always did when he was amused in a situation where mirth was inappropriate, then pondered the sardonic query earnestly. "Easy. Everybody knows Hollywood agents are all sociopaths."

Nolan scoffed and slowly made her way back to the house, eyes coursing the tall boxwood hedge that ran vertically from the pool area to the cliff. The tops had been pruned into crests and dips, presumably to mimic the movement of waves. There were deep cutouts that nestled additional teak benches for a secret garden effect. Nice. A triumph in landscape architecture.

She'd already scrutinized it on the way down, but a different perspective could sometimes yield a trove of missed evidence. A broken branch you couldn't spot from a certain angle, maybe a hint of color that could be plant blight, but might also be blood.

She stopped. "Al, come here."

He labored up the incline of the sweeping lawn. "What?"

Nolan walked into one of the privacy cutouts and pointed at a disturbance in the shrubbery she hadn't seen earlier. Some of the glossy green leaves were tinged with rust. Not plant blight, she was sure of that. The weathered teak bench had rusty speckles, too. Somebody had bled here, and Evan Hobbes was a compelling candidate. "Interesting, don't you think?"

"Blood is always interesting." Crawford looked at the Crime Scene caravan pulling into the courtyard. "I'm sure they'll think so, too."

Chapter Seventeen

DAPHNA WAS PROPPED UP AGAINST THE pillows, reading *Angeleno* magazine when Seth walked into the bedroom carrying a tray laden with Petrossian's finest and the bottle of Billecart-Salmon he'd lifted from the party. God, she looked sexy in that little silk camisole and lace-edged panties. *Good morning, sunshine.* "Caviar is served, my queen."

She tossed the magazine aside and clapped her hands together in delight. "Thank God you have champagne."

"You can't eat caviar without champagne."

They gorged on Special Reserve Kaluga Huso in bed while Daphna chattered happily about a location shoot in St. Petersburg and how great the caviar was in Russia. Or something like that. Seth was too captivated by the movement of her voluptuous lips to process the story fully. It was the most perfect morning he'd had in his life, and things were only going to get better . . .

And then her phone buzzed, ruining the precious moment.

"I'm sorry, Seth, it's my agent, I have to take this." She winked at him. "My soon-to-be former agent. I asked for a meeting tomorrow. I'll just be a minute." She jumped out of bed and went into the living room for privacy.

Seth was enlivened by her mention of "soon-to-be former agent," but unreasonably anxious about her departure, as if she was an apparition that might vanish if he didn't keep her in sight at all times. He quelled his apprehension by chugging another glass of pink champagne and powering up his own phone.

His heart rate spiked when he saw alerts for fourteen texts and eleven missed calls from Essie. That kind of compulsive phone abuse was SOP for most of the people he dealt with, but not for his sister. She answered before the phone even rang on his end.

"Seth, where the hell are you?"

Her voice sounded thick and wobbly. Something was definitely wrong. "At home. I slept in . . ." Sobbing interrupted him. "God, what's wrong?"

"Evan is dead. He fell off our cliff. The police and crime scene people are here now, all over the property, it's so horrible. Please come now."

She hung up before he could respond. Not that he would have been able to. His blood had drained to a faraway place, taking his voice with it.

Daphna breezed back into the bedroom, then stopped abruptly. "Seth, what on earth happened?"

He looked up from his phone and tried to focus on her face, but his head was pounding, gonging, blurring his vision to washed-out gray. "That was Essie. They found Evan Hobbes dead."

Her eyes grew into two celadon saucers and filled with tears. "Oh my God, Seth. That's the worst possible news! Do they know what happened?"

"All she said was he fell off their cliff. She's losing it." His stomach soured and it was only the price tag on his breakfast—even though he hadn't paid for it—that prevented him from vomiting on his silk Kashan rug. "Fuck. They don't have a fence. If it's ruled an accident . . ."

Her mouth dropped incredulously. "You're worried about them getting sued?"

"Yeah. No. Fuck, I don't know what I'm thinking. I have to go . . ."

The gonging in his head had migrated to the door. He heard the frantic rattle of the handle, then more pounding, more rattling.

"OPEN THE DOOR YOU SON OF A BITCH I KNOW YOU'RE IN THERE WITH SOME SLUT!"

Jesus Christ, how was this possible? How had things gone south so far, so fast? Daphna looked at him with a blank, teary expression. "Psycho ex. Ignore her."

"Should I call security? The police?"

Seth steadied himself against the headboard so he didn't tip over. The neighbors were probably calling both right now. This building and its residents weren't accustomed to déclassé domestic brawls. He would probably get kicked out. Shit. The world really was flat, and he was about to fall off the edge. "No, she'll go away."

Daphna's face shuffled through a catalog of emotions, then stilled with resolve as she manipulated her phone. "I'm recording this in case she doesn't go away. She sounds violent."

"YOU MOTHERFUCKING LIAR! OPEN THE GODDAMNED DOOR AND SHOW ME THE WHORE WHO'S EATING MY CAVIAR SO I CAN KICK HER SKANKY ASS!"

Daphna moved so fast, Seth barely registered her sudden flight. He reached out his hand as he rose from the bed to chase after her, catch her. It was all a murky, slow-motion, underwater shot.

"No . . ." His voice was a distorted croak, like vinyl on the wrong RPM setting. He froze as he witnessed disaster unfold: Daphna pulled open the door in her camisole and lacy panties to greet an enraged Amber.

"I'm not a slut, a whore, or a skank. And someone close to Seth has just died, so collect yourself and show some respect."

He watched in horrified fascination as Amber's pale skin turned the color of borscht. After the full force of celebrity recognition set in, she leveled an inferno gaze on him. "You're going to pay for this, Seth."

"Did you hear me?" Daphna asked incredulously. "Seth is grieving right now. Leave him alone."

"You're going to pay for this, too, bitch, I don't care who you are."

"Is that a threat?"

"It's not a threat, *slut,* it's a promise."

"The police will be interested to hear that. Please leave and don't come back."

"Seth, you pussy! You're just standing there letting your new whore do all the talking! Don't you want to say something to me?"

"Calm down, Amber . . ."

She lunged forward with the crazed eyes of a berserker, but Daphna intercepted her. With polished, action film moves, she turned her out firmly but gracefully. Seth had never seen such delicacy in physical engagement.

"Ouch!" Amber screamed, flailing her arms. "My hair!"

"You mean your extensions."

Oh my. Daphna knew where to find a vein. He loved her even more.

"We're calling the police, but we won't press assault charges. Consider yourself lucky."

"Fuck—"

Daphna slammed the door on "you" and turned with a stupefied expression. "Unbelievable. Who is she?"

He willed his mouth to move, his larynx to work. "Amber Harrison. She's vicious and vindictive, and she's going to spin this in some warped way and put it all over the web—"

"She's not going to advertise her humiliation."

Seth thought about the earlier scene in Petrossian. "That's never stopped her before."

"Who cares what she does? I don't, and you shouldn't, either. We belong together, and she belongs in an institution. Or maybe rehab, she reeked like alcohol." Daphna arched a gently reprimanding brow. "Maybe she's not an ex?"

"She's in denial. She has trouble with rejection."

"Well, if she wasn't an ex before, she is now. Don't look so distressed. It's not like she's going to hunt you down and kill you."

"I'm not so sure."

"You're being histrionic again. First, Becca's going to kill you, now Amber Harrison." She shook his arm. "Look at me, Seth. Listen to me. Evan is dead. Essie needs you. I need you. Pull yourself together, because I'm not letting you drive anywhere until you do. And I'm going to call the police. This has to be reported."

Seth thought about how ironic it was that he'd been lying to Amber an hour ago about how much Essie needed him, and now she really did. He had to be there for her; be strong for her, like she'd always been for him. "Yeah. Okay. You're absolutely right."

Daphna took his arm and led his slack, wobbling body into the bedroom. She kneaded his shoulders with force, divining subterranean knots he hadn't known existed. The unexpected release finally freed him to puke up several hundred dollars' worth of caviar on his Kashan rug.

Chapter Eighteen

SETH DIDN'T REMEMBER DAPHNA PUTTING A fresh bandage on his injured hand that had dented Becca's wall, didn't remember leaving his penthouse or driving to Malibu. He didn't even remember walking into the house. All he knew was that he was now sitting in front of a lifeless fireplace on Essie's vast, curving sofa, staring at the deranged painting of Medusa. He hated that painting. It reminded him of Becca.

Essie was resting her head on his shoulder. She'd stopped weeping, but her chest still hitched every few minutes. "It's going to be okay, Ess." What a stupid, ineffectual thing to say.

"Not for Evan."

He felt his throat tighten. Evan's death was starting to feel real, and it hurt. He was going to miss his endless kvetching and verbal italics. "No. Poor Evan. Goddammit, I shouldn't have left him. I should have shoved him in my car—"

"Don't you dare blame yourself, Seth. There were a hundred other people here, too. Nobody could have anticipated this."

He glowered at Medusa. He hadn't killed Evan, but he didn't know if he'd ever get over the wretched sense of complicity. If he'd shadowed his every move, things would have turned out differently. Essie probably felt the same way. "Do you think he could have . . . I mean, the video was a huge blow."

She straightened and wiped her eyes with a mangled tissue. "Done it intentionally? Absolutely not, you know him better than that."

"Yeah. I do. Did."

Essie drooped at the tense correction. "It was an accident. A tragic accident that was nobody's fault. I told the detectives that. Detectives Nolan and Crawford. They were very kind and compassionate, so be polite when you speak with them."

Seth's mouth sagged open. Holy shit. If life was a bad script—which it seemed to be—the chance meeting at Bristol Farms had been ham-fisted foreshadowing. "What else did they say?"

"That they're looking at everything. They brought up suicide, too, and homicide."

"Homicide? That's ridiculous." Seth's thoughts faltered. Was it ridiculous? Becca had made clear her wish for Evan's future. *He's a corpse now. Unfortunately, not literally—that would spare some ongoing unpleasantness, and possibly WIT's image.* He had a recording of her vitriol in his pocket.

"That's good that they're looking at everything, it's their job. They'll figure it out."

Essie had exhausted her emotional strength and sagged back against his shoulder. He stroked her soft hair, wishing he could make everything better for her.

"I can't reach David. He's going to be shattered."

Seth doubted that. David didn't care about anybody except David. "He'll call back as soon as he gets your messages."

She clenched her fists in frustration. "He's never here when I need him. What's the point, Seth?"

He sensed an impending meltdown. Essie was already falling apart under the stress of her tanking marriage. It was the worst-kept secret in Hollywood. Fuck, even Amber knew. He was certain her affairs were meaningless and pure retaliation, but if David knew about them, he wasn't bothered. The kleptomania didn't bother him, either, because he paid lawyers and therapists to deal with that inconvenience. Those truths, combined with Evan's death, were swamping her, and it infuriated him.

"Maybe this will get him to pull his head out of his ass. I know you don't think divorce is an option, but being miserable isn't, either. The money isn't worth it, and you'd have plenty of it coming your way, even with the prenup. Besides, you're an amazing designer, look at the magic you did with this house." Medusa notwithstanding. "You could build your own empire."

She wiped her eyes and looked at him with Shakespearean tragedy. "It's not about the money, Seth. I still love him."

Incomprehensible, but that was something for her and her shrink to sort out. "Essie, why don't you go upstairs and rest for a while? You need your strength to get through this. I'll talk to the detectives, you keep trying David."

She squeezed his hand. "Thank you, Seth. Can you try to get in touch with Becca, too? I haven't been able to reach her, either."

"Who cares about Becca?"

"I do. She's one of my best friends, and she needs to know her flagship client is dead before it's all over the news." She sighed impatiently. "I wish you two could just get along."

Best friends since when? She'd said it too defensively, and her indignant expression chilled Seth to the core. Sweet baby Jesus. Was that Machiavellian harpy double-dipping in the sibling gene pool? "Essie, please don't tell me you're involved with her."

"What a thing to say. Becca supports me as a *friend*. In fact, I'm thinking about investing in the agency."

Seth stared at her, horror-stricken.

"And don't tell me I'm being stupid. I've heard enough of that from David."

"I think the agency is in trouble . . ."

She made a curt, chopping motion with her hand. "Just call her. She wasn't feeling well last night, and she left the party without saying good-bye."

"She was at the party? I never saw her, and she makes sure she's always seen."

"She must have left before you got here. I'm worried something's wrong."

There was definitely something wrong with Becca. But Essie couldn't handle the possibility that her maybe-lover was a cold-blooded demon who might have killed one of her best friends, so he kept his thoughts to himself. "The video hit her hard, just like all of us. She was a mess yesterday."

"Oh. Of course. I'm not thinking straight." Essie started to whimper, like a child too traumatized to scream.

"Upstairs, sis. I'll take care of everything."

"Will you pour me a drink first?"

"Whatever you want."

"A vanilla vodka tonic with lemon. A double."

Seth went to the generously stocked bar and examined the rows of polished bottles. It didn't seem like enough alcohol to get through this day. He didn't think there was enough alcohol in the world to help with that. He reached into a cupboard for the glassware and recoiled when he saw a pair of gold cuff links tucked behind a Baccarat highball. *His* cuff links, the ones he'd been missing for months. Jesus. Essie was stealing from her family now. He stuffed them in his pocket and tried to push away the suffocating sense that his sister was in a downward spiral that was gaining momentum.

Chapter Nineteen

WILL CORRIGAN HATED WELFARE CHECKS. IN his six years with the Santa Barbara PD, he couldn't think of more than a handful that hadn't ended badly. He'd been a sorry witness to ODs, suicides, and elderly folks without med alert devices, lying broken on their floors, waiting for someone to miss them. He'd saved a few, and those had been his very best days on the job.

Then there was Clarence Ruehl. A hemorrhagic stroke took him down, and nobody missed him—not for days. His dog, Fredo, finally got too hungry, and the poor thing's mind snapped because of it. That was five years ago and Will still had night terrors, still looked at his own sweet golden retriever in a different way.

He cranked on the squad's air conditioner against the sweat that greased his brow and trickled down into his collar. It was a cool morning, but his dark memories always stoked a poisonous internal furnace. He was still a young man, but some days, he felt too old for this job. Or maybe he was just getting soft with his first child on the way. How could he look into the eyes of his innocent baby girl with all the ugliness he had stored in his brain? Wouldn't she see it?

Over the past few years, he'd considered making a career change in the sluggish way he'd thought about joining a softball league, but he needed to get a lot more serious about it. Clear his mind before the baby, so she wouldn't see the ghosts in his eyes. He loved being a cop, but he loved carpentry and woodworking, too, and he had the skills to make a living at it if he got credentialed. Never once had he heard of a carpenter who'd walked onto a job and found . . . the things he had.

Will pounded the wheel of the squad, jolting the recurring nightmares out of his head and bringing reality into focus. He could hope and wish all he wanted, but the truth was, he needed some schooling and an apprenticeship to join the union, and it would take a few years to graduate to journeyman and earn at his current level. Time and money were two things he didn't have, and Milly and Baby Girl were the only things that mattered.

He turned off the PCH and picked up a narrow road that led to a sheltered enclave of jaw-dropping beachfront property. You couldn't necessarily tell from the street—some of the façades looked downright modest—but if you walked this particular beach like he and Milly did on some weekends, you'd see how monolithic the backsides of these places were.

He would never make enough money in his lifetime to buy a hundred square feet of a house here, but it didn't make him jealous. Some people just had the talent and the drive and the willingness to make the big sacrifices that brought them to a certain apex in life. But he had reached his own personal zenith, and he wouldn't trade it for anything. His existence was uncomplicated, stable, and rewarding. He was married to his high school sweetheart and soul mate; Baby Girl Corrigan would arrive in five months and be the most-loved child the world had ever known; and there was no drama beyond the friendly marital quarrel over what color to paint the nursery.

Will pulled into the driveway, almost forgetting the reason for his visit here as he crafted a new, persuasive defense of Aloe versus Alyssum. He'd spring it on Milly tonight, and she would be giggly and helpless in the face of his refined argument for neutral green.

He was thoroughly enjoying the respite of his internal dialogue; even felt a smile on his lips. Until he saw the closed gate. That brought him right back to his grim purpose, and what he might find behind that gate.

No drama. Except the memories. The damn memories.

He called in his arrival, got out of the squad, and pushed the gate buzzer multiple times, even though he knew there wouldn't be an answer. Time to find another way in.

He did easily, by skirting the edge of the property to the end of the fence. He had to tangle with some shrubbery, but no harm done to himself or the flora. He followed a flagstone path through an arbor of grapevine laden with plump pendants of fruit, straight to the front door.

When he reached it, he wished he hadn't. One more nightmare to add to the list.

* * *

Will started at the rap on his squad's window. He hadn't even noticed Detective Jenny Wyler approach. He liked her a lot and respected her more, and her look of concern told him he wasn't doing a great job concealing his anxiety. She knew about Clarence Ruehl, and it made him feel ashamed. Weak. He rolled down his window and tried to keep his voice strong as he greeted her.

"Are you okay, Will?"

"Yeah." He mopped his brow. "Just hot. Might be catching something."

She nodded sympathetically. "You think you can take me on a walk-through now?"

"Sure." He stepped out of the car and ignored the vertigo and the nausea. Lemon trees obscured the front entrance from this angle, but he knew what was there. "It's just . . . she's so young."

"I know. I'm sorry."

Chapter Twenty

NOLAN WATCHED A TECH TAKE CASTS of the cliffside footprints under the watchful eye of Ross, who was in much better spirits now that his supervisory position placed him well away from the edge. The plaster made obvious what hadn't been to the naked eye: there were two distinct sets, one much smaller. "A man and a woman?"

Ross shrugged. "It looks that way to me. But women usually wear something with heels to a luxe party. Something that would spike the ground, and there's none of that here."

Nolan thought of the sexy sandals in her trunk. They were flats to compensate for her five-eleven stature. "Not necessarily."

"You would know better than me."

"She could have been barefoot, too. If you're wearing a thousand-dollar pair of heels, you're not going to walk in wet grass. At least I wouldn't."

"Good point." He sighed. "Turf is a shit medium, but the impressions will give us some information because they're deep. Al was right about that."

"What kind of information?"

"If any of the prints belong to Hobbes, we'll be able to get a credible size match with his footwear. And maybe there are distinguishing marks or some trace. Pure conjecture, but I'm envisioning a lovers' spat out here."

Nolan could see it, too, even though Essie Baum had told them Hobbes had put a moratorium on relationships. Maybe one had come back to haunt him. A drunken, cliffside contretemps could definitely end in an accident. Or a crime of passion. Pushing somebody off a cliff was arguably a near-perfect murder under the right circumstances.

She looked over at Al, who was conversing with another tech near the boxwood. Blood and footprints. Neither worth a damn without context or more evidence. Her phone rang, and she apologized to Ross as she retreated to the privacy of the pool house to take Remy's call. Poor form, but the compulsion to answer was stronger than her will to be imminently professional, and she couldn't control it. Horrifying. Bad Maggie. "Hi."

"You answered. Am I wrong to assume that's a good sign?"

"Unfortunately, yes. Evan Hobbes went off a cliff at a party, but we can't call it yet. Crime scene is just wrapping up and Weil is handling the autopsy. Are you boarding yet?"

"My flight was canceled, so I rebooked for tomorrow. On my way home now. Sounds like I don't have a prayer of seeing you."

"It's unlikely." Nolan saw the patio door slide open. Seth Lehman stepped out unsteadily, a drink in his right hand, which was bandaged. Interesting. He'd arrived a half-hour ago and darted straight into the house, never even glancing at them or the grim carnival despoiling his sister's beautiful yard. She and Al had given the grieving siblings some private time, but it looked like he was ready to talk. "Sorry, I have to go."

"Good luck, Maggie. Keep me posted."

"I will." She signed off and looked around the pool house. It was as beautiful and richly textured as the main house, with the same sense of care and permanence, which made her both jealous and

embarrassed. She didn't even have any pictures on her walls. Yes, she
had global trinkets from her life as a military brat abroad, but they
signified nothing more than a transient childhood. The only meaningful thing was a dedicated table that held Max's ashes, photos, and
the vase of flowers she always kept fresh. A dead man was the only
life in her house. Pathetic.

Maybe if she made an attempt to personalize her space, she would
at least like where she lived, even if it was an inglorious mutt she
didn't own. It might give her and the house a little self-esteem.

Crawford appeared in the doorway, interrupting her elegiac me-
anderings. He rocked back on his heels, taking in the pool house ap-
preciatively. "Some news?"

"No, just Remy checking in about the case," she admitted in the
new spirit of transparency.

"Lucky bastard is on his way out of town, otherwise he would
have been up next instead of us."

"His flight was canceled."

"So maybe he wants to take this case so we can go home and soak
our feet in honey."

That seemed oddly specific, but Nolan definitely didn't want to
pursue it further. "I think he'd rather walk to New Orleans."

He gestured toward the closed gate at the end of the driveway.
"News vans are crawling all over. The patrols are keeping them back,
but the bastards will be planted here long after we leave, waiting to
ambush Essie Baum."

Nolan reflected on the hard, cruel fact that surviving victims of
an untimely death, whether accidental or intentional, often ended
up prisoners in their homes. It wasn't fair. "What about the blood?"

"They found more, deeper in the hedge. Said it looked like a spray
pattern. There were quite a few broken branches, too, like somebody
took a dive. They found hair and fibers, too."

"It wouldn't be the first time a drunk stumbled into the bushes at a party."

"The spray pattern sounds like somebody socked him in the face. And Seth Lehman's hand is bandaged. Let's go talk to him. He looks like he could use a friend. Or a pharmaceutical."

Chapter Twenty-One

IN HALF AN HOUR, DAPHNA HAD sketched a mental portrait of Officer Shannon Birchard's life. She was a single mother juggling a demanding, emotionally draining job, a myriad of parental obligations, and the associated financial challenges. A good mom who had no support structure in her life and worried constantly; still young, but aging quickly. Single mothers couldn't afford preventative skin care.

Daphna recoiled suddenly from the legend she'd conjured. Speculating about the hardships of this stranger didn't make her feel content; in fact, it made her feel anxious and uncertain. Inexplicably, she wanted to rewrite the whole story so it had a happy ending: Shannon Birchard was married to a successful man who was devoted to her and the children. He bought roses for birthdays and anniversaries and sometimes for no reason at all. They had regular date nights and never fought. The children were well-adjusted and intelligent and went to a good school. A prep school, maybe Harvard-Westlake. Their future was shining brightly on a limitless horizon.

She felt an unaccustomed infusion of warmth fill her soul. It was so strange—her lifelong psychological safety net of negative transference was fraying, which should have catalyzed a monumental crisis. Instead, it ushered in new and wondrous feelings.

How could her psyche transform so profoundly from one day to the next? How was that even possible? The only thing that had changed was Seth's reappearance in her life—it was the obvious explanation. He'd not only shifted her inner contours, but the terrain of her future. He loved her unconditionally, and she believed she could trust him without reservation. What she'd always been missing.

Or could she trust him? She'd sacrificed too much and been hurt too many times for blind devotion to come easily. If she let herself go and he betrayed her, she might never recover. But if she didn't embrace the possibility of rebirth, she might never find the opportunity again. The quandary was distressing.

"Are you alright, Ms. Love?"

"Yes. Sorry, I'm just nervy. This situation . . . it was a shock, and on top of everything else."

"I understand. I see too much of this kind of thing and it's always very disturbing."

"I'm grateful for your time, Officer Birchard. I hope I'm not overreacting, but Amber Harrison frightened both of us." Amber Harrison had also obviously trusted Seth once, and she was a train wreck.

"It wasn't an overreaction at all, Ms. Love. It was smart to call, and to record the encounter. You and Mr. Lehman were clearly threatened. Several residents in the building called in reports of the disturbance, too. We'll have a word with Ms. Harrison. I don't think she'll be bothering you again."

"And if she does?"

"Regardless, I recommend a restraining order."

"Which is just a piece of paper."

"True, but it's an official record of hostile behavior, and if she violates it, you have legal recourse. Please call your lawyer and Mr.

Lehman should do so as well, as soon as possible. I know it's a terrible time for him, but it's important."

"Thank you very much, Officer Birchard."

"I'm here to help." She offered her card and stood. "I'm sorry for your troubles. Call anytime if you have further concerns. We take domestic incidents very seriously—they can escalate quickly. Please be vigilant, both of you."

"We absolutely will."

"Have Mr. Lehman call me for a follow-up interview when things settle down for him. And please pass along my condolences on the death of his friend."

"I'll do that." Daphna walked her to the door. "Do you have children, Officer?"

Her pretty, prematurely aging face lit with maternal pride. "I do. A girl and a boy."

"How old are they, if you don't mind me asking?"

"Not at all, that's kind of you. They're eight and ten, and huge fans of yours. So am I." She blushed. "Obviously, I won't tell them I met you."

A smile bloomed on Daphna's face. "You don't have to tell them *how* you met me. Would they like an autograph?"

"Ms. Love, it would make their year. Mine, too."

Chapter Twenty-Two

AS NOLAN AND CRAWFORD APPROACHED LEHMAN, she noted that his complexion had a bilious cast, and his eyes were vacant. Not the same callous, arrogant vacancy she'd seen in Bristol Farms, but the thousand-yard stare of a shock victim. Even when he recognized her—a bizarre coincidence that should have elicited at least a flicker of emotion—he didn't visibly react. Zombies were more expressive.

"Detective Nolan. This is very strange, seeing you here."

"It is. Mr. Lehman, this is my partner, Detective Crawford. We're very sorry for your loss."

He sank into a patio chair and drained whatever dark liquid was in his glass. Not straight Coke, Nolan was certain of that.

"Thank you. God, I can't believe Evan is gone."

"What happened to your hand?"

He cringed sheepishly. "I punched a wall."

Or Hobbes's face. He clearly had a temper.

"It was stupid. Embarrassing. I've been under a lot of stress."

"Your sister said you were looking after Mr. Hobbes last night at the party."

"Trying to, but he was totally in the bag. Evan had cut way back on the alcohol months ago, but that fucking deepfake was killing him." He wiped his mouth. "Shit. Bad choice of words."

"He had an issue?"

"He was a life-of-the-party guy, and overindulged sometimes. I wouldn't categorize it as an issue."

Nolan would, but her opinion didn't matter.

"Do you think suicide is a possibility?" Crawford asked.

"If I'd been worried about that, I wouldn't have left him. I wouldn't have left him if I'd thought he might fall off a cliff, either."

"You believe that's what happened?"

"Of course. He was stoned and drunk and obsessed with those stupid agave plants. Like you don't see them everywhere in LA. He kept wandering out to look at them."

Nolan caught Al's look and nodded. "You were out there by the cliff with him?"

"Yeah. I dragged him back to the party a few times, and he finally forgot about them. At least I thought he did."

"Was anybody else out there?"

"No. It was too cold last night for ocean- and stargazing."

"You said you dragged him. Was he resistant or combative when you were trying to redirect him?"

"Figure of speech. I guess you have to take everything at face value in your line of work."

Nolan tried unsuccessfully to keep the irritation out of her voice. "Yes, we do."

"Evan was high-strung—charismatic, I'd call it—but never combative. He was a lamb, especially when he was stoned."

"What time did you leave?"

"Around midnight. I was bored and exhausted." He clasped his hands at his chin and bowed his head like a penitent. "If I'd stayed . . ."

His voice fizzled away, leaving his wish for twenty-twenty hindsight understood but unspoken.

Nolan scribbled that addition to the timeline in her notebook. "What was Mr. Hobbes doing the last time you saw him?"

"Chatting with people. It was a party."

She added *dickhead* to her notes. Which was highly biased and probably unfair. He was having a really bad day. "Had he been arguing with anyone?"

"Not that I saw. Like I said, he was a lamb, and the party last night was friends and colleagues. Everyone was supportive of Evan. We all knew he was deepfaked." He deflated with a sigh. "Why do you think he was combative or arguing with somebody?"

"Because we found some evidence that suggests he may have been in a physical confrontation."

"Like what?"

"Bruises on his neck. Did you notice any?"

"No. If you fall off a cliff, you're going to have bruises, right?"

Nolan underlined *dickhead* twice, leaving room for more underscoring if necessary. "Can you think of anyone who may have wanted to harm him?"

"You can't seriously be considering homicide."

"We haven't eliminated the possibility."

Lehman gazed into his empty glass morosely. "The person who posted that video wanted to harm him."

"We're looking into that. Anybody else?"

He finally showed some cognizance, and emotion in the form of disgust. "Yesterday, my boss and I had a damage control meeting about the video. Essentially, she said Evan would be better off dead, and so would the agency. She's always spewing outrageous statements for the shock value, it's her signature personality trait. She's said worse, but I thought I should tell you anyhow. I have it recorded on my phone."

"Let's hear it."

Lehman cued up the recording and played the offensive snippet.

"Your boss's name?" Crawford asked tightly.

"Rebecca Wodehouse. Wodehouse International Talent."

If Rebecca Wodehouse had said worse, Nolan wanted to hear it. "Why would she say it was better for the agency if Evan Hobbes was dead? That doesn't make sense. He made money for her."

Lehman shrugged. "I don't think the agency is doing well, and that video was a death knell, at least in her eyes. Maybe she thought a tragedy would improve her bottom line with all the press coverage. But who knows how that woman's mind works? I'm sure she wasn't serious about it."

"Normal people don't say things like that."

"She's not normal."

"She was at the party?"

"I never saw her, but Essie said she was, and left before I got here."

"Do you think she's capable of killing?"

He considered the question gravely. "She's a Krav Maga brown belt; she's definitely capable of killing, at least physically. Mentally? I don't know."

"Why did you record that particular conversation?" Crawford asked.

The question caught him off guard, and he shifted uncomfortably in his chair. "I record all of our private conversations."

"Why?"

"We don't have a good relationship. I worry about what she might do if I piss her off."

Nolan was having trouble keeping her expression impassive. She noticed Al was struggling, too. "You're painting a picture of a very unstable person."

"That's why I quit this morning. The comments about Evan were the end for me. Look, I'm out of my head and painting a picture of a madwoman. That's probably not the fairest representation."

"Sounds fair to me," Crawford remarked sharply.

"But if she left the party before I arrived, she couldn't have killed him."

"You don't know for certain that she left before you arrived. Or came back to the party after you'd gone home."

"Well, no. I don't."

A strange keening sound suddenly emanated from the house, rising in pitch until it swelled into a wail of agony. They were all on their feet when Essie Baum lurched out onto the patio and collapsed.

"David is dead. Murdered."

Chapter Twenty-Three

SAM HAD GIVEN UP ALL HOPE of sleep after the tremors. They were too reminiscent of the concussion of a distant bomb, and none of his recently acquired coping skills could override the adrenaline mania of fight or flight. Therapy *had* kept him from a full-blown, ravening panic attack, so there was some positive news on that front.

Diversion was an important part of de-escalation, so he'd gotten up and wandered the house with intense focus and a flashlight, scouting for any new cracks in the walls. The tremors hadn't scrambled his foundation, at least structurally. He'd stretched and gone for a pre-dawn jog through his Mar Vista neighborhood. He'd showered and fried eggs he couldn't eat and brewed coffee he couldn't drink.

As the rising sun washed the sky with pastels, he'd raked fiery red, sweet gum leaves off his lawn—one of LA's few purveyors of autumn color. Had the neighbors been watching him, speculating about the disfigured hermit doing lawn work at sunrise? It would be something to talk about at the next cocktail party.

Hours later, Sam was still wired for disaster, but too drained to do anything else. Except water the persimmon. He put the hose at the base in sorry recompense for the summer's neglect, but he was way too late. The fruit had already dropped before ripening, which the omniscient internet said was a sign of underwatering. He could almost hear Yuki excoriating him.

He'd never had the heart—or maybe the guts—to tell her he hated the cloying taste of persimmons. Every autumn, they would show up in salads, sauces, and baked goods; and he always made appreciative sounds while stifling his gag reflex. Now, he'd give anything to have to choke one down to make her happy.

He saw Melody's pea-green Beetle pull up to the curb. An unexpected but welcome surprise. She bounced out with a bakery box and waved. He had to admire her fuzzy pink sweater with a skull on the front—fashion was just full of irony. She looked great, glowing, healthy; not remotely like a relapsing addict. Shame on him.

"I found a fabulous new bakery with croissants to die for, Sam. I had to share."

"Then I'm doubly glad to see you."

"Have you been watching the news?"

"Never. Too depressing."

"There was a huge rockslide after the tremors that shut down part of the PCH this morning and there was a body in the rubble. I'm pretty sure I saw Nolan and Crawford in an aerial shot. Not a great way to spend a Sunday."

Sam thought about Maggie's abrupt departure from the golf tournament yesterday, presumably for a homicide. Too soon for the body in the rockfall. She'd had something else going on. Remy came to mind. You'd have to be sightless not to notice the frisson between them. "Maggie was saying yesterday they hadn't had a callout in a while. I'm sure they're thrilled."

She snickered, then eyed the foundering persimmon skeptically. "It's not dead, is it?"

"I hope not. How was band practice last night?"

"Fantastic. You should come sometime."

"I'd love to." Melody wasn't capable of being giddy, but she was infused with energy and exuberance. She was clearly doing something she loved. Something she was meant to do. He wished he had a touchstone like that; at least one that didn't involve weapons. "Come in, I'll make a fresh pot of coffee."

The croissants *were* to die for, and his brew had vastly improved since Melody had turned him on to Tanzanian peaberry. At his urging, she chattered happily about the band, the material they were working on, and the managers already courting them before they'd even dropped a single.

"They're all vultures," she concluded. "But a necessary evil if you want to be a working band."

"How do they know to court you if you haven't released anything yet?"

"They sat in on some sessions. We're all pros, and the rest of the band has been in the biz a lot longer than I have. They made some calls."

"That's great."

She smiled, but her verve flagged as she started picking at a callus on her finger—Sam's first clue that everything was not all sunshine and lollipops.

"Isn't it great?"

"Yeah, of course it is."

"I thought you said you're never supposed to pick at guitar calluses."

Melody dropped her hands and eyes into her lap. "You're not. Nervous habit."

"You weren't nervous before I asked about the managers. Let me guess—they know you were Roxy Codone of the notorious band Poke, which almost got you killed by a psychopath. They want to use that as a promotional gimmick."

"Something like that," she mumbled.

"If you don't want to be fan bait, Mel, don't. Roxy is long gone."

She looked up at him with emerald eyes that betrayed a latent misery beyond vulturous, opportunistic managers. "But you're worried she isn't, aren't you?"

The moment was intolerably uncomfortable. He didn't want to confess, but he couldn't lie. "I was, a little. But not because I doubted you, because I cherish our friendship. I was being stupid and selfish. And overprotective."

She started twirling her long blond hair with the finger she'd been picking at. Anxious displacement behavior. "Okay, so here's the straight dope: use Roxy Codone and get a huge promo leg up. Or refuse to exploit my past and fade off into the sunset of a record label's memories."

"It's not an either-or proposition. You're talented, and the past is the least you have to offer. Give yourself some credit."

"A lot of people have talent who don't get noticed without a salacious backstory. It's all about social media buzz, any way you can get it. Or going on some stupid TV competition. Material doesn't matter anymore. Half the musicians you know about don't even write."

"It matters to you. Is the rest of your band riding on this?"

"No. It's my decision. They're great guys and they support me a hundred percent." She let out a tremolo sigh and brightened, halfway back to her normal self. "Thanks for listening, Sam. Now it's my turn. Tell me what's going on with you."

"Straight dope?"

Her mouth quirked up a little. "Uncensored."

"You're not the only one at a career crossroad—I have three viable choices—electrical engineer, a consigliere for my friend during his political campaign, or a consultant for LAPD SWAT."

"You didn't tell me about SWAT!"

"It's kind of recent."

She didn't hesitate. "SWAT. You're not a desk guy, and politics suck, whatever side you're on."

"That easy?"

"Nothing is that easy. But I cherish our friendship, too, Sam, and I want you to be happy. You're wired to fight bad guys, and you can't switch it off just because you're back home."

It was a far more concise, rational analysis than he'd been able to manage over countless hours of agonizing. But was he really wired to fight bad guys, or just trained to do a job? Would Peter have had a better outcome as a modern warrior? "I'm overthinking this."

"That's better than underthinking things, which is what most people do."

"I'm not so sure."

She squeezed his arm and gave him a puckish smile. "Let's do something stupid and forget we're adults on the precipice of life-altering decisions."

"Go to Disneyland?"

"I was thinking Malibu. Half the town has been there gawking all morning. I feel left out."

"I'm sure there's nothing left to gawk at."

"Actually, I just want to go to Malibu Seafood and walk Corral Beach."

A Sunday drive. If he was lucky, a giant squid steak. Why not?

Chapter Twenty-Four

ESSIE'S FULL-BLOWN HYSTERIA WENT STRAIGHT through Nolan's bones and into the marrow. She thought she'd seen spontaneous grief in all its forms, but this display had dark, ugly power far beyond her experience. Essie's face was contorted in a grotesque simulacrum of a beautiful woman; her preternatural wails of agony were the sounds of a world being destroyed; an atom bomb vaporizing somebody's life.

Seth stunned her by playing against type. The callous, self-absorbed Hollywood player she'd judged so harshly transformed into a compassionate caretaker. He scooped his sister off the patio stone and rocked her in his arms, smoothing her hair and whispering in her ear until she settled enough to be carried inside. The display of love and devotion was too spontaneous to be anything but genuine. They stayed until the tranquilizer worked its magic, then slipped out unceremoniously. Seth followed them out, thanking them with poignant, sincere gratitude. It was remarkable how people could become better versions of themselves in times of crisis.

Disturbed and distracted, Nolan accelerated aggressively past the media jamboree as she and Al decamped from the Baum residence. They were finished here, and Essie and her brother had a trip to Santa

Barbara to make, a new tragedy to deal with. Their bad day had gotten a lot worse.

"Really horseshit day for that family." Crawford echoed her thoughts. "What are the odds two people in the same family, in the same time frame, get scotched?"

"Somewhere between a lightning strike and a shark attack. But both of those things happen. Scotched? You're in the Hobbes homicide camp now?"

"I've always been in Switzerland, but now I can see it from the Alps. Especially after hearing that recording. Even if she didn't kill him, Rebecca Wodehouse should be locked up on general principles."

"No kidding."

"But you're right, Mags, it doesn't make sense for somebody to whack their client, no matter what kind of money he was or wasn't bringing in. Same goes for Lehman. Maybe he's a jerk, but he's not a killer."

"I don't think so, either. As much as I want him to be. Essie never got around to that guest list. Not that I blame her."

"Hopefully, Hobbes was an accident and we won't need it. I'd rather shove pins under my fingernails than vet a hundred people plus staff."

Nolan checked her rearview mirror and saw a news van following a few cars behind. Time to practice those evasive driving maneuvers she'd spent so much time perfecting on the course, just to piss them off. Look out, Formula One.

She picked up the 10, merged into the left lane, and stomped on the pedal. Traffic was light and speed was a good way to exorcise the triple-threat demons of media, crime scene, and notification. Crawford was uncharacteristically silent; probably rendered speechless by her skills. That, or praying the rosary. Did lapsed Catholics still pray the rosary reflexively in stressful situations? She'd have to ask him later. "Call Santa Barbara, see what they have to say."

Crawford seemed grateful for the distraction. While he was on the phone for a protracted length, she enjoyed the challenge of weaving through traffic while fielding calls. Talk about distracted driving. But dangerous multitasking was an important part of being a cop, whatever your rank. It was also super fun in a subliminally self-destructive way, and playing footsie with your mortality was another important part of being a cop. At least that was her take.

Otto Weil would perform the autopsy tonight; Ike, LAPD's resident computer geek, had gotten into Hobbes's phone; and the captain was giving an official statement in an hour and requested their presence in his office before that. Nothing from Darcy Moore or Ross. Patience might be a virtue, but it wasn't hers.

Al finally hung up as she pulled into the police parking garage. "Hollywood always brings the sauce. My life is so boring."

"At least you still have one. Dish the sauce."

"David Baum was found naked in bed at their other beach house. Shot in the back of the head twice with a small-caliber weapon."

"Who found him?"

"It was a welfare check. Essie couldn't reach him, so she called Santa Barbara. They estimate he's been dead around thirty hours or so, since Friday night sometime," Crawford recited from his notes. "A young, unidentified female was found dead outside the home. Also small caliber, but the gunshot was to the face. The mouth, more specifically."

Nolan's stomach lurched as gruesome visuals filled her mind. She'd seen it before and desperately wished she hadn't. "Murder-suicide?"

"No gun. Maybe a jealous boyfriend or an interrupted robbery. There's a laptop charger in a wall, but no computer. No other electronics were taken."

"What about cameras?"

"All security was disabled with the code Friday morning. Probably to make sure there was no footage of the girl. Sheriff Sembello thinks the place was a stag retreat."

"Based on?"

"Multiple complaints from neighbors over the years. Loud parties. Nudity on the beach. 'Young actress types' was how she put it. No calls on Friday night, though."

Nolan's heart contracted for Essie Baum. And for the girls. "So, he was a dirty dog with a casting couch love shack. How cliché. Whatever happened to Me Too?"

"Still going strong, but nothing will ever eradicate all the predators. There are too many young, hungry kids out there who would give anything for a shot."

She knew it was the sorry truth, and it incensed her. Would the human race ever improve? It seemed doubtful. "So, no linkage between Hobbes's and Baum's deaths."

Crawford shook his head. "Aside from the family connection, I don't see it. But they'll update us once they've processed things. Who called?"

"Weil. Autopsy tonight. Ike got into Hobbes's phone. No anomalies, no calls or texts to or from unusual phone numbers in the past month. The last ones he received were at five thirty this morning, from Seth Lehman, who also sent him an attachment of the press release he was planning to distribute today. And the captain—he's giving a statement in an hour. His office, pronto. Not a suggestion."

* * *

Captain Lou Mendoza was an oval man with an oval, russet-colored face that was partly from his Mexican heritage, partly from his love of whiskey. At least if you believed the gossip. He was perpetually jittery, and his plump, soft hands constantly sought out objects he could fiddle with to allay his anxiety. Today, it was a leaky fountain pen, and he seemed oblivious to the stains on his fingers that had transferred to his shirt cuffs. He wasn't remotely slovenly and would notice soon enough, which would cause more angst.

It was hard to imagine him as the fearless rebel he'd been back in his early days with LAPD, challenging policy and institutional defects with vigor. But his ambition had enabled the grinding machinery of politics to chew him up and regurgitate him as a model department apparatchik. Rebels ultimately became autocrats.

Mendoza's transformation had inspired ambivalence in the ranks. There were loyalists and there were haters, but most fell somewhere in between, the place Nolan comfortably resided. She kept her head down, did her work, and ignored the rest. The dead had no use for department politics.

"I appreciate your hard work, Detectives. I only wish there was something more equivocal I could tell the press."

"We won't have that until the autopsy tonight, sir," Crawford said apologetically. "Hopefully. As we mentioned, his body was in bad shape from the fall."

Mendoza sighed his disappointment, then dropped the fountain pen like it was a rattlesnake when he finally noticed the damage it had done. "Up-to-the minute updates, please, day or night."

"Of course, sir," Nolan assured him. "Do you want us at the presser?"

"No. Having homicide detectives present would give the wrong impression. The media wants a murder because an accident is too mundane. And we won't give it to them. Not unless that's what actually happened, and from your briefing, it doesn't look like the most obvious conclusion." He started rearranging his desk. Apparently, the photo of his wife and three children was in exactly the wrong place. "I'll wait to hear from you. Let's get this wrapped up."

Encounters with the captain never lasted long—Nolan considered it one of his stronger qualities. She and Al found an empty conference room and watched the live stream from her laptop. She had to admit Mendoza was good in front of the press—polished and grave as he delivered the message that would throw Hollywood and fans world-wide into paroxysms of grief and turmoil. Excluding the people who believed what they'd seen in the video. They would be rejoicing. Would Rebecca Wodehouse be one of them?

At this juncture, we have no reason to believe foul play had any part in Mr. Hobbes's death, but the investigation is ongoing, so I can't comment further. I assure you LAPD is working around the clock to bring this to a swift conclusion. Our thoughts and prayers go out to the family . . .

Etcetera. Mendoza wouldn't take questions, but that didn't stop the media from pummeling him with queries about the video, as if they hadn't just learned the man was dead. He let them know it wasn't LAPD's case in an urbane way that would shame any one of them with a conscience. Apparently, none of them fell into that category, because the questions didn't stop, even after he'd stepped away from the mic.

Chapter Twenty-Five

DARCY MOORE HADN'T SLEPT IN FORTY-EIGHT hours and her body needed nourishment and a stimulant that wasn't caffeinated—she'd puked up her last pot of coffee, along with some fluorescent-orange Flamin' Hot Cheetos. Not a great combo meal. Real food would be good, but a cigarette would be better. It pissed her off that she had to retreat to her car like a felon, then drive off the FBI campus just to indulge her reviled habit. At least smoking wasn't a federal offense. Yet.

She checked her computer again. The source of the Hobbes video was obscured in the fathomless labyrinth of the Tor onion router's end-to-end encryption, along with a VPN privacy bubble—virtually impenetrable, even with the world's most sophisticated tools at her disposal.

Everybody thought the FBI and the NSA had magic wands, but the truth was, their work was equal parts skill, dogged determination, and luck in the form of human error. That was a cybercriminal's greatest vulnerability. People were nothing if not fallible, and there were dozens of tiny, insignificant ways to make a fatal mistake that would de-anonymize you. A substantial portion of Cybercrimes' successes were in part the result of somebody's carelessness. All she had to do was keep poking the soft parts and wait for a fuckup. It happened all the time. If an established cryptocurrency platform could accidentally disburse $90 million to subscribers because of a glitch in their software, some low-level weenie with no life except ruining others could miss a notification that his VPN failed, or download the poisoned pill Tor update she'd sent.

As she shrugged on her jacket in preparation for the long journey to a nicotine fix, Anong glided into their cubicle with a huge takeout bag that smelled like Bangkok and heartburn. Anong meant "beautiful woman," and her birth name had been prescient. The genetic blend of her Thai mother and American father had resulted in stunning offspring, and Darcy was still crushing on her, even though she was arrow-straight and engaged to a Coast Guard officer.

"You're going home to shower?" she asked hopefully.

"Smoke break. Unless there's tom kha gai in there."

"There is, so eat with me instead. Any news?"

Darcy shook her head dispiritedly. "Our shark is way too smart to take our chum or buy child pornography on the dark web with a credit card. I'm just waiting for this guy to screw up."

Anong began unloading fragrant containers and lining them up on the desk in her methodical way. "You know what I was thinking about while I was waiting for my larb?"

"I never know what you're thinking unless you tell me."

"This video is quality work. Our guy is a pro, which means he probably won't screw up. But all of these people have Leviathan egos; think they're the next Michelangelo. And egos need to be stroked."

Darcy conceded with a shrug. "True. But not for something that could land him in prison."

"No. But he's not just an egomaniac, he's an artisan. Artisans need to perfect their craft, and that requires peer feedback. If we identify his stylistic nuances and set up a search, I bet we find his fingerprints on other deepfakes he showed off 'in the open' before he created this hideous masterpiece."

Darcy smiled diffidently. If she wasn't so besotted with Anong, she would have been jealous of her insight. "Ego is the root of all human error. That's why I didn't think of this myself."

Anong let out a chiming laugh and handed her a cardboard cup and a warm foil packet of garlicky roti. "Eat your soup before we go back to work, *teerak*."

Darcy tried not to bolt her tom kha gai and roti, which was a rigorous exercise in self-control, but she didn't want to see it again in a toilet. Meanwhile, the imperturbable Anong picked list-lessly at her larb, her expression distant. The woman never stopped thinking.

"Somebody must really hate Evan Hobbes," she finally said. "His public persona is pristine, so lovable, nobody would randomly do this to him."

"Or they might do it just because of that. Or a million other stu-pid, petty reasons that make no sense to a normal person. You have to stop looking for justification for bad behavior, because there usu-ally isn't one. Goodness isn't inherent."

Anong gave her a crestfallen look. "You're so cynical."

"And it amazes me that you're not."

She continued undeterred. "We didn't find anything that says Evan Hobbes was a bad man. But if he was and never suffered any con-sequences, the video would be good revenge. Killing him would be the ultimate revenge. Humiliate him and make him writhe before he dies."

"Wow. Remind me never to piss you off."

"I'm just an observer of human nature."

"We don't know that he was murdered. Besides, the how and why isn't our problem. We find the bad guys and let the criminal justice system and God sort it out."

"You have an interesting philosophy on life. Very compartmentalized."

"Our job is compartmentalized. Life is easier that way."

Chapter Twenty-Six

SAM RECLINED ON ONE OF MELODY'S blue-and-white-striped beach chairs, enjoying the aerobatics of keening gulls as they fought for fish in the surf and scraps of human food on the beach. Survival of the fittest in action.

Forevermore, gulls would remind him of the blood on Lenny Jesperson's boat deck and the horrific events that had transpired after that. But the ending had ultimately been a happy one, so their raucous presence didn't spoil the atmosphere of Corral Beach. Pronounced "coral," not corral, just like Rodeo Drive was pronounced "ro-day-oh," not rodeo. Diction could be tricky in LA.

It was cold and windy down here at sea level, but the air was fresh and briny and cleansing, and the sun was warm when it peeked out between the gathering banks of clouds. It was peaceful, too—there was nobody else around, not even any idealistic tourists in shorts, willing to freeze their gams and nuggets off for some California dreaming.

He glanced at Melody, who was poking at her phone. It annoyed him that she wasn't taking in the majestic scenery—Malibu had been her idea, after all—but he was happy to have the quiet of a conversational respite. He watched the languid, frothy surf tumble in and recede back to the depths with soothing regularity. It was the pulse of the earth, steady and never-changing. And what mysteries did those blue depths hold? He would never know, and that was part of the magic. Men and women had been to space countless times, but the bottom of the ocean was still an unexplored frontier.

As a kid, playing on the beach, he'd always waited for a bottle to wash up. There would be a note in it—an important, life-changing note that had traveled the currents thousands of miles to land at his feet; or a genie who would grant him three wishes. But he'd only found beer bottles, containing nothing more than the dregs of some beach party. Still, a small piece of that childish hope still lingered in his heart. He could really use three wishes at this point in his life. Actually, he only needed one, and that would be for some semblance of internal peace. Once he had that, everything else would fall into place.

"Oh my God, Sam, Evan Hobbes is dead!" Melody startled him out of his reverie and waved her phone in front of his face. "That was the body in the rockslide!"

Melody was not particularly expressive, and certainly not melodramatic. She was genuinely upset, and he said so.

"I *am* upset. I had the hugest crush on him when I was a kid." She breathed out a gloomy sigh. "He wasn't immortal after all."

"Nobody is."

"But you believe it when you're young. Remember when he'd come into Pearl Club? I almost had a meltdown every time."

Sam was as surprised as he was amused. "You fooled me. There were always celebrities at Pearl and you never paid any attention, even when you waited on them. You must have really had it for him back in the day."

Her cheeks turned a ripe shade of pink. "I had posters of him all over my bedroom, and I practiced signing my name 'Melody Hobbes' more than I practiced guitar."

Sam tried to imagine her as a besotted tween, snapping bubble-gum as she worked on perfecting her married signature. "I think it's cute. Did you ever confess your youthful obsession and ask him for an autograph for old time's sake?"

She gaped at him. "God, no!"

"Why not? I'm sure he would have loved it."

"Too humiliating. Besides, he was never at the bar, just in the dining room, usually with some guy in a suit. Ashley said it was his agent."

Ashley, the Hollywood-obsessed floor manager. She would know. "You missed an opportunity, Mel."

"I know." She scowled. "I don't think that video is real, do you?"

"I don't trust anything I see on the internet."

"I wonder what happened to him."

"We'll find out eventually. But I'm not going to bother Maggie in the middle of a case."

"Of course not." She rummaged in the cooler for another can of sparkling wine. "You're on a first-name basis with her now, what's she like?"

"She's a good golfer."

"Come on, you know what I mean."

Sam sensed a burr in her voice he'd never heard before. Jealousy? Melody had missed out on a lot when she'd summered in Chicago, so it was possible. "She's terrific, but guarded. I don't really know her much better than I did when she wanted to throw me in prison for murder."

"Her job probably makes it hard to warm up, seeing the worst in people all the time."

Sam thought that was certainly a part of it, but observing first-hand the complex Nolan family dynamics, he knew that was a component, too. "She has a self-effacing sense of humor. That surprised me a little bit."

"Just like you. Humor can be armor. Look at comedians. It seems like the better they are, the more miserable they are. Anecdotally, anyhow. Evan Hobbes died miserable, with the worst kind of pall over his head. That's sad."

"Unless the video is real, then he got what he deserved."

"I don't believe it was." She started fidgeting with the tab on her can. "Were you happy or unhappy when you almost died?"

Colloquies with Melody had a tendency to bounce around, and sometimes he had trouble following the threads. But he was always honest, maybe more with her than with himself. "I was happy because I was going home in two weeks, and Yuki was waiting for me. Make plans and God laughs."

"What about now?"

"I'm grateful to be alive. That's progress." Sam cocked a brow at her. "You seem very happy, like you got your groove back."

"It's the music. I lost it for a while, but it's like rediscovering an old friend I always went to when things sucked, which was most of the time. I know now I can't live without it. But I wonder about what's next, don't you? Like what else is waiting out there."

Sam succumbed to the temptation of a beer. The dialogue required it. "Why so introspective?"

"My teenage idol died before he hit forty. Ever since I got clean, I'm always thinking about my future like it's limitless, but it isn't. Rolf Hesse should have taught me that, but he didn't."

"Understanding you're mortal isn't necessarily a bad thing. It makes you more careful with your life."

Melody finished her bubbly and tossed the empty into the cooler. "You haven't been very careful lately, running into gunfights."

Sam was about to protest, but he didn't want to argue the finer points of her erroneous statement. Nobody ran into gunfights. "Can we talk about something lighter, like World War Three or another pandemic?"

Her sweet face crumpled in apology. "God, I'm an idiot sometimes. I'm sorry, Sam."

"Don't be, and you're not an idiot."

Melody tugged her cardigan tighter around her shoulders. It also featured a skull, this one on the left breast. A skull sweater set. They never went out of style, not with the rock 'n' roll crowd.

"It's cold, Sam, let's go."

The conversation was over, but it had left wandering footprints in his mind. What *was* in his future? He'd had a purpose-driven life for so long in the military, the civilian world seemed empty and colorless sometimes. What would a new happiness look like, feel like? He couldn't see it from Corral Beach, as serene as it was on this brisk October day.

He brushed the sand off his chair and folded it carefully. "Want to cap the day off with a hot toddy at my place?"

She gave him her cute, crooked smile, but it radiated melancholy. "I thought you'd never ask, but I'd like to have more than one. Mind if I spend the night?"

Sam looked up at the sky, now entirely blanched with clouds. Yuki had been a tarot card dabbler, and he remembered her telling him cards with clouds represented things hidden; the doubts and confusion caused by lack of clarity.

He offered his hand and pulled her up. "The sky is telling me it's a very good day to get drunk with you. And that you shouldn't drive home."

Chapter Twenty-Seven

SETH HAD NEVER LIKED DAVID, BUT he'd grown to loathe him over the years for treating his sister like chattel. Seeing him gray and dead on the steel table in the morgue hadn't softened his opinion. The gutless, soulless prick had died the way he lived, making promises he never intended to keep to naïve young starlets so he could screw them—the dead girl was unassailable evidence. But he'd ruined his last life and Essie had suffered her final humiliation at his hands.

Only she didn't see it that way, and she was tearing his heart to pieces. He kept glancing at her as he sped down the 101 toward LA, just to make sure she was still breathing. Her tears had dried up an hour ago, and she was basically catatonic. He'd had to take away her bottle of Ativan so she didn't self-medicate into a coma. That had been an ugly scene that he would probably replay in his mind for the rest of his life.

"Ess, are you . . ." Okay? No, she wasn't fucking okay. "Why don't you come stay with me tonight?"

She rolled her head languorously to look at him with tranquilized eyes. "I really did love him."

"I know, Ess."

"We had so many good times, back when he was still working his way up. He used to be wonderful."

"That's what you have to remember. We'll go to my place, and you can tell me some stories."

"No. I want to go home. To Beverly Hills, not Malibu. That's the last place we were happy."

That was more than he could say for a lot of people he knew who lived in Beverly Hills. Good zip codes didn't guarantee a lifetime of contentment, although Seth was going to be very content spending time there with Daphna at the home she'd just purchased. "Then I'll stay with you there."

"I want to be with my friends."

Seth wasn't insulted by the rejection. He got it. Her girlfriends knew the rub, and they would circle the wagons, and concurrently keep her from an accidental overdose, which was his concern at the moment.

"The detectives are coming there for David's computer. And Becca will be there soon."

That was a bombshell that made his stomach roil. When the fuck had she called? Maybe when Essie was in the bathroom at the coroner's after seeing David's body. But Becca wasn't his problem anymore. The lawsuit would be, but he and Daphna would handle it. Which reminded him, he needed to call his lawyer—ask him about a restraining order against Amber, warn him about Becca, have him set up an LLC—Seth Lehman Talent sounded good—and draw up a contract for Daphna to sign. His life was imploding and expanding at the same time. He just had to keep his shit together and get through this wrinkle in his timeline, just like a beleaguered movie hero. "Disney needs to be informed, Ess. Can I call them for you?"

She bobbed her head and turned to stare out the window. "Yes, please. Will you come over tomorrow afternoon and help me with the arrangements? David wanted to be cremated and his ashes interred at Forest Lawn. We have plots there."

Seth didn't want his sister to be buried next to her primordial scum husband, but it wasn't a good time to bring that up. Hopefully, she'd eventually come to that conclusion on her own. "Of course, whatever you need."

"Maybe you could help me write the obituary, too."

David Michael Baum was an irredeemable pig dog . . . no, that's an insult to pigs and dogs. David Michael Baum was an amoral, reprehensible golem, universally hated by anyone who had to suffer his company, and he should have been shot in the head a long time ago . . .

"Maybe your girlfriends can help you with that. I don't know that I could find the right words."

She reached over and put her cold, cold hand on his shoulder. "I wasn't honest with you before. You're right, Becca and I are together."

Seth almost veered off the road, but he shouldn't have been jolted by the confirmation of what he'd already suspected. What was that psycho scheming? It had to be something about money, there was nothing else in her wicked little world. She'd used him to get to Essie and David, and now she was using Essie, who was more vulnerable than ever. He was going to make that deranged bitch suffer . . .

"Say something, Seth."

"Sorry, you just caught me off guard."

"Are you upset?"

Hell yes, he was upset. Furious. Disgusted. "It's okay, Ess. Thanks for telling me. And I need to be honest with you, too. Daphna and I reconnected last night. We're keeping it on the down-low for now, but we're together as a couple, and I'm going to represent her."

"That's wonderful," she slurred. "Becca will be thrilled."

Becca, Becca, fucking Becca. "No, she won't, because I quit this morning."

"Seth! Why?"

He had to get his sweet, naïve, trusting sister's mind right. Plant the seeds of truth and let them germinate. Essie had no idea who and what she was dealing with. "Becca said some really horrible things about Evan, and about me, and then threatened to fire me. I had to make a preemptive move, but I didn't know at the time . . . I didn't know it would be so complicated. There's going to be a lawsuit, and it won't be pleasant. I'm really sorry."

She attempted to pound her fist on the console, but it was an uncoordinated maneuver. "How could she do this to me?"

"It doesn't have anything to do with you, it's just business. We hate each other, we always have, and the bough was going to break eventually. Put it out of your mind, it's the last thing you should be worrying about."

"There will be no lawsuit, I won't let that happen," she said with groggy petulance. "I have power. Leverage."

Seth was astounded by the words, so absurd coming out of her mouth. She was an art history major, for God's sake. She'd spent her senior year running around Italy in Birkenstocks, drinking espresso and going to cathedrals and museums. Not exactly meek, but definitely mild.

He thought about her leverage: *sue my brother, and I won't put a dime into your business.* He doubted her relationship with Becca factored into it at all, because it was just one of many retaliatory salvos against David. No, her leverage came from pure family loyalty, which touched him in a deep part of his heart that had been dormant for most of his life. His entire life?

But as tempting as her offer was, he couldn't let it happen, because Becca would turn it around on her, just to hurt them both. *Did you know I've been fucking your brother? Did he tell you* that?

"No, Ess, please don't bring it up. This is a problem between Becca and me, and I'll take care of it. I shouldn't have even mentioned it."

"I can do whatever I want now. Let me handle it."

He wiped at the film of flop sweat that had erupted on his upper lip, but it was a Sisyphian endeavor. Life's dominoes were tumbling toward irreparable disaster. "Let me talk to Becca about this first. Please. I'm sure we can come to a civil agreement. No reason to burn bridges, especially now."

Essie's shoulders slumped in unison with a sigh. "I suppose you're right."

"I am, believe me. You need to focus on you. Nothing else. And please don't say anything to her about me and Daphna. It could affect the lawsuit." He doubted that, but it sounded good. The less Becca knew about his personal life, the better.

"Okay."

Seth took a deep, quivering breath and flicked his eyes in her direction before returning them to the road, because he was pushing a hundred and ten miles per hour. Although flying into the ditch didn't seem like such a horrible idea anymore. Shit. She was crying again.

"Ess?"

"We need to make arrangements for Evan, too. We're his family, he doesn't have anybody else."

"I'll take care of everything. Rest now. We'll be home soon."

She leaned back in her seat and closed her eyes. "I've always liked Daphna. You two belong together, you always have. I'm happy for both of you."

Seth blinked away the unexpected sting in his eyes and took Essie's hand; the kind and loving and nonjudgmental hand that had always been there for her selfish, shitty little brother, no questions asked. He had to step up, do better. "Ess, it's my turn to help you."

She whispered something incoherent then fell asleep as his phone erupted. LAPD had just released the news that Evan was dead. If he could be any animal right now, he would be a bear so he could hibernate until spring. Or a tiger, so he could rip Becca's throat out, then eat her.

Chapter Twenty-Eight

WILL CORRIGAN WAS SITTING IN THE den of his tiny house, staring at the earring in the evidence bag that had the potential to make his life better, or completely destroy it. Through the plastic, he rubbed his thumb across the large diamond he'd learned was set in the highest-quality platinum from the hallmark on the back. He'd spent a lot of time online, surreptitiously researching fine jewelry and how much he could get for it. It was a substantial amount, enough to pay off some bills. Enough to make things a lot easier when Baby Girl finally came into the world.

He kept telling himself nobody would ever know. In a home invasion, things got stolen. A quick trip to Vegas and he could come back with some cash in hand, scot-free. But *he* knew, and God knew, and his actions sickened him to the core, to the point where he couldn't eat or sleep. Milly thought it was because he'd once again been the first responder to an ugly scene—she knew about his nightmares and struggles after Clarence Ruehl better than anybody.

He was a devout man, but the devil had found him anyhow. He'd never stolen anything in his life, or even committed the most venial sin, but he'd stepped over a very bad line, and his fallen soul was shriveling with each passing hour.

"Will?"

He shoved the bag in his pocket and busied himself with some papers. "Hi, hon, what's up?"

"How are you doing?"

He forced a smile. "I'm doing okay."

"If you want to talk about it, I'm here, you know."

Why did women always want to talk about things? "I know. Thanks."

Milly folded her arms across her burgeoning breasts. "I've been thinking. I like Aloe."

His high school sweetheart, wife, and soon-to-be mother of his child smiled her glorious, sunrise smile, and Will felt like the lowliest amoeba on the planet. God had blessed him with this excellent woman and a career as a trusted law enforcement officer, and here he was, strategizing about how to fence stolen property in Vegas. "Really?"

"Yes, really." She walked over and sat on his lap, guiding his hands to her pregnant belly, just beginning to swell into something noticeable. "Let's start today. I'll go get the paint."

Will wrapped his arms around her and held her close, caressing the bump that would soon be a living, breathing person. A person who deserved to be proud of her daddy, just like Milly deserved to be proud of her husband. "I'll get the paint. I have to stop by the office anyhow."

"But it's your day off."

"I just have to file some paperwork," he lied.

She kissed him loudly on the cheek. "Don't be too long."

"I'll be back before you know it." Unemployed and disgraced, with a couple felony charges hanging over his head. This was going to kill her, but he realized now that he didn't have a choice. He'd fallen hard, but it wasn't too late to salvage a piece of who he'd been before a diamond had caught his eye.

* * *

Will was drenched in his bad sweat when he sat down across from Sheriff Sembello; another excellent woman he'd betrayed.

"Are you okay, Will?"

"No. I'm not." He let out a shaky breath and pushed a paper across her desk, along with the earring. "That's my resignation. I'm so sorry, Sheriff."

She fixed him with dark, startled eyes, then picked up the bag and examined it. "What is this?"

"From the Baum crime scene. It was on the floor of the bedroom where I found him. It was the worst decision of my life, and I don't deserve to be an officer. I stole, and I tampered with evidence, and I'm ready to accept the consequences."

She leaned back in her chair, and her scrutiny made his cheeks burn with shame. "But you're returning it."

"I'm hoping to make things right. I know they won't ever be right here on Earth, but I pray they will be with God."

She placed it in her desk drawer. "I'll turn it over to Detective Wyler."

Will looked down at his hands curled in his lap. Hands that belonged in cuffs. He would never be able to look Jenny in the eye again. Or anybody else on the force. A comfortable, happy life reduced to ashes of greed. He and Milly couldn't stay here, that much was certain. Life as a carpenter had been a nebulous imagining of the future, but now it was a necessity. "I hope it helps."

"I do, too. Right now, they're at an impasse, and there are two families that deserve answers."

He hadn't even thought about denying justice to the families of

David Baum and Kira Tanner until now. Every crime, small or large, resonated far beyond the scope of the act, and it destroyed people and their lives. It was far worse when there was no closure. Another violation of his oath, another black mark on his dying soul. "I'm sorry," he repeated with an agony that had lodged deep into his marrow and would be with him always.

He watched despondently as Sheriff Sembello stood and paced tight circles by the window that overlooked Calle Real. Real Street. Yep, he was on real street, alright.

"I'm extremely disappointed, Will," she finally said. "More than that, I'm shocked. But the fact that you came to me isn't a surprise. You're a good man. And a good cop."

"I used to be. I did an unforgivable thing."

"Did you conceal evidence with an intent to change the outcome of the investigation?"

"No, of course not, ma'am. It just . . . happened. I don't even know how I got to that place."

She sat down again and gazed over his shoulder as she drummed her fingers on the desktop. "I know you've had some issues with trauma in the past. You clearly weren't in a good frame of mind."

"I wasn't. But that's no excuse."

"I wonder. How's Milly?"

Will was taken aback by the question. "Uh . . . she's great, thanks for asking. We were going to start painting the nursery, but when I tell her what I did . . ." His voice suffered sudden death.

"I think she would be proud that you're here now. Humans make mistakes; sometimes bad ones. If mistakes defined our character, we'd all be in trouble. Whether or not you tell Milly is your decision."

"I . . . I don't understand."

"I want you to take a week off and think about why you became a cop; and if you still want to be one. Go home and paint your nursery and hug your wife. She needs you, and so does your baby. Not everybody deserves a second chance, but it's my judgment that you do. So does your family."

"But—"

"Get out of here before I change my mind, Will."

Chapter Twenty-Nine

EVAN IS DEAD. GONE FOREVER.

Daphna had done twenty laps in her pool, but it hadn't changed reality. If she did forty more, it still wouldn't change. Evan had definitely never been a friend, but he had been a colleague, and Hollywood was, at its heart, a very small town. The shocking, sudden death of one of your own hit everyone in the community hard.

His fans were equally stricken, flooding social media with outpourings of sorrow; already making the pilgrimage to his star on the Walk of Fame to leave flowers and stuffed animals. Candlelight vigils were being planned. And sadly, concomitant to modern attention spans, he would be forgotten in a week by all but the most stalwart devotees, because there would be some other shocker to capture their attention. The media would move on in less time.

She stood on the pool deck and watched the droplets of water she was shedding. They spread on the stone, briefly darkening it before evaporating under the gaze of the sun. In the lurid fog that followed death, she saw every drop as a life, disappearing before her eyes. Those capsules of water were her; they were everyone. They would all disappear eventually, it was just a matter of when.

She toweled off and sank into a chaise. She had to focus on something more positive, and her future came to mind—framed not just by success, but by freedom. Gone was the baggage of desolation; gone was the ache that could only be alleviated by imagining emptiness in others. Seth had banished those bad things, just like that. And if he was an instrument of her liberation, she couldn't live without him, could she? It was all a matter of trust at this point, which would be hard to marshal, because her mother was still a relentless presence in her life—maybe even more so after her death. The wounds she'd inflicted wouldn't close; her past words wouldn't be silenced.

You're both too young to destroy your lives, Daphna. You have such bright futures, and there's plenty of time to have children. Trust me, once it's over, you'll thank me.

Not only was marriage a business arrangement, children ruined your life. Unless they became rich and famous. Then they were useful, because you could move to a mansion in Palm Beach and drink yourself into an early grave on their dime. Her mother's last thought had probably been how fortunate it was that she hadn't aborted Daphna, too.

Despair and loneliness were seeping back in as she thought of her and Seth's child getting sucked up into a tube and drained into a biohazard container. *Trust me, once it's over, you'll thank me.*

Nauseated and trembling, she grasped for the lifeline of her phone. Finally, *finally,* there was a message from Seth. He answered immediately when she called back, and from the tightness in his voice, she feared some new, horrible thing had further darkened this dreadful day. "I've been so worried. What happened today?"

"It's bad, Daphna. David is dead. He was murdered."

"*What?*"

"We had to go to Santa Barbara to identify the body and talk to the police. I just got home."

She clamped a hand over her mouth and mumbled through her fingers, to herself more than Seth. "Oh, my dear God, I can't believe it. Do they know who did it?"

"No. A girl was killed, too."

So, the rumors about David Baum's beach house were true. Of course, they were. That son of a bitch. "Essie must be absolutely gutted. What can I do?"

"I don't think there's anything either of us can do. I haven't always been the best brother, Daph, and I feel so shitty. Helpless."

She caught the hitch in his voice and her heart squeezed painfully. "I'm so sorry, Seth. Where is Essie now?"

"She's at the Beverly Hills house. She wanted to go home."

"But you're staying with her tonight, right?"

"I offered, but she wants to be with her *friends.*"

Daphna frowned. "Why the sarcasm?"

"Friends meaning Becca. They're sleeping together and I know that bitch is using my sister for her money, and probably to get to me. She's evil, Daph, and I'm freaking out. I don't know what to do."

"Did you talk to Essie about it?"

"I can't now. She's a wreck. So am I."

"You're in a bad place now—the worst—but it will get better. Come here, stay with me. You shouldn't be alone."

She heard a shaky sigh. Seth was clearly at the end of his tether, and it was distressing.

"I would really like that, but I have a lot of phone calls to make. And I'm exhausted. Can you come here instead?"

"Absolutely, but I can't stay the night. I have an early breakfast with my agent tomorrow and I need to prepare. It's not going to be pleasant."

"That's okay, just seeing your face will make things better. Give me a couple hours to get some things sorted."

Daphna hesitated for a moment. Bad timing, but the question had to be asked. "Seth, does Amber have a key to your place?"

There was a brief silence; the silence of a liar, scrambling for the right answer? "She wouldn't give it back to me when I broke it off."

"Then you should get your locks changed. I called the police and they talked to her today. We have no idea how she'll react."

More silence. "Yeah."

"Bolt your door until I get there. I'll see you soon."

"Can you bring some Klonopin? I have a call in to my doctor, but it's Sunday."

"I will, Seth. Just be calm and take care of yourself until I get there." She signed off and stared out at the placid turquoise water of the pool. David was another droplet of water; another life gone. Seth was ensnared in calamity on multiple fronts, but Essie was fully entrenched in a nightmare. It was almost like somebody was trying to ruin the poor woman's life.

Chapter Thirty

NOLAN HADN'T EXPECTED GUY JOHNS TO call, because his client was dead, obviating the need for a defense attorney. She put him on speaker and she and Al listened to a lengthy monologue that was a mélange of practiced sorrow and righteous indignation. He was an actor, too, in his own milieu.

"I believe that video directly resulted in my client's tragic passing, and I am duty-bound . . . no, honor-bound, to clear his name and preserve his legacy," he concluded dramatically.

As far as Nolan knew, defense attorneys like Guy Johns didn't have any honor, but that was probably just sour grapes. They were on opposite sides of the justice fence. "I agree that the video may have set the circumstances of his death into motion, but I don't know how we can help you."

"That video is bullshit, but the FBI isn't talking. Perhaps they've been more forthright with you. And don't deny you've been in contact with Agent Moore. A good detective covers every angle, and you've proven yourself to be one."

"Our investigation has nothing to do with the veracity of that video."

"Have you determined a cause of death?"

"No, Mr. Johns, not yet."

He sighed irritably. "I'll be giving a press conference tonight. I'd appreciate any information you can give me. You know damn well people will be coming out of the woodwork, claiming to be victims so they can sue his estate. I'd like to forestall a media smearing. Evan doesn't deserve that."

What an asshole. "That is a really shitty thing to say. How do you know there aren't victims?"

"Evan's character is unimpeachable."

"Spoken like a defense attorney. Listen, Mr. Johns, the FBI will make a statement when and if it's appropriate, and LAPD will do the same. I'm sure you'll plead a compelling case for Evan Hobbes's innocence to the public without any further information. You're also good at your job. Too good, in my opinion."

Johns chuckled smugly. "Touché, Detective. Maybe I'll see you in court again soon."

Another dickhead. She hung up and looked at Al, who was pensively munching a bite-size Snickers bar.

"Honor and duty. Who said defense attorneys don't have a heart?" He tossed her a mini KitKat. He'd obviously been raiding the Halloween stash.

"Yeah, right. Why did he even call? He already has his speech written. We heard part of it."

"He wants us to tell him the video is bullshit, and how Hobbes died, so he can spin his rhetoric for maximum impact. What I can't figure out is why he's so vested in Hobbes's postmortem."

"Easy. He's sitting on a nice retainer that he wants to deplete before probate catches up with him. Or more likely, bleed what he can out of the estate. He's probably praying for lawsuits against Hobbes that he can defend."

"Your cynicism is inspiring, Mags."

Nolan checked her watch—a Baume and Mercier she'd inherited

from her maternal grandmother, who'd made caramel rolls and cherry pies and planted spectacular flower gardens just so she and Max could decimate them for bouquets whenever they were back from abroad.

The watch made her an anachronism to anybody who paid attention to her wrist, but smart watches didn't do it for her. Not when she had a Swiss beauty with a deep, emotional connection. "Ready to go to an autopsy?"

"Nothing better to do, except go home to Corinne, eat a real meal, and go to bed."

"Go for it, Al, I've got this."

"No way, Mags. Besides, 1104 Mission Road is the most peaceful place in LA."

Chapter Thirty-One

NOLAN PULLED UP TO THE REDBRICK-AND-concrete building in Boyle Heights that housed the Los Angeles County Department of Medical Examiner-Coroner. It was impressive and ironically beautiful for a temple of the dead—transitional neoclassical, Beaux Arts, or Austrian/German Secessionist, depending on what historical architecture enthusiast you spoke to.

A wind had picked up, and she could hear the gentle tones of the three hundred hand-blown glass bells of *Pentimento,* a meditative art installation in the garden area between buildings. The voices of the dead, spoken through white plastic ringers that resembled toe tags. The sound always filled her eyes.

In the lobby, an elderly woman clutching a manila envelope wept in the arms of a younger friend or relative. She'd just said good-bye to someone she had loved. This place was filled with sorrow, but also with reverence and compassion; yin and yang, the enduring truth of the universe.

A woman in scrubs led them to an autopsy suite where Otto Weil was ministering to his patient. Nolan could never shake the disturbing impression that all the scales, sinks, and stainless utensils could belong in a kitchen. Possibly the reason she didn't like to cook.

The harsh tang of chemicals combined with the lurking odor of de-composition also brought tears to her eyes, for a very different rea-son than *Pentimento*'s poignant song of human fragility. But she'd smelled much worse at crime scenes.

The doctor clicked off his recorder and offered an abstracted greeting. He was on a different plane now, where living things were of little interest. "I'm almost finished, Detectives. Come." He waved them toward the table.

Hobbes was dismantled—a truly disturbing and unnatural sight—and Weil hadn't gotten around to putting him back together yet.

All the king's horses and all the king's men . . .

"The split lip, the broken nose and jaw, they could have been from the fall," he said without preamble. "They could have also been from an assault. Difficult to say decisively. Same with this . . ." Weil stretched open Hobbes's eyelids to reveal pinpoint hemorrhages. "Petechiae is relatively common in the dead, and is not in itself diagnostic. But com-bined with the retropulsion of the base of the tongue, the fractures in the laryngeal skeleton, the ruptured venules in his brain—among other things I will detail in my report—my preliminary conclusion is that he died from both blockage of the airway and blood flow to the brain."

"Could those have been a result of the fall?" Crawford asked.

"No."

"Strangulation, then?"

"Yes. More specifically, a choke hold. Detective Nolan, you men-tioned the bruises on his neck, which would account for the blockage of blood flow. The collapsed larynx and cartilage damage accounts for the blockage of the airway. A choke hold could do both."

Nolan thought of the small footprints by the cliff, of the blood on the boxwood. *The spray pattern sounds like somebody socked him in the face.* A fight first, then a strangulation and a trip off the cliff. "Could a woman do this?"

Weil lifted a shaggy brow inquisitively. "Certainly. Manual strangulation requires a large disparity in physical strength to be effective, but choke holds don't. They're far superior if killing is on your agenda. Even a small woman with self-defense training could easily do this, especially given the blood alcohol level present in the victim. He probably lost consciousness far sooner than would be normal. He may have already been on the verge of losing consciousness from intoxication."

Self-defense. Martial arts. Krav Maga. Rebecca Wodehouse, who thought Hobbes would be better off dead. "Were there any defensive wounds?" Nolan asked.

"Impossible to tell with the multiple contusions. And the freshly dead can bleed and bruise, which complicates things. Perhaps Ross can tell you something from the fingernail scrapings."

"You said freshly dead."

"Yes. If he was deceased when he went off the cliff, it hadn't been for very long."

Chapter Thirty-Two

THEY FOUND ROSS IN HIS LAB, hovering over a microscope. Empty bottles of Mountain Dew filled a wastebasket by his desk. Old-school midnight oil.

He looked up and smiled wearily. "I was wondering when you two would show up." He wheeled away from his workbench and gestured to chairs stacked with files. "Throw that stuff on the floor and have a seat. Weil filled you in already?"

Nolan smiled back. "With meaningful and appreciated brevity."

"I'll do the same. First things first: the blood in the bushes is a match for Hobbes. Blood on the grass and bench, same. Enough that I'm pretty sure he got smacked around there, but he wasn't injured badly, because there was no blood trail from there to the cliff."

"What about the fibers?"

"Fibers from his clothing were present on the benches in the box-woods and by the cliff, along with his fingerprints. Fragments of the champagne bottle also have his fingerprints. That was a foregone conclusion at the scene."

"Right," Crawford said.

"I found a bunch of different human hairs on him, too. Exactly what you'd expect after a party, so that's a nonstarter."

Nolan narrowed her eyes. "But you have a surprise for us, I can tell by your sparkly, glassy eyes."

Ross smirked. "Mountain Dew and exhaustion. But we also found light-colored mink hairs at both locations, and we're looking for a woman with tiny feet, right?"

Nolan hated to disappoint him. "Essie Baum has a pearl mink throw on her sofa. The hairs could have come from anybody at the party who sat there. Including Hobbes."

"That's such a buzzkill, Maggie. I was thinking a femme fatale in a mink coat. Find her, case solved, à la noir."

"There still might be a femme fatale in a mink coat out there, don't lose hope."

Ross brightened. "Do you have somebody in mind?"

"We do. What about the footprints?"

"Like I told you, turf is a shit medium. The men's prints are Hobbes's size, an eleven, but his shoe soles were smooth leather, so they didn't leave any identifying tread impressions. But you were right about the woman being barefoot, Maggie—we found a couple toe-marks in the casts we made. Faint, but definitely there. Small feet, size six maybe."

"Weil mentioned fingernail scrapings."

Ross flicked through some papers. "Some skin cells that weren't his, but no blood, so he wasn't clawing at anybody. Give me a suspect and I can tell you if they match, but that's beyond weak as far as evidence goes. Everybody has all kinds of stuff under their nails they don't know about. Other than that . . . damn, I thought the mink was good. Sorry to disappoint, but there's nothing more."

"This is good, Ross," Nolan reassured him. "From the bloodwork, we know he probably got in a fight with somebody at Point A. There were no drag marks, which means he ended up at Point B of his own accord. Point B was where somebody put him in the choke hold that rendered him unconscious and possibly killed him before he went over."

Crawford sagged back in his chair and stared up at the ceiling. "Now all we have to do is interview a hundred party guests plus staff and pray we find a witness who saw him with a barefoot woman by the cliff."

Ross opened up a fresh bottle of Mountain Dew. "And I thought my job was tedious."

* * *

"Rebecca Wodehouse is looking pretty good," Crawford observed as he climbed into the car. "It's getting late, what do you want to do about her?"

"I say we catch her in the morning at the office. Nobody knows Hobbes was a homicide yet, and if we show up at her door at this hour, we'll tip our hand."

"Yeah, I agree."

Nolan glanced over at him. He was navel-gazing as he rubbed his thumbs together methodically, one of his tics that presented when he was wrangling with a theory, or pondering a new one. "What?"

"I was thinking."

"Obviously."

"Weil can't say for sure Hobbes was dead or alive when he went off the cliff. And Ross can't say for sure that those men's prints belong to him."

"Yeah, so?"

"What if he was killed in the fight in the boxwoods—accidentally or intentionally—and was carried to the cliff for a body dump? That would explain the lack of drag marks, and the lack of a blood trail, which hit me as a little odd. If a totally crocked guy is bleeding, he's not going to be meticulous about using his hankie to keep the blood off the lawn while he saunters off to his date with death. And who carries a hankie anymore?"

Nolan reoriented her thinking to sync with Al's fresh approach. "You're talking about an accomplice."

"That would be ideal. As they say, two people can keep a secret if one is dead. They're easy to sweat."

"It would have to be somebody close to the killer, and if we're looking at Wodehouse, good luck with that. From the sound of her, she probably doesn't have a real friend in the world."

"People's standards can be incredibly low. I'll call the captain so he can spend the night worrying about tomorrow's presser, then we go home and sleep on it."

"You go home, Al, I'll run background on her."

"No point until we talk to her. Maybe she has an ironclad alibi, and then you ran yourself into the ground for nothing. Get some rest, Mags. There's nothing we can do tonight, and that's a rare opportunity, so take it. If you can stir your brain with a straw, it's not much use, and we're both there."

Chapter Thirty-Three

SETH WAS MELTING INTO HIS BED, becoming one with the mattress as Daphna worked on his back. Her talents weren't just limited to the screen. In this small slice of time, the world didn't seem like the monumental shit show it actually was. Nobody was dead, and Becca and Amber had never existed. Daphna truly was a source of light, shining brightly, dispelling the chaos, and continued to inspire his maudlin inner poet. "You're amazing," he mumbled into the pillow.

"Feeling a little better?"

"I can almost forget today ever happened, so yeah. Thank you."

She was silent as she continued her magical ministrations, and he felt himself drifting into the buoyant, peaceful state that preceded sleep . . .

"I think we should get married, Seth."

Wide awake now. *Married?* Where the hell had that come from? It was a dream come true, but he didn't dare believe it. He rolled onto his back and searched her face, waiting for another deflating punch line, but her expression was sincere, her eyes imploring. "You really mean it?"

"I really mean it. I've been thinking a lot about this."

You couldn't think a lot about anything in twenty-four hours, let alone make a life-altering decision of such magnitude. It was a Goliathan leap that no sane person would make. And he was pretty sure Daphna was sane. At least in contrast to the other women in his life. "This is . . . very sudden."

"I know." She touched his cheek. "But it's a horrible time and it will save us both. We've wasted too many years as it is."

It was a lot to take in—almost too much—but why not? Marrying Daphna wouldn't be the worst life-altering decision he'd made. Far from it. "I think we should get married" wasn't exactly an impassioned proposal, but who was he to criticize her delivery? She was offering him everything he'd ever wanted, and he had to show some enthusiasm. "It's an outstanding idea! A spring wedding? Essie could plan it, nobody does events like her, and it would give her something to look forward to."

"Actually, I was thinking tomorrow."

Oh, God. Maybe she wasn't sane. Had she really just said that? No, there was no way. He wasn't processing things correctly because he was a basket case. But in times of extreme mental exhaustion, it was helpful to play along with a stress chimera and see it through. "We can't, Daphna, not when things are such a mess. It would ruin the best day of our lives. And it would be inappropriate. We have to bury the dead first."

Daphna looked inconsolably sad, and it crushed him. "I was thinking it would make things better."

He took her hands. "I love you, Daph. More than anything. But now isn't the right time for a celebration. And our wedding should and will be a celebration."

Her lips trembled. "You're right. I'm too impulsive, and you're exhausted and emotionally ragged. I shouldn't have brought it up."

"No, no, no, I'm over the moon about this, Daphna. I'm the luckiest guy in the world. We don't have to wait until spring. I just thought you'd want a big wedding."

"No. It's not anything I ever dreamed of, even as a little girl. My mother made marriage sound like a death sentence. Nothing worth celebrating."

Teenage flings didn't engender frank personal discussion over coffee and scones, so he didn't know much about her family or up-bringing. It didn't sound like it had been a particularly happy one. If she thought marriage was a death sentence, then why . . . was this some kind of a test? Shit. Her eyes were drifting. He was losing her. "It *is* worth celebrating, Daph! And we'll do it any way you want. We can elope, but we wouldn't get any wedding presents."

"All we need is each other."

Seth *was* exhausted and emotionally ragged, but his rapture allayed his misery. "That's exactly right. Let's talk more about it tomorrow and we'll make plans. I just have to go to the office in the morning to clean out my desk and face the wrath of Becca. I'm helping Essie with funeral arrangements, but not until later."

She lay down next to him and rewarded him with a soft, sweet kiss. "Perfect. I'll be finished with my meeting by then. I'll come over after that. Ten o'clock?"

"Ten o'clock."

"Go to sleep, darling. I have to leave soon."

"I'm too excited about getting married to sleep. Did you bring the Klonopin?"

She leaned over, rummaged in her purse, and shook a small hand-ful out of the bottle. "Don't take more than two tonight."

Was that on top of the Ativan he'd already purloined from Essie's stash? "Thanks, Daph. I love you."

"I love you, too, Seth. More than anything. Bolt the door after I leave."

"I will." Seth wasn't going to get out of bed for anything, but she didn't need to know that. She was obviously a worrier.

* * *

Daphna left at midnight, disappointed that they wouldn't be getting married tomorrow, but some things weren't meant to be. And it really would be inappropriate, what had she been thinking? But she was worried about Seth. He was under an unimaginable amount of stress, and not thinking clearly. The smallest thing might send him down a dark, destructive abyss.

As the elevator coasted down to the lobby, she thought about a life with Seth. Their futures had always been entwined, and it seemed as if fate had forged an inexorable path for them to walk side by side. The question now was where that path would lead them. She thought of the script she was reading and her spirits sank. Love always ended in tragedy.

She greeted the doorman named Archie, an older gentleman with a rough, sun-cured face and a nice smile. He'd been on duty when Amber had stormed the ramparts, and he'd also spoken to Officer Birchard. Security had been informed not to let that maniac through ever again, but if she still had a key, she could get into the building through the parking garage, couldn't she? Daphna asked him.

"Sure, if she has the garage code, Ms. Love."

Daphna didn't know if she did or not. "She could still get into the garage on foot, couldn't she?"

Archie folded his lips together as he considered her question earnestly. "I guess she could."

"Are there cameras?"

He hesitated. "We're installing a new system, so they're not up and running yet, but we do regular checks. I don't want you to worry about her, Ms. Love, she wouldn't try it. She's had some time to cool off. Plus, when people like her get a visit from the cops, that's a big reality check. I've seen plenty of this sort of thing."

"People like her?"

Archie shifted uncomfortably. "I don't want to speak out of turn, Ms. Love."

"I promise you anything you say is between us."

"Amber Harrison thinks she owns the world, thinks she can do whatever she wants. When she came around—it wasn't often, mind you—she always treated me like something on the bottom of her shoe. She got knocked down a few notches and I'm sure she's feeling it."

"I know the type, and it makes me sad. I'm sorry, Archie."

"You're good people, Ms. Love, nothing like her."

"Watch out for Seth, will you? Just in case."

"I promise I will, ma'am, and I'll let my relief know, he'll be here soon. And I'm on duty again tomorrow morning, so don't let it trouble you anymore."

"Thank you, I feel so much better. Have a nice night, Archie."

He grinned at her, then blushed and looked down at his feet. "You, too, Ms. Love. It's really an honor to know you. I mean, to meet you again."

"The honor is mine. Do you have children?"

"That's really flattering." He chuckled. "I have grandchildren. And all of them are crazy about you and your movies."

Chapter Thirty-Four

NOLAN SAGGED AGAINST REMY AS HE pulled her close, her guilt for knocking off before solving a murder instantly ameliorated by the relief of letting go. She could only do that with someone who understood. He knew what she'd been doing for the past twenty hours. And like Al, he also knew there was a point of diminishing returns.

"I ordered in, Maggie. Your favorite—cacio e pepe with lobster from the Bel-Air. Disparagers of seafood and cheese be damned. The Latour Montrachet is optional, but I did sample it to make sure it wasn't corked. It wasn't, in case you're interested in a glass."

Wow. Lobster again. And Montrachet. She swooned as her salivary glands outpaced anything Pavlov's dog could have mustered on his best day of begging. "Hell yes, I'm interested in all of the above, but I need to shower first. I've been at the morgue."

He hugged her tighter and sniffed her hair. "That's odd. You smell like rose petals to me. Go do what you need to do while I warm up dinner. If you fall asleep, which you should by all rights, I'll put in a feeding tube."

She laughed against his chest. What an alien feeling, having someone greet you at the door with promises of spectacular food and wine, hug you, and make a joke, all without any intimation of sex. It felt like all the makings of a real relationship, but since she'd never had one, she couldn't be sure. Besides, everybody was on their best behavior at the beginning. In a month, Remy could be drinking dinner in front of the TV while she threatened to brain him with a cast-iron skillet.

"Why are you giggling?"

"I don't giggle," she huffed in ersatz offense.

"I disagree. You *laughed* at my poor joke about the feeding tube, but then you started *giggling*. There's a difference. Care to share the source of your amusement?"

That was a hard no. "Al said you shouldn't work if you can stir your brain with a straw."

"Ah. Article 209.57 in the Homicide Special Section charter, I'm sure you've read it. It's an encumbrance sometimes, but a rule that must be followed."

Nolan felt the traitorous giggle rise up again. "I'm going to shower now."

Remy's voice followed her up the stairs. "You'll tell me why eventually."

The shower revived her, along with the gustatory promises to come. Ensconced in a thick guest robe, she entered Remy's room-sized closet. She had a few pieces of clothing here, all cheap, utilitarian things, hanging next to his wardrobe of Italian suits, summer linens, and workout gear. Seeing her own humble clothes in this exotic, strange place set a tiny seed of panic. If you started leaving pieces of yourself, you couldn't ever get them back. But that was a stupid way to think, wasn't it?

She slipped on a sweater and jeans and walked into the bedroom, half-expecting Remy to be there naked and ready to ravish her, but he wasn't. That said volumes about the man she was reluctant to trust, a man with a reputation. But she'd seen him with his sister and niece, and that kind of love and compassion belied the rumors and gossip. God, life was complicated. Why was she even trying to make sense of it?

The heady aromas of her favorite meal rose up from the kitchen, and she cleared her mind and followed her nose downstairs, where Remy had set a table with candles and flowers. He always had flowers in the house, so it wasn't anything special, meant just for her, but his care and consideration was. "This is nice. Thank you, Remy."

He measured Latour burgundy into crystal glasses and pulled out a chair for her. "You deserve to be pampered." He lifted his glass to hers. "I'll be right back with our main course."

The wine was sublime, the cacio e pepe above praise, and she indulged in too much of both. Still, she couldn't resist popping the last, succulent chunk of lobster in her mouth. "What time is your flight tomorrow?"

"Ten a.m. But after this excellent evening, I'm finding it difficult to muster any enthusiasm for the trip. You might need me to feed you until your case is solved."

Nolan smiled and set down her fork. "I'll manage. Charlotte and Serena are waiting for you."

"And you don't think you're as important as my sister and niece?"

His onyx eyes were penetrating, pinning her to her chair. He was serious. "No. Besides, you have a lot of lost time to make up. I'll be here when you get back."

He gathered their plates. "I was hoping I could convince you to join me in New Orleans, once your case is closed."

She blinked at him, which probably made her look incredibly stupid. She felt incredibly stupid, like she'd missed an obvious joke. "Why?"

"You haven't had a vacation since you started Special Section. And Charlotte and Serena ask about you all the time. You were wonderful with them after the kidnapping. They haven't forgotten it, and they never will. But the real reason is a selfish one." His smile was inscrutable. "Do I have to explain it?"

Nolan's vision fragmented, like she was looking through a kaleidoscope. Shock? Exhaustion? Both? "I don't know what to say."

"Don't say anything, just think about it. Go to bed, Maggie. Sleep. You only have a few hours before you're at it again, which might give your brain enough time to resolidify."

Nolan walked up the stairs on rubber legs, thinking she must be having delirious, auditory hallucinations. Even more disturbing was that her hallucinations involved an advancement in relations with Remy. She decided there was no point in belaboring it, because things would be normal again after her body and brain rested for a while. She wouldn't even remember this, it was all part of her delirium, and not at all wishful thinking when she was at her weakest and most vulnerable.

She woke up facedown in bed, still in her sweater and jeans. She felt Remy next to her and heard the soft, even susurration of his breathing, which immediately lulled her back to the threshold of sleep. As she transitioned from conscious to unconscious, a wildly disjointed cinema played in her mind: she was on Ladera Road in Ojai, watching olive groves being harvested. She was golfing the links with Max and her father at St Andrews in Scotland. She was a little girl marveling at the Glockenspiel on Marienplatz in Munich, holding her mother's hand. And then a projection, not a memory: she was standing with Remy outside the Acme Oyster House in New Orleans. Nothing after that, until her phone woke her up at five.

Mortified by the puddle of saliva on her pillow, she wiped her mouth and groped her way to the bathroom in the dark so she didn't wake Remy. "Al. Where are you?"

"In my kitchen, mainlining coffee. Santa Barbara called."

She flicked on the light and squinted at her reflection in the ornate mirror above the marble his-and-hers sinks. Really bad bedhead, dried drool frosting her mouth, raccoon eyes, pillow creases denting her pale face. A raving beauty if you were into horror movies. "Why?"

"They ID'd the girl. Kira Tanner, model-actress."

AKA "mattress," Nolan thought bitterly. That was the cruel moniker for the ones who weren't going to make it, but kept trying any way they could. "And?"

"Same gun killed them both, but it hasn't turned up."

"Toolmarks?"

"Don't match anything on the registry. But that poor thing, bless her soul, just shook up our case."

"How so?"

"Santa Barbara found a flash drive in the pocket of her jeans. A virtual photo album of Baum with young girls, no doubt uploaded from his missing computer. He started them out with basic headshots, model-type poses, but then they got graphic, as in pornographic. And here's the real kicker: Hobbes was in some of them, too. Not so unimpeachable after all. We've been looking at that deepfake as a random act of cruelty, but maybe it was a message. Or a warning."

Nolan braced a supporting hand against the vanity as alarm bells rang and her thoughts churned the wicked brew. "Kira Tanner was planning blackmail."

"Yeah, but she's dead, and so are Hobbes and Baum. That kind of closes the circle."

"Their killer is still alive, presumably in possession of the computer. And so is Essie Baum, who's worth a ton of money. Her brother mentioned Wodehouse might be in financial trouble. We have to look at it."

"You want her for three murders in two days? That's a stretch, no matter how crazy she is."

"They have to be connected."

"I can't see a straight line, Mags, not with two different MOs. And how would Wodehouse even know Baum was a pervert?"

Nolan dug through her toiletry kit for a hairbrush and dragged it through her snarled halo of strawberry blond. "Through her agency, maybe. Kira Tanner could be a link."

"Possibly, but Baum isn't our problem, Hobbes is. Have you heard from Darcy Moore? The deepfaker is at the top of my list of potentials."

Nolan checked her phone. "No. But I'll call her on the way to the office."

"Let's meet up at the Wodehouse agency. They open at eight, so we get there early and stake things out, see what we can see. I've got coffee, and bagels from Barney Greengrass."

As much as Nolan loved Barney Greengrass bagels, her stomach protested the thought of more food. It was still working on the lobster. "See you soon."

"Say hi to Remy for me."

Al was turning into an annoying psychic. "I'm actually at one of my other lovers' houses. Don't tell Remy." Nolan hung up on his laughter and started when she heard Remy's voice from the bedroom.

"How many other lovers do you have, Maggie?"

She stifled a giggle. What the hell was the giggling thing about? She had to get over it, it was degrading. "Four. Or five. Hard to keep track."

"I'd like to meet them. Maybe we can all go to New Orleans together."

Chapter Thirty-Five

SAM DREAMED THAT HE SHIFTED IN bed and draped his arm over Yuki like he always did when dawn's emergent light stirred his hypothalamus. Except Yuki felt different—the contours of her body were all wrong. And she smelled different—not like the expensive shampoo and soap she used.

He opened his eyes and remembered everything when he saw Melody's tangled blond hair; her shapely shoulder with the dragon tattoo; the generous rise of her bosom beneath the sheets. They'd been drunk last night, but not memory-killing drunk, and without a full complement of inhibition, something finally gave. It had only been a matter of time, and apparently, last night was the time.

As he entered a full state of wakefulness, he recalled that it had been very good—caring, loving, and genuine. For all the guilt that plagued him incessantly, it wasn't darkening his world now. Hopefully, Yuki's ghost wouldn't suddenly appear and crush his head or another part of his anatomy farther down the torso. But he didn't think her ghost would do that; her ghost would understand.

Melody mumbled groggily and rolled over, then her half-mast eyelids flew open on startled green eyes. "Oh . . . God. This happened."

"It did. A long time coming, I guess."

She started crying. Sam had never known how to console a tearful woman, and when the lachrymal glands let loose in bed, it was even more bewildering and distressing. But the one thing he had learned was to be unconditionally supportive and never ask what was wrong, so he pulled Melody close and held her. Her body was taut and un-yielding and poised for flight, which he didn't take as a good sign. "I hope it wasn't that bad."

She snorted at his pathetic and probably inappropriate attempt at levity, then buried her face in his chest, her tears fast and hot against his skin. "Did we screw things up?"

"I don't know how."

"You're my best friend, Sam. I can't lose my best friend over a hormonal, drunk roll in the hay."

"Is that how you see it? Do I need to be offended?"

She looked up and wiped her eyes. "I'm not kidding. Let's pretend this never happened."

"That would require a lobotomy."

"Stop joking, I'm serious."

"But it did happen, Mel, and I feel good about it. I wish you did, too. We didn't do anything wrong."

"Then why do I feel that way?"

"You tell me." He already knew why—she was struggling with her own bitter brand of PTSD. Her long history of abusive relationships had rewired her brain to accept culpability for anything—even things that didn't exist—but if she was forced to vocalize her unfounded guilt, she might realize how ridiculous it sounded. It was one of the tricks he'd learned from countless hours of therapy with Dr. Frolich.

"Because . . . Yuki. It hasn't been that long."

It hadn't been long since she'd died, but it had been a very long time since the relationship had. She'd left the marriage for a better sit-uation and a better man to suit her needs, he just hadn't known about it. In retrospect, he didn't blame her. "If it was too soon, it wouldn't have happened. There's no predetermined time frame for moving on, but it's important that we do, whenever it feels right. She would agree, and I'm pretty sure she'd be happy for us."

"You don't feel guilty?"

"No. And you shouldn't, either." Sam kissed her hair, which smelled like sun and coconut. "I will always be your best friend, Mel, and you'll always be mine. This doesn't change things; it only makes them better."

She squirmed in his arms. "You need to think about this."

Sam was amazed to realize that he didn't. For the first time in two agonizing years, something felt perfectly right. He'd been mired in a noxious world of lassitude and self-destruction, in limbo between Scylla and Charybdis, but he'd finally taken his first step out a door that had opened just a little. He'd always known when that happened, it would be easier to take the next step, and then the next. Suddenly, making decisions about his future didn't seem so overwhelming. Maybe this was the internal peace he'd wanted a genie to give him; the thing that would finally set him free. "I don't. Do you?"

She shook her head and softened in his arms. "No."

"Good. Let's go to Pink's for a bacon chili cheese dog later to mark a new beginning."

Her smile was tentative, reluctant to fully form. "Do you think it's pathetic that our special place is a glorified hot dog stand on La Brea?"

"Somehow it seems appropriate."

"Yeah, it kind of does. It'll be way better than a giant squid steak. Yuck."

Chapter Thirty-Six

DARCY MOORE SOUNDED MANIC AND BREATHLESS and a little giddy when she answered her phone, and Nolan knew instinctively the cyber chase was approaching some kind of climax. She wondered what it was like for her when she finally came down from the intense high of adrenaline overload after an enemy was conquered and a case was closed. Did she become as depressed and aimless as Nolan did when faced with the deadening tedium of day-to-day life?

She'd never equated her feelings with those of her brother, Sam Easton, or any warrior, back from the battlefield to grapple with grocery shopping and laundry, because it seemed like an insult. But she realized that the emotional impact was analogous—just further down on the spectrum of intensity.

"Detective, I was just about to call you. We finally have a bead on the deepfaker. In Studio City, right in our backyard."

"Great, fast work. How did you do it?"

"I'm assuming you don't want the technical answer."

"Absolutely not."

"It was a simple screwup. People with gigantic egos don't always think things through like they should. We're deploying a team now, and I'll be with them to secure the equipment. Hopefully, the press on Hobbes's death didn't send her packing, but these fuckheads are so arrogant, they usually don't bolt."

"It's a woman?"

"There's no gender inequality in cyberspace. Her name is Brianna Cornish, former honors student at Cal-Tech, computer engineering. Somebody we might have hired. Hell, we still might, depending. How is the Hobbes situation progressing?"

"Confirmed homicide. Not public knowledge yet."

"Do you have any suspects?"

"We have a serious person of interest."

"Oh, yeah, I keep forgetting that's what we're supposed to call all the aforementioned fuckheads."

Nolan smiled. Darcy Moore talked like a street cop, and her rough edges were probably frowned on in her specialized division, at least among people who didn't have flatfoot experience. It made her intensely curious about her background. Maybe they'd grab a drink sometime—no bullshit, no political correctness, just frank law enforcement talk between two women in a man's world. James Brown, look out.

"There's a backstory to this you need to know about, in case it comes up in the investigation on your end."

"Hit me."

"David Baum was murdered at his home in Santa Barbara—"

"I heard. And Hobbes bit it at one of Baum's other homes in Malibu, at some big party. Sounds like you bought yourself some more craziness, Detective Nolan."

They had a solid rapport now. No reason for titles anymore. "Maggie. And the craziness is always free in this job."

She chuckled. "Don't I know it. I also heard there was a girl and that it was probably murder-suicide."

"Kira Tanner. And no, they were both homicides. Santa Barbara found a flash drive in Tanner's pocket with pornographic photos of Baum and Hobbes with young girls. Aspiring actresses, more specifically. We're working blackmail and revenge elements now, and a possible connection between the two, but nothing's popping at the moment."

Moore was atypically silent for a few moments. "So, Hobbes was a scumbag after all. And so was the big Disney exec. That's a disappointment."

"Do you have a bio on Cornish?"

"We're still building it." Her keyboard clattered as her fingers flew. "I'll take a look at what we have so far. Hang on a couple."

Nolan stopped for gas on the outskirts of Beverly Hills while she waited. At almost seven bucks a gallon, she was glad LAPD would be picking up the tab.

"Still there, Maggie?"

"Still here."

"Got something. Cornish was a working actress in her tweens. Did a few low-budget films that got limited distribution, then fell off the radar. Don't know if they had anything to do with Hobbes, but there you go."

"She could have been a victim."

"Yeah, but it's a long drive from victim to murderer. My partner and I don't agree on this, but why do the video and ruin his career, then kill him? Assuming she could even get into the party. That's a huge risk to gild the lily."

"It doesn't feel right to me, either. Does your coverage mention whether or not she traveled to Malibu or Santa Barbara recently?"

"No. All records have her in Studio City for the past month, actively using her credit cards and phone that follow her usual pattern. I'm not seeing Kira Tanner on the list of known associates, either. But I'll let the agents in charge know. This is all a little too cozy for comfort."

"Is Rebecca Wodehouse on that list of known associates?" Nolan heard more keyboard abuse.

"Negative on that, too. I take it that's your serious person of interest. I'll make a note in the file."

"Thanks."

"Don't worry, Detective, things will get a lot clearer once I have my hands on her machine and the agents have her in an interrogation room. Did I just say interrogation? I meant interview. She's probably not your killer, but she might know who is. Let me know if you want to talk to her at any point."

"Thanks, Darcy." She heard a clamor in the background, and Darcy Moore's muffled voice directed at somebody else.

"Wheels up here, gotta run, Maggie. I'll call once we finish in Studio City. Intra-agency cooperation, right? It's a beautiful thing."

Chapter Thirty-Seven

SETH WOKE IN A STUPOR TO the strident, relentless clanging of his phone alarm. He scrabbled for it on the nightstand and squinted to bring the display into hazy focus. Five o'clock. Jesus. He'd slept through it by almost fifteen minutes. Only the dead could sleep through such an obnoxious alarm tone for that long. Maybe he *was* dead. He felt like it.

He silenced the phone and tried to get out of bed, but his limbs were leaden; unmovable. How many tranqs had he taken on top of the whiskey? Clearly too many—the last thing he remembered was Daphna leaving, which terrified him. Had he popped more pills in his pharmaceutically induced sleep? Isn't that what had happened to Elvis? And he'd been worried about *Essie* overdosing.

The urgency of his bladder finally propelled him out of bed and he tottered unsteadily to the bathroom, every step flaying his brain with white-hot pain. Tylenol didn't work for shit—ask any medical professional—and normally, he'd take an Ativan or a Xanax to smooth the edges of a hangover, but not this morning. Oh, hell no.

After a marathon piss and a hot shower, he felt partially human again, but still fuzzy and tired. He skipped the shave and suit, dressing instead in beat-up jeans and a UCLA sweatshirt. A final fuck you to Becca, who took grooming and wardrobe far more seriously than her job. Now he just had to work on a strategy to get that vile bitch the hell away from his sister.

His phone was bloated with texts and messages from her, none of which he listened to or read. He didn't have to. She was engorged with rage, and ignoring her only threw more gas on the fire. The longer he was silent, the more pissed off she would get, hopefully to the point of self-destruction. Or at the very least a psychotic break. He'd just stroll in when the agency opened, smug as you please, and try not to sustain any injuries while he cleaned out his desk.

The scenario made him indescribably happy. He was Teflon now, and she was helpless. In fact, maybe he'd just go back to bed and not show up at all. Daphna would be here at ten and they had a wedding to plan; there wasn't anything in his office he couldn't live without.

While coffee brewed, he transferred some files from his phone to his computer and backed them up on an external drive. You couldn't be too careful when you had a lawsuit in your future. Then he pulled up the *Los Angeles Times* and read the stories on Evan and David. The hacks were frothing at the mouth with potential for scandal. They rejected the notion of coincidence and conjectured about possible connections. Such inflammatory bullshit, there obviously was no connection. He hoped Essie would be staying away from the news for a while.

She wouldn't be up for hours . . . oh, God, was Becca sleeping next to her right now? Or had Essie confronted her against his advice? The thoughts congealed his blood. He composed a supportive, loving text to her and asked for a callback when she needed him. Before he sent it, he ruminated over sharing the phenomenal news about his forthcoming union with Daphna. Why not tell her? It might leaven this desolate time in her life a little. Yeah, she'd be happy for them. And if Becca saw it, oh well. It was going to come out eventually.

Next, he wrote a borderline saccharine text to Daphna. She was his fiancée after all. It still didn't seem real. Maybe they *should* get married right away, before any misgivings could subvert her thoughts. No one had to know about it until the time was right. What happened in Vegas stayed in Vegas, at least if you were smart about it. The honeymoon was the best part of matrimony anyhow, and they could take their time planning it once they were husband and wife. A week at the Four Seasons on Bora-Bora, or maybe the Maldives. They had a Four Seasons *and* a Ritz-Carlton there.

After researching some possibilities, his empty stomach started complaining bitterly. Daphna's comment about smoothies was still lodged in his brain, so he instead retrieved the leftover caviar from the fridge and finished it off at the kitchen counter with the unwashed mother-of-pearl spoon still in the sink. Better to eat caviar with the proper, dirty utensil instead of a clean metal one—that would be a crime against fish eggs. It never occurred to him to wash it himself.

His phone chimed a new text, and he grinned, certain it was from Daphna. But his smile dissolved when he saw Amber's name. Dammit, things had been too crazy yesterday, he'd never even thought about blocking her number. His finger hovered over the screen for a long time, then against his better judgment, he opened it.

Watch TMZ. And watch your back, too. Fuckhead.

Chapter Thirty-Eight

NOLAN AND CRAWFORD WERE PARKED ACROSS the street from Wodehouse International Talent, sipping tepid coffee and gnawing on heavily schmeared bagels. Not quite accurate—he was gnawing, she was nibbling around the edges because her stomach was still turbulent.

Last night's rain had scoured the sky of clouds, making way for a burnished October sun that augured a warm, autumn day. Despite the pleasant weather, there wasn't a lot of action this early on Robertson Boulevard, and like all stakeouts, it was 99 percent boredom, which irritated her more than her surly digestion.

"What exactly are you hoping to see, Al?"

He shrugged. "Something interesting. Like Wodehouse in the middle of the street with a bullhorn, confessing to blackmail and triple murder. Or the homeless guy who used to sell his poetry at stoplights. That was on Robertson, wasn't it?"

"I only saw him on Wilshire."

"I miss him, he was a character. Always cheerful, never hustling too hard. I bought a few."

Nolan raised a brow at him. "Never figured you for a softie."

"He was offering something in exchange for a couple bucks instead of just looking for a handout. I admire initiative."

"Fair enough. How were the poems?"

"Robert Frost's estate doesn't have anything to worry about, but he made an effort. They always ended with 'Thank you for helping me on my way, have a nice day.' Then a big smiley face. I hope he got off the streets instead of dying on them."

"That's depressing."

"It was meant to be uplifting."

Nolan checked the clock. It was exactly two minutes later than the last time she'd looked. It was going to be a long morning. She scrolled through her phone for distraction—nothing pertinent to the case, but she saw a new text from Remy. She knew she shouldn't open it, but did anyhow. He'd stripped her of all self-control. His closet had taken possession of part of her wardrobe. His consuming presence had burrowed under her skin and into her thoughts like an insidious, tropical parasite. Not a great way to think about your paramour. What the hell was wrong with her?

On the way to the airport. Are you thinking about what I said, Maggie?

No, she wasn't thinking about it, because going to New Orleans was a horrible, ridiculous idea. He had family business to take care of, relationships to mend and nurture. And maybe that's why he really wanted her there—as a buffer and a diversion from difficult things. That, and sex. Nothing wrong with any of it, in her opinion. But New Orleans was still a horrible idea.

She felt Al's eyes on her and pocketed her phone. "Dry cleaning's ready to pick up."

"You're a shitty liar, but don't worry, I'm not asking."

She felt her cheeks blaze; the heat spreading down her neck. So busted. Again. "Remy asked me to meet him in New Orleans," she blurted out. God, he'd taken away her discretion and privacy, too.

"Yeah? If he asked me, I'd go. Take a vacation, relax, enjoy Crescent City. See where things go. It's not a summit on nuclear nonaggression, Mags."

He made it sound so simple. But nothing ever was, especially when it came to matters of the heart. "I can't believe I even brought it up. Sorry, I didn't mean to drag you into this."

"That's what friends are for. And after eighty years of marriage, I consider myself something of an expert on relationships."

Nolan felt her diaphragm tighten again with the mysterious giggling affliction. Maybe she should see a doctor. "Corinne would kill you if she heard that."

He smiled. "Yeah, but I know you won't say anything to her, just like you know I won't say anything to Remy. Hey, look at that." He jabbed a finger against the passenger window. "We have some action."

Finally. A smartly dressed, well-shod young woman with black, bobbed hair approached WIT and keyed open the door. She had the demeanor of a convict on the way to her execution, which spoke volumes about the workplace environment. Ten minutes later, Rebecca Wodehouse stalked through the sparkling glass doors of her eponymous agency in a swirl of cashmere and toxic energy.

You could basically write a psychological profile on any stranger, just by the set of their head, the way they moved, the expression on their face in a moment they believed was unobserved. In this case, the phrase "Hell on wheels" came to Nolan's mind, although her judgment may have been skewed by their interview with Seth Lehman, and his recording of her coolly wishing a client dead.

"Reminds me of Cruella de Vil," Crawford remarked through a mouthful of bagel. "Better clothes and hair, though."

"She has the carriage and attitude, but she's a lot prettier."

"Deadly combination. Maybe literally." He pushed his door open. "Let's take a stroll. If she comes out with the decapitated head of that poor girl, we'll be able to take her down faster."

Nolan smirked. "I'm sure Rebecca Wodehouse is a very lovely woman, just misunderstood."

They crossed the street and walked a block up Robertson past boutiques not yet open for business; a man washing the windows of an art gallery; a young woman in workout clothes being tugged along by a bossy French bulldog.

They circled back and slowed their gait as they approached WIT's granite façade. Nolan admired the potted boxwood topiaries that flanked the door, trained into obedient spirals. Not a speck of blood on them. She glanced through the window casually and saw the reception area, where the queen of the realm was gesturing viciously at her employee. "She's raging about something."

"I see that. Can't hear a damn thing, though. We'll wait for her to storm off somewhere—which you know she will in about a minute—then we go in and meet our new best friend. She obviously takes a lot of crap, so she might be willing to dish a little."

Chapter Thirty-Nine

CRAWFORD'S STRATEGY WAS A GOOD ONE. Wodehouse disappeared and the reprimanded, scarlet-faced girl sat down at the reception desk and started texting furiously. Nolan could only imagine what it said. Probably not that her boss was a lovely, misunderstood woman. She jerked her head up when they entered and stashed her phone.

"I'm sorry, we're not open yet."

Nolan badged her. "LAPD. And you are?"

The girl shrank in her chair. "Lily Suhr. This is about Evan, isn't it?" Her eyes filled with tears she tried to blink away.

"Yes. You obviously knew him."

She nodded gloomily. "I can't believe he's dead. He was so nice, so sweet."

They'd heard a lot of that, from the media and people who hadn't been aware of his well-concealed dark side. Lily obviously hadn't been a victim. Too old—she was at least twenty-four. "We'd like to ask you a few questions, if that's alright."

"Yes, of course."

"Were you at the Baums' party Saturday night?"

"Not a chance. I'm just an assistant, but I wish. I hear they have legendary parties." A few tears crawled down her cheeks. "And now David is dead, too. Murdered. That poor family, I'm sick about it. One of our agents—Evan's agent—is Essie Baum's brother," she explained.

"We know, we've spoken to Mr. Lehman and Mrs. Baum."

She wiped her eyes carefully and looked up at the ceiling. Gravity was your enemy if you were trying to keep tears at bay. "God, I feel so bad for Seth, and even more sorry for Essie. She's such a nice woman. She comes here occasionally."

"Did you know David Baum?"

"I've never met him, but everybody knows who he is."

Nolan glanced at the window washer. He probably didn't know who David Baum was. Hollywood was so egotistical.

"He was well-liked for a studio exec," she added. "Who would murder him?"

A shrill, infuriated British voice suddenly reverberated down the hall, as if in answer, at least in Nolan's suspicious, overactive imagination.

"Seth, where the fuck are you? Ten minutes, otherwise don't bother. Hope you called your lawyer, you prick."

"Ms. Wodehouse sounds very upset." Crawford stated the obvious. "Is she like this often?"

Lily looked over her shoulder, then leaned forward and whispered, "She's always angry. Especially when it comes to Seth."

Nolan had been feeling slightly guilty about prejudging Rebecca Wodehouse, but she didn't anymore. "Perhaps she's not aware that he's just lost his brother-in-law in addition to Evan Hobbes."

Lily Suhr's face turned stormy. "Oh, she knows, she's friends with the Baums. But she and Seth hate each other."

"Hate is a strong word, Ms. Suhr. Did something happen between them?"

"For one thing, Seth quit over the weekend, and I know why. TMZ just broke that he's romantically linked with Daphna Love. That would drive her insane."

"Why?"

"Because if you're an agent sleeping with a star, you're going to be representing them, and Love is a hot commodity. But for the three years I've worked here, it's always been that way between Becca and Seth. I can't believe Seth hasn't quit before now." She looked over her shoulder again, whispered again. "She's a snooty toff, always reminding us her dad was a sir or a lord or something, as if anybody cares. She makes it clear that we're not good enough for her. No one is."

They'd hit a nerve, and Nolan was surprised *she* hadn't quit. Al was clearly pleased by her candor and the direction of the conversation—he'd predicted it—and he turned on the charm in the interest of furthering trust and amity. "I've worked for a lot of people with that attitude, they're everywhere, blue blood or not. And they're all a pain in the ass. Sorry, I meant 'butt.'"

The corner of her mouth ticked up in a tiny, grateful smile. "Yes, they are. Some people feel so entitled, and it doesn't matter if they have money or not. This agency is broke, Becca just pretends it isn't. Like her pedigree is going to pay the bills." She shrugged. "Or maybe it will, I wouldn't know about her personal finances."

Nolan thought of the idiom about keeping your friends close, but your enemies closer. A stupid saying, because the safest course of action was not to make enemies in the first place. "But you know about the business finances."

She scoffed. "I'm Asian, of course I'm good with numbers, right? That's what she thinks, anyhow. So, she assigned me the daily books. I enter every dime that comes into the agency and every dime that goes out, then send the spreadsheets to the accountant each month." Her hands suddenly fluttered to her mouth in horror. "Oh my God, I shouldn't be saying this. She would kill me if she found out."

"It's okay, Ms. Suhr, whatever you say to us is confidential," Nolan reassured her. "You mentioned Ms. Wodehouse was friends with the Baums."

"Good friends with Essie, for sure. I never really got how she could hate Seth when she was close to his sister, but who knows about family dynamics?"

Nobody, Nolan thought. "What do you mean by close?"

"They went to lunch a lot, and Becca gets invited to all their parties. And all the big premieres."

A true measure of friendship, LA style. "How was Ms. Wodehouse's relationship with Mr. Hobbes?"

"She's always nice to clients. She has to be." Her eyes suddenly sparked. "You're asking a lot of questions about her."

"We ask a lot of questions about everybody who might be relevant in an investigation. It's good to get the lay of the land," Crawford said.

"But Evan's death was an accident, right? I mean, there isn't much to investigate, is there?"

"Follow-up," Crawford dodged the question. "Can you let Ms. Wodehouse know we'd like to speak with her?"

Lily Suhr seemed disappointed the dialogue was ending, and even less enthused about speaking to her boss. She nodded dolefully and put in an earbud. "Ms. Wodehouse, I'm sorry to bother you, but the police are here to see you about Evan."

Chapter Forty

REBECCA WODEHOUSE HAD TRANSFORMATIVE powers. Her endemic bile turned to charming gentility during Nolan's and Crawford's short walk down the hall to her office. She ushered them in courteously and offered them tea or coffee, which they declined with equal courtesy. Her expression approximated a combination of warmth and solemnity, but her eyes were vacuous. Nolan knew instantly she was a woman unoccupied by emotion. Either something had emptied her, or maybe she'd always been this way.

Up close, she gave the impression of a shiny, new razorblade—silver and sharp, with the ability to cut. She was coldly beautiful, in a much different way than Essie Baum, who was wholesomely beautiful. It wasn't hard to imagine her as a ruthlessly efficient Krav Maga master, dispatching an enemy without chipping her chrome manicure.

But what piqued Nolan's interest most was the dent in the wall by the door, accented with dried bloodstains. Somebody had been very angry, and there hadn't been time to repair it. Wodehouse's hands were creamy white and unblemished—no indication of anything more strenuous than working a keyboard.

I punched a wall. Stupid. Embarrassing. It's been a stressful time.

Seth Lehman hadn't been lying, and he'd left his mark here.

Relations between the two really were in the sewer. She turned her attention to the woman's feet, visible beneath the mirrored glass desk where she held court. Her stiletto-heeled boots were much larger than a size six—not the feet that had left impressions in the spongy, cliffside lawn in Malibu. It was a disappointment, but that didn't mean she hadn't killed Hobbes, it would just make it harder to prove.

"We're all gobsmacked by Evan's death and a bit on edge," she was saying. "It's been quite terrible."

Much more terrible for Evan Hobbes, but Nolan swallowed her sarcasm. "We're very sorry for your loss, Ms. Wodehouse." She couldn't count the times she'd said that. It was starting to sound insincere, like something off a teleprompter. Maybe it was time to come up with another line, but what else could you say?

"Thank you. How can I help?"

"We understand you were at the Baums' party Saturday night."

"Yes, but I didn't stay long, I wasn't feeling well."

"What time did you leave?"

"Around ten."

"Did you see or speak with Mr. Hobbes?"

"Briefly, before I left. He was quite upset. And quite drunk."

"What did you discuss?"

"He was concerned about his career, and I reassured him that the agency would stand behind him."

The first lie. "Was he with anyone when you spoke to him?"

She couldn't contain a moue of disgust. "Seth Lehman. Evan's agent. He was looking after him."

The second lie. Lehman said he hadn't seen her, and Nolan believed him.

"Where did you go after the party?"

Her eyes narrowed slightly. "I went home and went to bed. As I mentioned, I wasn't feeling well. What is this about?"

"Can anyone corroborate that?" Crawford asked.

She gaped at him. "Are you asking me if I have an alibi for an unfortunate accident?"

"Turns out, Evan Hobbes was murdered. So, we'll be asking everyone who was at that party if they have an alibi. That's our job."

Nolan watched Rebecca Wodehouse's simulated warmth and concern regress to snotty indignance. Not the typical response of someone shocked by the unexpected news of a homicide.

"I find it difficult to believe that Evan was murdered, but if he was, it's your job to find that person, not harass innocents. What you're implying is outrageous." Her eyes narrowed shrewdly. "I can see you're both very interested in the hole in my wall. Seth did that. He has a violent temper. Perhaps you should be looking at him."

"You don't seem surprised that Mr. Hobbes was killed."

She raised her chin contemptuously. "You're incredibly rude, Detective Crawford. Do you treat all victims of a crime this way?"

"Evan Hobbes was the victim of a crime," he snapped. "And you believed his death would be beneficial to the agency, so you can understand our interest in your whereabouts Saturday night. Did you know Mr. Lehman recorded that conversation?"

The purest rage Nolan had ever seen ignited in her eyes. If Seth Lehman ended up dead, they'd know where to go.

"I did *not* kill Evan Hobbes."

Al was hot and ready for battle, and Nolan decided it was time to step in with a velvet glove. "Still, you can see how that looks to us, Ms. Wodehouse. Which is why we're asking you for your cooperation. Can anyone corroborate you went home after you left the party? It's a simple question."

She stood abruptly. "You can speak to my lawyer."

"We could do that. Or you could end this now without drawing unwanted attention to yourself. Evan Hobbes's case is extremely high-profile, as you know. The media is watching closely, and that scrutiny will intensify when news that it was a murder is released.

Incidentally, we're counting on your discretion. It would be unfortunate for you if the news got out before the captain gives his press conference this morning."

"I have a live-in housekeeper," she spat with venom that matched the rage still burning in her eyes. "She brought me soup and tea in bed and checked on me several times." Rebecca Wodehouse ripped a sheet of paper off a notepad and scrawled on it hard before shoving it across her desk. "Her name and phone number. While you're at it, call my goddamn security company, too. I set the alarm when I got home and it wasn't disabled until Sunday morning."

Crawford stood and smiled jovially. "We appreciate your time and cooperation, Ms. Wodehouse. Thank you for helping us on our way. Have a nice day."

"You're both beasts. I'll be speaking with your captain," she seethed as they exited the office.

"Your parting shot was priceless," Nolan commented as they got in the car. "Too bad she didn't get it."

"Meant for you, Mags. Glad you appreciated it."

"You had way too much fun."

"And you didn't? Come on, that was like throwing water on the Wicked Witch of the West. I've never been called a beast before. It was kind of a turn-on."

She snickered. "I won't tell Corinne that, either."

"Bummer that her alibis are probably going to check out. If they do, she's not good for Hobbes."

Nolan had a feeling the alibis would check out, too. But she really didn't want to let go of Rebecca Wodehouse as a villain, because she was so perfect for the role. "She lied to us twice."

Crawford grunted. "Stupid, pointless lies. The kind psychopaths and narcissists tell for shits and giggles, and she checks both boxes."

"We know the agency is broke, and she has access to the Baums, so she still might be good for David. Santa Barbara needs to know about her, and the possibility of a connection to Kira Tanner."

He unclipped his seat belt and pushed open his door.

"Where are you going?"

"I'm going to help out Santa Barbara. Be right back."

Nolan watched him duck into the agency, then emerge a few minutes later with a befuddled expression that scarified his forehead with wrinkles. "Lily said Kira Tanner signed with the agency six months ago."

"Why do you look so confused? That sounds like a nail being pounded into Wodehouse's coffin."

He excavated his half-eaten bagel from the bag on the console. "If she was already using Tanner to get something on David Baum, why would she go up to Santa Barbara and kill them both? That's a huge risk with nothing to gain."

"Maybe she found out Tanner was planning her own blackmail scheme and didn't want to share the money."

Crawford shook his head. "The killer didn't take the flash drive. Which means they didn't know about it."

"That could have been part of a setup." The words were a lame rejoinder to a good point, and they resonated distastefully in Nolan's mind. She'd been nurturing an unhealthy fixation on Rebecca Wodehouse, and personal sentiment was obstructing systematic analysis. Yes, the woman was a full-on bitch and very likely a psychopath, but it was possible she hadn't murdered anyone. Not all psychopaths killed, and not all killers were psychopaths. She draped her hands over the wheel and sighed. "But you're right, our only job is Hobbes. Apologies for losing focus."

"You were expanding your focus, not losing it, and I caught your bug. We're missing something."

"We're missing the person who killed Hobbes. If it's not Cornish, that person is on Essie Baum's guest list. I'll call her while you check on the alibis and fill in Santa Barbara." She looked over at Al, who seemed engrossed in some inner monologue, or else he'd slipped into a trance. "Why are you checking out? The party's just starting."

"Wodehouse, Hobbes, the Baums, Seth Lehman . . . they're all twisted together in some freaky Gordian knot. Let's talk to Lehman again. He seems like the most stable of the group, at least among the living."

"That's an unflattering distinction," Nolan muttered.

Chapter Forty-One

IN DARCY'S EXPERIENCE, THERE WERE TWO types of cybercriminals: ones who worked for hostile foreign governments or organized crime and didn't part easily with information, if at all; and the young, arrogant jackasses who started wailing like croupy infants and flipping everybody they'd ever known when they realized they had prison time hanging over their heads.

Brianna Cornish fell into the latter category, but she didn't have anyone to flip. She was a solitary freelancer who advertised her services on the dark web; she'd been anonymously solicited there; and likewise, anonymously paid five grand in cryptos when Evan Hobbes's deepfake was approved and posted. That had been easy to confirm with a cursory exploration of her computer—people lied, but machines didn't. And she didn't think Cornish was lying about anything at this point in the interview. It was painfully obvious she wasn't a career criminal worried about getting whacked by her bosses, she was just a terrified young woman who'd really fucked up.

But Darcy didn't feel sorry for anyone who broke the law, for any reason. In fact, she was thoroughly enjoying watching the spectacle from behind the one-way glass. Cornish lost her mind when the agent informed her that she could be charged with the morally reprehensible act of distributing child pornography. All for a payday—ironically, one that wouldn't even put a dent in her student loans. It wouldn't pay three months' rent on her Studio City apartment. What an idiot.

She glanced at Anong, sitting next to her with a stoic, unreadable expression. "Greed incarnate, right in front of our eyes. Anything for an easy buck."

"She'll lawyer up now."

"It doesn't matter, we have her cold."

Anong was contemplative as usual. "I believe her. She never worked with Hobbes, there is nothing personal here. The deepfake was pure illicit commerce. She didn't kill him."

"What I've been saying all along. But it *is* personal for whoever paid her five g's, and we might be able to follow the cryptos if her employer was as careless as she was. You said somebody had a hard-on for Hobbes—"

Anong scolded her with a look. "I didn't say it like that."

"No, you were much more refined about it. But you were right, and he might be the killer Detective Nolan is after."

Darcy watched the sobbing woman being led out of the room, and wondered if she had already spent her proscribed earnings. "Let's go finish taking apart her cyber world."

She nodded and stood. "Call the detective, *teerak*. She's been waiting very patiently for an update."

"She knows I'll be in touch the minute we have something."

"We do: Cornish wasn't the mind behind the video. Communication is important in a murder investigation. This new information might help her."

"What might help her is telling her who paid for the deepfake."

Anong shook her head like a long-suffering parent disappointed by a wayward offspring's life choices. "This compartmentalization of yours is a problem."

"Hey, I had a nice chat with Maggie Nolan about this. Batted a few opinions back and forth."

"Not good enough."

Darcy rolled her eyes. "You can be an insufferable nag."

She smiled mischievously—a rare thing for someone so habitually serious. "Yes, I can be. Aren't you glad I'm straight?"

Chapter Forty-Two

NOLAN SIGNED OFF WITH DARCY MOORE and briefed Al as she parked on the street in front of Lehman's building. Wilshire Corridor was an odd assemblage of high-rise luxury residences that were anomalous to LA and seemed awkwardly transplanted from another city. This one featured a dramatic glass-and-stone-clad façade, circular cobblestone drive, black oval fountain, and a white-gloved, liveried doorman that belonged not just in a different city, but a different century.

Seth Lehman's choice of habitation made a statement about his financial achievements, and his deceased client had certainly been a contributor. But that particular gravy train had reached the end of the line. Daphna Love would be appropriating that position.

Al was assessing the property with a critical eye. "This place is way over the top."

"Did you hear anything I just said?"

"Yeah. Is she sure Cornish doesn't have a past with Hobbes, from back in her acting days?"

"No connection to him or any other players on our roster. They're positive she was just a gun for hire; positive that the contact and transactions were completely anonymous. Whoever paid five grand for a felonious deepfake wanted it bad. That video was revenge, and I think the murder was, too."

"It's also a big, fat, dead end, Mags. The only reason there's a dark web is to keep the people who use it anonymous."

She shrugged. "Moore was cautiously optimistic about tracking down the exchanges between the two of them. There was the initial contact, approval of the final video, and the disbursement of cryptos to her e-wallet when the job was done. 'Lots of opportunity for mistakes' is the way she put it. What did you find out?"

Al flipped through his notebook. "That we hit another dead end. The housekeeper confirmed Wodehouse got home feeling sick around ten thirty p.m., when Hobbes was still stumbling around at the party. She also confirmed bringing her soup and tea in bed, and provided a couple additional details that shore up her alibi and the woman's atrocious character."

"Like?"

"Like Wodehouse threw the teapot at her because the water wasn't the right temperature. Then she woke her up at two in the morning to run her a bath and massage her feet."

"And she didn't drown her? Amazing."

"I thought so. The security company confirmed the system was armed at ten thirty-six and wasn't disarmed until six the next morning."

Nolan was disappointed, but also relieved to have one less thread to follow. "Then she's out of our lives. Thank God."

"Gone, but not forgotten. Santa Barbara is very interested in her, which should make you happy."

"It does. Why the interest?"

"They found a diamond earring that was initially overlooked at their crime scene. And it doesn't belong to Essie Baum—she doesn't keep any jewelry there. Hasn't even been to the house in over a year, which speaks volumes."

"They're sure it didn't belong to Kira Tanner?"

"They don't think so. For one thing, she wasn't wearing any jewelry except the kind of cheap, hippie stuff you pick up on Venice Beach. And this particular earring isn't the kind of thing a sleaze like Baum would give his underage plaything. It's vintage Cartier, valuable as hell, either a family heirloom or something acquired from an auction house like Christie's or Sotheby's. They're trying to track it down that way."

Nolan's pulse quickened as she considered an earring with provenance. A rich killer? A rich, jealous mistress? Both? She still desperately wanted Wodehouse to hang for something. "Even if Wodehouse is completely destitute, she probably hasn't gotten around to selling all the family treasure yet."

"I mentioned that. They're also working the revenge angle on their end, too, trying to identify the victims off the flash drive."

"There still might be a dovetail between Baum and Hobbes."

"Could be. Did you reach Essie Baum?"

"Left a message, but with what's going on in her life, we're going to have to show up at her door to get that list."

"Maybe Lehman can help us out with that." He closed his notebook and returned his gaze to the building. "Wilshire Corridor is a weird place. And an eyesore."

Spoken like a proud native who didn't want a piece of Manhattan intruding on one of the most distinctive, self-styled cities in the world. "Maybe so, but it's prime real estate. These places go for millions."

"For that kind of money, they could live anywhere. Who would choose a soulless condo?"

Nolan thought of her tiny San Fernando Valley rental: a needy, antediluvian ranch house inconveniently located far from the heartbeat of Los Angeles, and priced accordingly. Houses were a pain in the ass, even if you didn't own them. "People who want to be close to the action, but don't want the hassles of home ownership. Single people, old people, and smart people." Her phone interrupted their banal conversation about LA real estate with a text alert. Another incursion from Remy.

Flight delayed. Update when you can.

"Dry cleaner again?" Al asked nonchalantly.

"Yeah. The dry cleaner's flight is delayed."

He grinned at her. "He's going to get you to New Orleans if he has to drag you there himself. I told you a long time ago he was a persistent son of a bitch."

She redirected the conversation to things more salient, and something that had been needling her. "You said Essie hasn't been to Santa Barbara in over a year, so there was obviously trouble in paradise. Do you think she knew what her husband was?"

"I'm sure she knew he was a cheater, but not a pedophile. No way she knew Hobbes was tangled up in it, either. She made it sound like he hung the sun and the moon. That's one of the reasons I want to talk to Lehman again."

"If he knew what was going on, he isn't going to tell us. That's obstruction and a trip to a fed pen."

"Yeah, but I'm betting he knows something, even if he doesn't know he knows."

While Nolan pondered the grammatical abomination of using three "knows" in one sentence, a Porsche Cayenne parked across the street and disgorged a severely underweight woman in a fur-trimmed suit that was in vogue even though the temperature in LA would hit the upper seventies before noon. Fashion was dictated by runways in cities with four seasons.

The woman glanced at them briefly as she passed, did a double-take, then continued up the walk toward Lehman's building.

Crawford's jaw went slack. "That's Daphna Love. How could she possibly be more beautiful in person?"

Nolan had been in close proximity to enough film stars to know that they were very different from regular people. They all seemed to be imbued with the ethereal glow of a demi-deity; unmistakably human as they walked among mere mortals, but far more perfect in an impalpable way. Probably where the sobriquet "star" had originated. "She's so tiny. The camera really does put on weight."

"I wonder why she didn't valet."

"Probably because she realized what an ass Lehman is and wants to make a quick getaway after she dumps him."

Crawford snickered. "Yeah. She's way out of his league. Man, she's got great hair. You think it's her natural color?"

"I don't know, Al," she said irritably. It wasn't jealousy, exactly; but there was something demoralizing about seeing the breathtaking apogee of beauty and knowing you would never scale those lofty heights. "If she really is Lehman's lover, she may have been at the party. Try not to hit on a potential witness."

Chapter Forty-Three

JENNY WYLER PUSHED AWAY FROM HER desk and rubbed her burning eyes. She'd already parsed through hundreds of captioned photos on Kira Tanner's Instagram account, but so far her search hadn't yielded anything but double vision and profound depression. It was a daily chronicle of a beautiful, naïve young girl from Oklahoma who wouldn't be making a big splash in Hollywood, because some son of a bitch had shot her in the face.

Nothing distinguished it from any other Instagram account, except the sudden silence of death. No more posts about favorite beaches or clubs or restaurants; no more photos of celebrity sightings or LA landmarks. But if there was a single pixel that might provide a clue, Jenny was going to find it, or go blind trying. There was nowhere else to go at this point, and she wasn't pinning all her hopes on an earring and a woman named Rebecca Wodehouse.

She returned her attention to the monitor and recommenced the misery-inducing search. Kira Tanner had lived in a shabby studio apartment in Koreatown, but she seemed to have an endless budget for eating out at hip, high-end places that were celebrity magnets. Places to see and be seen. No doubt courtesy of David Baum, who would dole out petty cash to keep her fantasy alive as long as she was useful to him; before another prettier, more talented young wannabe deposed her.

Ten minutes later and a year into Tanner's postings, a captioned photo of security escorting two men out of a restaurant caught her eye: EVAN HOBBES GETTING BOUNCED OUT OF PEARL CLUB!!!! BIG FIGHT!!!

Baum's twisted accomplice in pedophilia. Her gut told her their deaths were somehow connected, but so far, there wasn't a shred of evidence to prove it, and a fight in a restaurant certainly wasn't going to break her case. But maybe the person he'd fought with was also the person who killed him. LA would appreciate a heads-up.

She looked at the clock on her computer and uttered an oath. She was late for her meeting with Sheriff Sembello. The call to Crawford would have to wait.

* * *

Anne Sembello had been the Santa Barbara sheriff for four years and Will Corrigan's grave misjudgment was the only discredit to the force during her tenure. Some type of disciplinary action was required—ideally, some unpaid leave and a few months on a desk—but her detectives were the ones who'd been stymied, and they deserved a say in the matter.

Will Corrigan was universally liked, but forgiving and forgetting were two different things. If he did stay on, there would naturally be lingering suspicion, and it would take time to rebuild trust. Could he live with that kind of scrutiny? He had his reasons for making a stupid mistake, and she had her reasons for wanting to protect him, but maintaining department morale superseded all. Unhappy cops were accidents waiting to happen.

Jenny Wyler was sitting across from her, in the same chair Will had been in when he'd made his confession. She was bright, intuitive, and worked harder than anybody else. Not because she had a chip on her shoulder, but because she was intensely empathetic and took every crime personally. This was only her second homicide because Santa Barbara just didn't get that many. Thank God.

"You're doing great work, Jenny. Nothing about this case is easy—it's ugly, it's high-profile, and there are a lot of moving parts—but you're handling it like a seasoned pro."

Her peachy complexion ripened. "Thank you, Sheriff. The whole team has been outstanding, and I promise we'll get there. Sorry we're behind on the reports."

"Doing the work is more important than filling out paperwork. Updates?"

She shook her head in frustration. "We still haven't found Tanner's personal belongings or Baum's missing computer—they could have been dumped anywhere. Nothing from the canvasses or camera footage from the neighborhood. Same with the autopsies, ballistics, and trace. It was very clean."

"Like somebody thought it out."

"Somebody who was familiar with the property. I think the killer came for Baum and the computer, and Tanner was collateral damage. They tossed a couple dresser drawers as an afterthought to make it look like a burglary. Right now, we've got blackmail and revenge for motives, but if it was revenge, why take the computer?"

"Maybe a victim didn't want to risk being identified as one. It might be why they didn't go to the cops in the first place."

Wyler scowled. "That's so infuriating. The abusers still have the power, even in this day and age."

"It's horrifying, but it's a reality. What about Baum's phone and home computer?"

"Nothing jumped out at us. He wouldn't keep anything about his disgusting secret life on any electronics his wife had access to. And Tanner's family—if you could call it that—was a bust. The father said she had a history of running away, hasn't seen her in over a year. Didn't seem upset about it, either. The mother died when she was ten."

Sembello felt something elemental drain out of her body. She knew there were good, uplifting stories out there. But in the job, you saw the sad, hopeless ones more often, and now Jenny Wyler was seeing them, too. "How about her apartment?"

"Grungy, Koreatown studio, barely lived in. The neighbors didn't know she existed. No computer, no red flags in her phone records, either. I'm still going through her socials."

"What do you think about LAPD's angle on Rebecca Wodehouse?"

"It fits, but it's conjecture. Unless that earring unequivocally belongs to her, or some other evidence turns up that connects her, we can't even justify an interview. We're still waiting on callbacks from SoCal estate jewelers and the auction houses. Hopefully something will pop on that end. It's a place to look, and we need one."

The moment Sembello had been dreading arrived. "About the earring. I have some decisions to make, and I'd appreciate your input. Will's actions set the investigation back, and that's inexcusable."

She let out a despairing sigh as her gaze drifted. "I've known Will for a long time—he's a good man, one of the best—and this isn't him. We're all shocked. Yeah, he screwed up, and sure, we're angry, but he ended up doing the right thing. I'd settle for an apology."

"You'll all be getting one. For what it's worth, this destroyed him."

Don't ever do something that makes you feel bad.

Her father's advice. Words to live by. "What's your read on where everybody else stands?"

"Same. Nobody wants to throw him on the third rail, we just want to solve this case."

When Jenny's phone rang, Sembello excused her and returned to the issue of Will. She hoped he would come back. Not just to a desk here, but to law enforcement in general. He'd burned himself badly and some cops didn't recover from that.

Jenny returned with a barely perceptible smile. "We just heard from Christie's. Those earrings were purchased at auction fourteen years ago by Sir Edgar Frederick Wodehouse."

She returned the smile tenfold. "Good work. I guess you're heading back to LA. From what I understand, Rebecca Wodehouse is a lunatic, so best of luck."

Chapter Forty-Four

NOLAN AND CRAWFORD GOT OUT OF the car and followed Daphna Love up the walk. It was more than a little surreal when she paused at the door and turned to watch them curiously as they approached; like she was waiting for friends to catch up. For some reason, it made Nolan feel like prey.

"You're Detectives Nolan and Crawford," she said with a warm, dazzling smile. "I thought I recognized you from the press coverage, but I wasn't sure. Seth is a friend and he said you've been extremely compassionate during this dreadful time. Thank you for that."

Nolan was impressed that her partner wasn't slobbering or prostrating himself at her feet. He managed a very professional, "Good morning, Ms. Love. It's nice to meet you."

"Same to you both. You must be here to see Seth, too. About Evan."

"We are."

Wow, Al was really keeping his cookies together. He wasn't even blushing. But Daphna Love wasn't so composed anymore. Her eyes suddenly glossed with tears and she pulled a tissue from her alligator bag. Or maybe it was lizard. Nolan wasn't great at identifying dead reptiles.

"Have you found out what happened to poor Evan?"

"We're working on that," Crawford reassured her.

"I'm sorry, that was a stupid thing to say." Love blotted around her eyes, careful not to disturb her makeup. "It was a tragic accident. But there are obviously some details left that you need to tie up, otherwise you wouldn't be here."

Nolan sighed inwardly. There were going to be a hell of a lot of shocked people when the captain made his statement this morning. "Were you and Mr. Hobbes close?"

"Not at all, but Evan and I have both been in the business for a long time. It's like losing a family member. And seeing him in such misery before he died . . . he was so drunk. Out of his mind drunk. It's a horrible memory."

Bingo. A new witness. "You were at the Baums' party?"

She nodded solemnly. "The only good thing about that night was reconnecting with Seth. I've known him since junior high, but we lost touch." Her gaze settled on a distant point, remembering happier, more innocent times. "We were sweethearts a long time ago. If you pay attention to the media gossip, then you know we're sweethearts again."

Love was painting a very different, very sentimental picture of Seth Lehman the Dickhead. The infatuations of youth left indelible prints and opaque blinders on the soul. Nolan knew this. Young Ernst Koppel had been the love of her life at the age of eleven, cruelly stripped from her when her family had left the Army base in Germany for good. Her parents had probably done her a favor. Ernst wouldn't be able to keep her in the Hotel Bel-Air's lobster cacio e pepe in Wiesbaden. "Do you mind if we ask you a few questions about that night, Ms. Love?"

"No, of course not, especially if it helps with Evan."

"When was the last time you saw him?"

"Maybe around eleven? He was talking to Essie in the kitchen."

"Did you speak with him?"

"I don't know if you could call it that. Seth was looking after him, and I was catching up with Seth, so we made small talk, but I'm not sure he even recognized me, he was so impaired."

That was hard for Nolan to believe, unless he was blind drunk. Which he may have been, according to Dr. Weil. "When did you leave?"

"Shortly after that. He kept going outside and wandering off, and Seth was trying to keep an eye on him. It was too cold for me. It was too cold for everybody, even with the outdoor heaters. The party had moved inside by then."

Nolan wasn't a skinny person, but she knew a few, and they were always cold. "Did you notice Mr. Hobbes spending time with anyone else in particular?"

Her eyes stormed over. "Rebecca Wodehouse. Seth's former boss."

"Not fond of her?"

"I don't know her, but she has a reputation for being hideous. Seth has told me some things, too. I'm so glad he quit. When I asked him how she would react to the news, he said she would probably kill him. Hyperbole, of course, but the way he said it made me think he wasn't being entirely facetious. Apparently, that's the kind of person she is."

Nolan was amazed that somebody hadn't killed *Wodehouse* by now. "Anybody else?"

Love shook her head sadly. "People were supportive of Evan at the party, and polite, but nobody wants to talk to someone in that condition. Seth was the only one who stuck with him, and I don't think he'll ever get over leaving Evan. But I'm sure he told you all this."

"Just trying to build a timeline, Ms. Love," Crawford said. "Thank you for your help."

"Certainly. Shall we go in?"

Nolan and Crawford drafted in her magnetic wake, and the doorman straightened and smiled broadly when she entered.

"Good morning, Ms. Love, nice to see you again."

"Hi, Archie. These are Detectives Nolan and Crawford, here to see Seth, too. They've been very kind to him."

He nodded a cordial greeting. "Archie Burgess, at your service, Detectives."

Love went from light to dark in an instant. "I hope there haven't been any further problems with Amber Harrison."

"No, ma'am, no sign of her. We're on high alert."

"Thank you, Archie."

Nolan made a mental note of the name as she took in the luxuriously appointed lobby. It was filled with plush seating areas and tables laden with elaborate flower arrangements in marble urns. An enormous, colorful tangle of a glass chandelier dominated the space. She was fairly certain it was a genuine Chihuly and not a knockoff.

"Shall I call up first, Ms. Love?"

"No, Seth's expecting me."

He opened a large glass door etched with palms and gestured them through to an elevator vestibule with an intricate mosaic floor, lots of shiny brass, and more flowers. "You three go on up. Have a good day."

"Amber Harrison?" Nolan asked once the elevator doors had closed.

Love sighed despondently and looked at her with troubled eyes the color of imperial jade. "A jealous ex-girlfriend of Seth's. She tried to force her way into the apartment and attack us yesterday. She also made verbal threats against both of us."

"Did you call the police?" Crawford asked.

"Absolutely. An Officer Shannon Birchard responded. She was very helpful and reassuring. I filed for a restraining order, but Seth hasn't had time. He was on his way to Malibu when Officer Birchard arrived." She shrugged; a helpless gesture. "Just when you think things can't possibly get worse, they do."

The elevator settled delicately on the penthouse level and emitted a refined ping. The doors opened directly onto yet another finely furnished, flower-filled vestibule. The place was starting to feel like a funeral home. There was a single, darkly lacquered door—this was obviously Lehman's very own foyer. You paid for privacy when you paid for a penthouse. Nolan looked for cameras but didn't see any. With the multiple layers of security in place, maybe the developers or the resident had deemed it redundant.

Love rapped on the door. "Seth, it's me." She waited for a few moments, and knocked again. "Seth? The detectives are here, too."

To forestall a possibly naked man answering the door. Nolan appreciated that.

"He might still be at work. He was going in this morning to clean out his desk and I'm early."

"We just came from the agency. He didn't show up while we were there."

Love frowned. "Seth told me he'd planned to be there when they opened. I guess he changed his mind. Maybe he's in the shower. Or out for a jog." She tried the handle and the door eased open. "He's supposed to keep this locked and bolted with that crazy woman running around," she mumbled disapprovingly. "Seth!"

The space was clean and contemporary—elegant bachelor pad décor—and the air was faintly scented with coffee and woodsy, masculine bass notes. A mug, an open laptop tethered to an external hard drive, and a phone sat on a black granite counter. Nolan didn't hear a shower running, music or a TV playing, or any of the usual morning sounds that accompanied somebody getting ready for their day.

Love sighed in exasperation. "Maybe he went back to sleep. He was so exhausted when I left last night. I'll check the bedroom."

"Lehman pisses off women," Crawford said under his breath once she was out of earshot. "You think he was sleeping with Wodehouse and dumped her, too?"

"One possible explanation for the ongoing hatred. Her relationship with the Baums would be trashed if she fired him and she'd lose all those movie premiere invites, so she was stuck with him."

Crawford grunted and looked around. "Nice place, even if it is in Wilshire Corridor. Not my thing, but I can see a single guy—"

Love's scream shattered the silence. It wasn't a movie scream, but shrill and primal, like Essie Baum's had been. And so very loud.

But not loud enough to wake the dead.

Chapter Forty-Five

THE SUN WAS HOT ON SAM'S shoulders as he watched the continual flow of Pink's customers carrying laden trays out to the red-floored patio. It reminded him of a documentary on migratory birds, flocking to feed. Melody was quiet as she focused intently on her Guadalajara dog. She was either starving or preoccupied.

He decided on preoccupation—Pink's held a lifetime of good memories for Sam, but their last visit here together had included an encounter with a charming psychopath who'd eventually tried to kill them both. And no less significant was the fact that she'd just slept with her best friend. Things like these were bound to consume a person's thoughts.

Oddly, he wasn't distracted at all. Instead, he found himself looking forward instead of backward—thinking about next steps, thinking about planning for a future that didn't seem quite so ambiguous anymore. That was progress. Dr. Frolich was going to be ecstatic.

He lifted his orange Fanta, hoping to dispel her trance. "Cheers to new beginnings, Mel."

She looked up with an ingenuous expression and smiled, like a child who'd just been wakened from a dream. "It feels good, doesn't it?"

"Like comfortable slippers that somebody just sewed a few se-quins on."

She tittered.

"You don't like my analogy?"

"You just called me an old slipper."

"I said 'comfortable.'"

Her demeanor shifted suddenly, from silly to serious, and she put her chin in her hands. "They say that a seismic shift in one area of your life carries over to everything else. Positive begets positive, neg-ative begets negative."

"I hope you're feeling positive."

"I am. And I've been thinking about what you said. About Roxy Codone being the least I had to offer. You're right. And if I can't make it as a commercial musician without a tawdry gimmick, then I don't want to be a commercial musician. I'll take my chances and be a starving artist if I have to."

Sam reached over and took her hand. "I wouldn't judge you either way, but that makes me very happy, Mel. And you'll never starve with your psych degree. There are enough nutjobs in the world to keep you in skull sweater sets for the rest of your life."

"Oh my God. You actually paid attention to what I was wearing yesterday?"

"I'm quietly observant. Plus, it's adorable." She rolled her eyes, but she was blushing. That was adorable, too.

"What about you, Sam? Is your future looking clearer? Shining on the horizon?"

"I don't know about shining, but it's partly sunny, which is a vast improvement over the last two years."

"And what do you see?"

Sam hadn't furthered his analysis of his work quandary, at least not with any serious cognition, so he was surprised by the words that tumbled out of his mouth. "I can't stay jobless forever, it's driving me crazy. But I see electrical engineering as too cerebral; SWAT as too visceral; and politics is an unholy union between both."

"At least you know what you don't want, that's good." She tapped a glittery red nail on her lips thoughtfully. "Maybe you need a change of scenery where you can refine your thoughts. Like a vision quest. Summer in Chicago was mine, but you're a man of action, so I'd suggest something more exciting."

"Like?"

"Like walking the Appalachian Trail barefoot, or free-climbing El Capitan."

Sam smiled. "You're trying to get rid of me already."

She squeezed his hand. "Not a chance. You already have something in mind, I can tell."

"How?"

"I just can."

Peter Easton had just popped unbidden into his thoughts and given him an idea. It was spooky that she could read him so well, even though half of his face couldn't express emotion. "Have you ever been to Pennsylvania?"

"No. Why Pennsylvania? Independence Hall? The Liberty Bell?"

"I think I need to look up somebody there."

"An ex-girlfriend?" she teased.

"A dead relative."

"Oh my. What precipitated this?"

"A door opened, so now I have to close one. Or at least try."

Melody frowned. "That's poetic, but vague."

Sam started to tell her about Peter and the letter, but a strident, surgically enhanced blonde at the next table rudely interrupted. She was barking into her phone like a drill sergeant, drawing disapproving glances from the patio's denizens. Pink's was a place for all people, from celebrities to meth heads to ordinary citizens, but there was a limit to the collective tolerance.

"There was just a press conference!" she screeched at the unfortunate person on the other end of the line. "Evan Hobbes was murdered!"

The crowd's attention immediately shifted from the obnoxious woman to their phones, Melody included. He was going to have to raise the topic of her phone usage at some point. A few minutes later she looked up, stricken. "It's true, Sam. How horrible."

Sam wasn't sure how to respond without sounding callous. The poor man was already dead, did it matter that he'd been murdered? It would to Maggie and Al, it was their job to care, but it also did to Melody, too, very much. Teen idols were essentially first loves, and he had to be sensitive to that reality. "I'm sorry. But Maggie and Al are on it, you know they'll find out who did it."

"Who would kill him?"

The blonde leaned over and tapped Melody's shoulder. "David Baum was murdered, too, in Santa Barbara. They're saying it's connected. But the cops don't know who killed him, either."

Sam cringed when Melody engaged the intrusive gossipmonger.

"Who is David Baum?"

"The head of Disney. Evan's boss. I heard a girl got killed, too. Maybe it's a love triangle." Her eyes glittered lasciviously. "And Daphna Love is shacking up with Evan's agent. Too bad poor Evan is missing all the excitement." She returned her attention to her phone as if she'd never even had a conversation with a stranger.

Nothing like the mingling aromas of hot dogs and schadenfreude, Sam thought cynically. He wondered if people in Lancaster, Pennsylvania, were gossiping about it, too. Probably. A meteor had killed all the dinosaurs; social media was going to kill off the human race one day. Likely from starvation, because the world would eventually become too distracted to eat.

Melody wrapped up the rest of her G-dog and put it in her tote, which also had a skull on it. With rhinestone eyes. He assumed she was too distressed to eat any more of it and wanted to leave so she could mourn Evan Hobbes in a new way. Grieving for a homicide victim was different than mourning a natural death. Sam knew all about that. But she surprised him.

"You *have* to go to Pennsylvania, Sam! And if you want a travel buddy, I'm all over it. Come on. Take me back to your place and show me that letter. I'm great at research, and I have an account with Ancestry.com."

Chapter Forty-Six

DAPHNA LOVE WAS INCONSOLABLE, POSSIBLY IN shock, and looked so diminished in her profound sorrow. Nolan was sitting with her in the entry foyer, waiting for backup to arrive—once again in the role of miserable witness to a devastation. She and Al had found her draped over Lehman's body, choking on sobs, and when they'd gently pulled her away, she'd crumpled to the floor like an irrevocably broken thing. Like most of this job, it hacked at Nolan's heart with mean, swift strokes and made her think about the wisdom of her career choice.

Baum had been a scumbag, and she'd had a real problem with Lehman, but they'd both had women who loved them; who were suffering beyond bearing, and would be far into the future. Al had it easy—he was just dealing with a corpse.

"Is there anything I can do for you, Ms. Love?" For the first time since they'd been sitting here, she looked up. Her face was ravaged, but still beautiful.

"Find Amber Harrison. Make her pay."

Nolan offered her another handful of tissues. She was running low. "We will. And if she didn't do this, we'll find out who did."

"If it wasn't her, it was Rebecca Wodehouse. There was going to be an ugly lawsuit over his quitting and he didn't think she could afford it. He also told me she was sleeping with his sister for her money. She saw him as an obstacle on multiple fronts."

The door on Nolan's depressive thoughts slammed shut and a new one opened on yet another convoluted neighborhood in Hollywood Babylon. "We'll take that into consideration."

Love's tears fell unabated. She didn't even try to wipe them away. "I had a meeting with my agent this morning. I had to part ways with him so Seth could represent me. Otherwise I would have been here. I should have been here. I could have stopped this."

"This isn't your fault, Ms. Love."

She looked down at her lap again, her thin shoulders shaking. "Seth and I were going to plan our marriage this morning. We both knew it was right—being together again after all these years, we realized our souls and hearts have always been one."

"I'm very sorry."

"We couldn't wait, so we decided to elope. No wedding, no Hollywood sideshow, just us." She rummaged in her bag, withdrew a miniature porcelain box clad in gold, and plucked out a round green pill. "I'm taking a tranquilizer."

Apparently, it was déclassé for luminaries to carry around orange plastic pharmacy bottles. The box was the modern-day equivalent of a Tiffany cigarette case, Nolan supposed. Vices deserved elevation, too. "That's a good idea, Ms. Love."

"This world has been very good to me, but sometimes I hate it." She dry-swallowed a pill like she'd been doing it her whole life, and closed her eyes. "I'm going to wake up every morning thinking Seth is still here; and every morning I'll lose him all over again."

Her insight was poignant, and made Nolan think of the endless marathon of grief. You always ran side by side with it, but it got easier the further you got into the race. "That's true. But one day, remembering him will make you smile instead of cry. It just takes time."

Her swollen eyes fluttered open. "You've lost somebody you care about very much, too."

"Yes."

Love was suddenly rapt, and the raging river of tears ebbed to a creek. She didn't ask, but Nolan knew she wanted more. And what the hell, why not? It might make her feel infinitesimally better, and she could almost hear Max screaming at her to put in a good word for him. If he'd been younger, she would have been his screen saver. "My big brother. I know it's not the same, but he was a soul mate. We were a team. And he was a big fan of yours. Maybe your biggest."

"May I ask what happened?"

"Afghanistan."

"I'm so sorry he never came home."

"He did come home." Nolan tapped her heart. "He's here right now. And Seth will always be with you, too."

The tears resumed their relentless march down her cheeks.

"We'll need to speak with you later, Ms. Love."

"I know."

"I called Shannon Birchard, and she's coming to take you home. She'll make sure media doesn't see you leave, so your privacy will be protected. She'll also sit with you until we get there, if you'd like."

"Thank you, Detective Nolan. You've been so kind."

"You'll get through this, I promise. Even if it seems impossible now." Nolan heard the hum of the elevator rising, and felt guilty relief. She wasn't sure her attempts at consolation had offered any to Daphna Love, but she hoped so. Talking about grief was better than thinking about it.

Chapter Forty-Seven

CRAWFORD WAS STANDING OUTSIDE THE BEDROOM door with a fierce scowl when Nolan reentered the penthouse. "How the hell are we supposed to solve anything when the whole family is getting picked off one by one? I'm starting to worry a little about Essie Baum's life span."

"At least with this one, we've got a head start. You said it yourself, Lehman pissed off women, and there are two of them who wanted his head."

"That's for damn sure. While you were grief counseling I went through his phone. He has about a thousand texts and voice mails from Wodehouse, threatening most of his body parts; and one from Amber Harrison telling him to watch his back. Sounds like she's the one who squealed to TMZ. His alarm was set for four forty-five, so we have the beginnings of a timeline." His expression softened. "How is Love?"

"Bad, but I think she's tougher than she looks. Officer Birchard's taking care of her, so that's something."

"Yeah. A familiar face."

"She's sending her reports from yesterday, but she said Amber

Harrison was calm, articulate, and remorseful when she interviewed her about the incident."

Crawford shrugged. "Then she's not an idiot, but she's obviously volatile. She did a slow burn. Happens all the time."

"What about his computer?"

"He wasn't logged into his email account, but his recent searches from this morning were articles on Hobbes's and Baum's murders, and weirdly, a bunch of luxury beach resorts in exotic places like Fiji and Bora-Bora. And the Maldives, which really seemed to catch his eye. I had to look that one up . . . What? That's making sense to you?"

"Lehman and Love were planning to get married. Elope, more specifically. Those are prime honeymoon spots if you can afford it."

Crawford's brows jumped. "After hooking up at a party less than forty-eight hours ago?"

"They're old lovers, and she was expansive about how they were soul mates who'd rediscovered each other. It happens. You and Corinne tied the knot pretty fast, and you hardly knew each other."

"Yeah, but we were young and stupid."

"So are they. Love also told me Rebecca Wodehouse is sleeping with Essie Baum. Using her for money."

"You're *shitting* me."

"She said if Harrison didn't kill him, Wodehouse did. She thinks Seth was an obstacle on multiple fronts, was the way she put it." Nolan slipped on a pair of gloves. "Show me what we've got."

"You tell me. I'm your mentor, remember? Except the student already surpassed the teacher. Sucks getting old."

Nolan squeezed his arm affectionately. "You've been married eighty years, so that makes you, what? A hundred and something?"

"Laugh now, commiserate later. Time waits for no one."

Nolan took it all in from the doorway first, absorbing the scene as a whole before focusing on the main event. Lehman was on his stomach on top of the comforter, in a sweatshirt and jeans. His arms were splayed to ten and two, like he'd passed out drunk. He was cool, but not cold, and just beginning to stiffen. There was some blood in his hair, but nowhere else that she could see. It wasn't wet, but it wasn't fully dry, either.

"Just a scalp laceration," Crawford said. "No major damage to the skull that I could see. It probably didn't kill him unless it set off a bleed or knocked an aneurysm loose."

"Which is entirely possible."

He pointed to a small, white marble sculpture of a jaguar on the floor by the bed. The head of the cat was bloody—art imitating life. "How does a guy let himself get whacked in the back of the head without a struggle? At some point this morning, he was awake, made coffee, and showered. The towels are still damp and so is the tile."

"He was wiped out. He probably went back to sleep, like Love said."

"Yeah, but he's fully dressed. If you decided to take a snooze after your morning ablutions, wouldn't you strip down and crawl under the covers?"

Nolan didn't want to mention that she had collapsed fully dressed on top of the covers in that very same dead starfish position last night and slept for hours, completely unaware of the hot lover right next to her. "Not necessarily. Not if you're exhausted." She knelt at the nightstand and picked through the drawers. Behind a box of Trojans—half-empty or half-full?—she found a prescription bottle. Two-milligram Ativan tabs, prescribed to Esther Baum. "Or took a couple tranquilizers. These are high dosage."

Crawford opened it and peered inside. "A bunch of little white pentagons, but there are some green pills on top, too."

"Love just took one of those greenies. Looks like he was a collector of other people's benzos. Maybe he had a problem and his doc cut him off."

"In LA? I doubt it. It's harder to get cigarettes here than tranqs. There's more drug residue in the wastewater than there is *E. coli*."

Nolan watched him contemplate the broader issue while he rubbed his chin. He'd missed most of the whiskers on the left side of his jaw, making her grateful she only had to worry about her legs and armpits every few days.

"No sign of B and E, so let's say the crazy, pissed-off ex still has a key. She lets herself in, bashes him in the head while he's tranked up in bed, then bolts. The only problem with that scenario is the doorman said there was no sign of her and they were on high alert."

"I'm sure there's more than one way to get into this building, if you're familiar with it and have access. Anybody smarter than a toaster isn't going to announce themselves to the doorman in the wee hours of the morning, then go kill a resident."

He leaned over the body and turned the head to expose the neck. "What?"

"Looking for signs of a ninja choke hold."

"Wodehouse?"

"A very viable option."

"She was screaming pretty convincingly at Lehman's voice mail before she knew we were there."

"Establishing an alibi with Lily Suhr."

Nolan shrugged. She was beginning to think anything was possible at this point. "Let's take a stroll through the rest of the place."

They returned to the living room, and sun from a skylight hit something on the living room rug just right. Nolan stooped down and lifted a tangle of white-blond hair with a pen. "This isn't Daphna Love's color. Or Rebecca Wodehouse's."

"What do you bet Amber Harrison is a blond? But there was a scuffle here yesterday, it could be from then. Wodehouse is still in the running."

They slowly coursed through the rest of the penthouse like tracking hounds, which took some time—it was a big place, but clean and orderly. Lehman had a taste for Pop Art—she recognized a Warhol, a Haring, and a Lichtenstein. The rest were mysteries to Nolan's untrained eye. He also had a taste for black-and-white photography, mostly female nudes, which didn't surprise her.

They finally reached the end of their tour in a hallway that led to the guest bedrooms. The first was made up for company and undisturbed, and the second served as a home office. It didn't smell pleasantly woodsy like the rest of the house. This room smelled like something small had died in it.

Crawford's nose wrinkled. "Since I don't see another dead body lying around, I'm guessing mouse. Those little fuckers are everywhere, even in a Wilshire Corridor penthouse, and Lehman hasn't had time for restraining orders *or* housekeeping."

Nolan isolated the sickly sweet odor to a closet, and they both took a step back when she opened the door and a foul miasma drifted out like it had been waiting for escape like an evil spirit.

She didn't find a dead mouse, but she did find a garbage bag stuffed behind a rack of running shoes. Inside was a gray-checked Tom Ford sports jacket, crusted with blood. The plastic had kept in just enough moisture for organic matter to putrefy well.

"Holy shit." Crawford squatted next to her. "Lehman didn't have time for getting rid of evidence, either."

Chapter Forty-Eight

NOLAN WAS DUMBFOUNDED, HER MIND BACKPED-
aling furiously to their long conversation with Seth Lehman in Malibu. His answers had been natural, seamless, and convincing. "I can't
believe this. Neither one of us thought he did Hobbes. Everything he
said meshed with his sister's and Love's accounts."

Crawford was gnawing on his lower lip like he meant to eat it.
"Yeah. Maybe that's a red flag."

"How do you mean?"

"The two most important women in his life would cover for him,
and they both had plenty of opportunity to get their stories straight
before we talked to them."

"Come on, Al. Conspiracy?"

He shrugged and turned up his hands. "Why not? That second set
of footprints—*women's* footprints—always had us thinking accomplice. Not to mention the lack of a blood trail or drag marks from the
bushes to the cliff."

"One of the biggest stars in Hollywood wouldn't risk her career
and her life to aid and abet a murder."

"Why not? History is full of women who sacrificed their lives for
their lovers. Remember that Meatloaf song about doing anything for

love? Her real name is Daphna Katz, you think she pulled her stage name out of a hat? She's a romantic."

"Finish the lyric: *but I won't do that*. And Essie Baum wouldn't, either. Hobbes was like a son to her."

"*Like* a son. Blood is thicker than water. And a quickie marriage would disqualify Love from testifying against him."

Nolan wondered if Al was losing his mind. "It's a giant spitball. Lehman had no motive."

His eyes landed on the jacket again. "That says he did, we just don't know what it was yet. And guess what I learned? The Maldives don't have an extradition treaty with the United States. Of course, he doesn't need that now that he's dead, but he didn't know he'd be dead."

"You're turning a search for honeymoon spots into an international flight from prosecution?"

"You hated Lehman, now you're fighting for him with the evidence right in front of your eyes?"

Nolan felt confused. And pissed. "I'm not fighting for him. I'm just having trouble understanding how our judgment was so far off the mark."

He laid a reassuring hand on her shoulder. "Don't beat yourself up over it, Mags. The guy was in the biz. Acting is probably something you absorb by osmosis. And conspiracy or not, this blood belongs to Hobbes, I guarantee it. Lehman said he left the party at midnight, and he was slick, so I'm sure we'll be able to corroborate that with the valets. The last time anybody saw Hobbes alive was around eleven. That's an hour to kill somebody and toss them off a cliff. With or without an accomplice."

Nolan rubbed her eyes. They felt gritty and raw. "All true. But this blood could be from the fight. I can see Lehman punching his lights out, he was being a pain in the ass."

"That's true, too. But then why stuff it in a bag and hide it? Fighting isn't a crime. At least if it doesn't end in murder."

"It's quite a coincidence that Lehman dusts his client and then he just happens to get killed two days later."

Crawford puffed out a beleaguered sigh. "I'm not saying it isn't connected. In fact, it kind of has to be, doesn't it? But hell, I could be wrong about Lehman. Maybe it is from the fight. Or maybe he cut himself shaving and balled his bloody, three-thousand-dollar coat up in a plastic bag and stuffed it in a spare closet where he keeps all the other stuff that has to go to the dry cleaners."

"Don't be a dick, Al. You're hearing alarm bells, too."

"Yeah, but evidence is better than gut."

Ross's voice from the doorway startled them. "Did I hear something about guts?"

"Not what you're thinking. This one is low drama."

He shuffled in and recoiled at the unleashed stench. "Where's the body?"

"In another room. You're smelling this bloody jacket that's been moldering in a plastic bag in a closet for a couple days."

"The dead guy was a killer?"

"We think he killed Hobbes." Crawford slid his eyes to Nolan. "At least I do."

"And he ends up dead, too? Interesting. Who was he?"

"Seth Lehman. Hobbes's agent."

"That's a twist. From what I hear, clients in this town usually want to kill their agents. How did it happen?"

"That's the thing. We're not sure. He's flat on his face in bed, and there are no outward signs of violence or struggle. But there are definitely people who wanted him dead."

"Weil will love it. He's on his way."

"Hurry up and wait for the real detectives." Nolan buttered him up, and was rewarded by a grin.

"Real Detectives. Great name for a TV show, Maggie. I'll star and you can executive produce."

"God, no. I've had enough of Hollywood in the past two days."

Ross crouched down to examine the jacket, then pulled out a penlight and a magnifying loupe. "Tom Ford. Nice."

"Not anymore," Crawford mumbled.

"Did this guy have a cat?"

Nolan frowned. "No sign of any pets, why?"

"Because up close, this jacket looks like my sofa. It's a lot of hair to be wearing to an A-list party. Even the schlubs I hang out with have lint rollers. Actually, it looks more like fur animal than cat."

"Probably picked it up at the party, like Hobbes did," Crawford suggested. "Or it could have transferred from him."

Ross was silent for a long moment as he took a closer look with the loupe. "Huh."

"What?"

"This doesn't look anything like the mink I found on Hobbes's clothing. It's from another source. Transfer goes both ways, which means contact was probably after Hobbes was over the cliff."

"Nobody would cozy up to a guy in a bloody sports jacket," Nolan pointed out.

Crawford bumped her arm. "An accomplice would."

Ross looked at them curiously. "Wow, this keeps getting better and better. But I was thinking it came from Lehman's car, or maybe from here. I'll take a sharp look at everything, and I'll double-check Hobbes's clothing. Even I miss stuff. On very rare occasions."

Crawford squatted down next to him and borrowed his loupe. "That's definitely not silver mink."

"I told you."

"Can you test the blood as soon as you get back to the lab, Ross? We'd like to solve at least one murder today."

"Sure thing. I'll compare those men's prints to whatever shoes we find here, too. Walk me through and show me the body."

Nolan trailed after them, cursing Al for planting the seed of an accomplice in her mind. It was becoming a weed, the persistent kind that grew up out of a crack in the sidewalk. You could pull it out, but it would keep coming back. Essie Baum? No way. Daphna Love? Unimaginable.

But then there was the fur. She had no moral qualms about wearing it, that was clear from her suit du jour. It had been frigid in Malibu the night of the party—perfect weather for showing off an expensive, warm coat. Purely speculative, but the size 6 footprints by the cliff were a fact. She was damn near emaciated, so she gave the impression of being tiny, but maybe her feet were, too. *Would Daphna Love do anything for love?*

Chapter Forty-Nine

IT WAS IMPOSSIBLE TO MINIMIZE THE impact of crime scene activity, especially a body bag leaving on a gurney. You could cordon off a large perimeter outside to keep rubberneckers away, but you couldn't keep people from entering and exiting the building where they lived. Fortunately, most of them seemed to be at work, but there were a few residents clustered in the far corner of the lobby, trying to look inconspicuous as they craned their necks to catch a glimpse of the misfortune that had befallen a member of their privileged coterie.

One of the onlookers was a man much younger than the others, and appeared to have been chiseled out of a huge chunk of stone. But the man of stone was ashen and looked like he was on the verge of being sick. Nolan pegged this young, buff, affluent gym enthusiast as somebody in the biz; maybe somebody who'd known Lehman. "I'm going to have a word with that colossus."

"I'll track Archie down."

She introduced herself, and he dwarfed her shooting hand as he shook it gingerly, which she appreciated. A gentle giant with manners. Almost nobody shook hands with a cop, and she appreciated that, too.

"Derek Lohr, ma'am. Is that Seth?"

"I'm sorry, Mr. Lohr. Was he a friend? Colleague?"

His face went from ash to white. "No, but we ran into each other at the gym sometimes. Talked shop. I'm a stunt coordinator."

"What made you think it was Seth?"

"I live a floor below, and I heard the fight yesterday. I had a bad feeling about it. Domestics are the worst."

"They are. Did you ever hear any fights before?"

"No. I asked Archie about it, but he's a classy guy, he wouldn't say anything. But the cops were here. You probably know that."

"Did you hear or see anything unusual this morning?"

"No, nothing."

"Last night?"

"No." He shook his big head sadly. "I'm sorry for Seth. He had it all—penthouse, great job, Daphna Love, for God's sake . . . it's scary to think about how you can be on top of the world one minute, and gone the next."

"Thank you for your time." She gave Derek Lohr, the philosopher, her card. "If you think of anything."

⁂ ⁂ ⁂

Archie Burgess looked like somebody had drained all the blood out of him. Even his lips were a thin, white line.

"Mr. Burgess, is there somewhere private we could chat?"

"Uh . . . uh . . ." He finally gave up on verbalization, nodded, and led them to a small security office. He sat down at a cluttered desk and started crying.

"We're really sorry, sir. I know it's a shock," Nolan said sympathetically.

"I don't know how this awful thing happened. I wasn't here last night, but everybody on staff knew to watch for Amber Harrison. I have Jim's report and the guest and valet log right here. His shift was quiet. No sign of her. Nothing unusual at all."

Nolan would have offered him a tissue, but she didn't have any left. "We'd appreciate copies of those, and we'll also need all the security footage from the property, starting last night through this morning. Is that something you can help us with?"

"As soon as the manager gets in. He's still stuck in traffic." He put his head in his hands. "God, I can't believe this. I never thought she'd do something like this. I told that to Ms. Love last night, but I was wrong."

Told her Amber Harrison wouldn't kill her boyfriend? Not exactly small talk. "Tell us about your conversation with Ms. Love."

"She was leaving. Around midnight, I guess. She was very concerned about Seth. Afraid Amber Harrison could get in some other way than through the front."

"Is that possible?"

He nodded miserably. "Through the parking garage, but security does regular checks, so I reassured her. I was wrong," he repeated.

Nolan felt sorry for him. "In spite of what you see on TV, homicide is actually quite rare, and female killers even more so. No reason to expect it. Are there cameras in the garage?"

"Yeah, but we're installing a new system, so that whole quadrant is down. It was supposed to be up and running by now, but they're waiting on parts."

The story of the times. "How about exterior views of the entrance?"

Archie slumped like a rag doll who'd just been relieved of its stuffing. "Those are on the same quadrant."

"Do you know if Ms. Harrison had access to the garage?" Crawford asked.

"I couldn't say. It's gated, and she used the valet service whenever I saw her here, but Mr. Lehman could have given her the code."

"Do you know what kind of car she drove?"

"A blue Aston Martin. But we had an alert on that, too."

Chapter Fifty

MALIBU WAS HUSTLING AND BUSTLING WITH the return of the heat—residents, tourists, and surfers were out en masse to celebrate. You'd never know PCH had been buried in rubble just a couple days ago. The vibrancy partially distracted Nolan from the onerous reason they were here. Nothing but sun and fun—no nightmare notifications, no dead bodies piling up on their watch, just a beautiful SoCal day by the beach. Thoughts of Remy were another pleasant distraction she allowed herself. She wondered if he'd made it to New Orleans, or if he was back home, sitting poolside with a Cheshire grin, a cocktail, and new flight reservations for two.

Al was on his phone, swiping through Amber Harrison's social media. He'd been silent for a long time, so she apparently had an engaging online presence.

"What's her story?"

"A few thousand followers across the platforms, but no activity since yesterday, when she went on a wicked rampage about her cheating ex—unnamed. If there were pics of them together, she took them down. Apparently, she didn't know she'd been tossed over until she caught him with a half-naked woman. Sounds like Love spent the night there after the party, doesn't it? Maybe reminiscing about the thrill of the body dump."

Nolan made a face. "What else?"

"She's a highly narcissistic, platinum-blond bombshell—definitely her hair in the apartment—who posts a lot of provocative selfies in her bikini. Used to be a ballerina. And she has a little kid. Really cute. Name's Asad, which she says means lion in Arabic. There are pictures of them visiting the baby's daddy in Riyadh, but no bikini pics there, obviously. Looks like she's on good terms with at least one ex. Probably because he lives eight thousand miles away."

"The kid doesn't take her out of the running for Lehman, but it dials it down a little."

"Yeah, but she sounds like a whack job with anger issues and no self-control." His phone jangled and he lifted a finger. "It's Sembello."

Nolan returned her attention to the scenery as she jumped off PCH and navigated toward the Baum compound. Al wasn't saying much and the call was short, but he was grinning when he signed off.

"They traced the earrings. Purchased at auction by Sir Edgar Wodehouse for fifteen big ones, pound sterling. Wyler is on her way down here. Things aren't looking so hot for lovely daughter Rebecca."

Nolan should have felt elated, but didn't. It was a tawdry, anticlimactic ending to a tawdry, venal crime. Except it wasn't the end. One earring did not solve a case. "Do they have anything else that connects her to the crime scene?"

"No, not yet, but it's a good break." He frowned. "You seem oddly underwhelmed by this excellent news that vindicates your own theory. The very one I pushed back on."

"She was good friends with the Baums. There are a lot of reasons it could have been there. And it could have been there awhile."

"Now you're just being negative. The earring was right there on the bedroom floor where the body was found." He narrowed his eyes. "Oh . . . I get it. We're a mile away from looking Essie Baum in the eye and giving her more bad news. Probably the worst. That ruins everything."

Nolan felt her chest tighten. Al was right. He almost always was. "How much can a person take before they shatter?"

"Unfortunately, we're going to find out." His phone chirruped a new notification, and he resumed swiping. "I put an alert on Harrison's accounts."

"Anything interesting?"

"I'll let you know."

Nolan felt her foot lighten on the accelerator. Stupid, because there was no avoiding this, and postponing it was just prolonging the agony.

"Oh, shit."

"What?"

"Harrison just posted a ton of pictures and a couple videos: her at LAX with some girlfriends. On a plane drinking champagne. In front of a sunrise on Waikiki Beach with a bloody Mary. Here's some captions: 'On the way to Hawaii last night to heal my broken heart. My girls kidnapped me, got me drunk, and took my phone away. Keeping the party going this morning! Love them so much!' Lots of hearts and gal pal emojis." He shoved his phone in his pocket in disgust. "We'll check flight manifests, but I'm pretty sure our prime suspect just went bye-bye, literally and figuratively."

"At least it narrows down the field. I guess social media is good for something." Nolan pulled into the driveway with an overwhelming sense of gloom and an impulse to turn the car around and head to LAX herself. Anywhere was better than here right now.

Chapter Fifty-One

THE PLACE LOOKED ENTIRELY UNOCCUPIED—NOT a vehicle in sight—but Essie said she'd be there and had the guest list for them. She didn't tell her the guest list probably wasn't a priority, since her dead brother had most likely killed the man who'd been like a son to her. At least that was off the table until Ross could test the blood on the jacket. Besides, it was bad form to interrogate people you'd just notified. God, this was a mess.

Essie Baum answered the door in a black suit and heels. Her tawny hair was coiled in a severe twist and the only jewelry she wore was a delicate gold chain with a Star of David pendant. She was also wearing a glassy, doped-up expression of serenity. A visit to Ativan Land, Nolan suspected, and she was glad for that.

"Come in, Detectives." She led them to the sofa with the mink security blanket and settled into it bonelessly. "I slept at the Beverly Hills house last night because I couldn't stand to be here," she said dreamily, apropos of nothing. "But I felt a compulsion to come back this morning. It didn't seem right to stay away."

"How are you doing, Ms. Baum?"

"Nothing seems real. I guess that's a good thing." She reached into a patent leather handbag and withdrew a printout. "The guest list you asked for. And staff information. I hope it helps you find who killed Evan."

"We appreciate it, ma'am." Crawford folded it and shoved it in his jacket pocket.

She looked around and sighed. "I'm thinking of selling this place. Santa Barbara, too. They're just too sad now. Filled with bad memories."

And they were just going to get worse, Nolan thought. "But there are good memories, too. Don't rush into anything too quickly."

"No. I won't. Things will get better, it's just hard to see it right now."

Nolan's eyes were drawn to a plastic storage box on the drift-wood coffee table. Probably old photographs and memorabilia. Essie Baum noticed her scrutiny and something flashed across her face briefly before she lifted the lid. Nolan could have sworn it looked like guilt, but that made no sense. Why be ashamed of a trip down memory lane? Every bereaved did it after the passing of a loved one.

Of course, she was heavily sedated, so the look could have meant nothing at all. But she didn't think so, and it drew her gaze down to her feet—quite large, as one would expect of a tall woman.

"I always find the most interesting things after a party," she explained, gesturing to the box. "Jewelry, articles of clothing, sometimes people even forget their shoes. Surprisingly, handbags are the most commonly forgotten things. Most guests inquire the next day, but if they don't, I keep it all just in case. Like a lost and found. This is from Saturday night." She plucked out a bejeweled cupcake. "A Judith Leiber, can you believe it? It's a classic, a collector's edition. The first run hasn't been available for years. The owner must have been off her head, leaving this. There's no ID inside, but I'm sure I'll be hearing from her."

"That's a handbag?" Crawford was skeptical.

"A minaudiere. More like a jewelry piece that holds a few small items."

Wow. They'd just been schooled in rich. "May I take a look?" Nolan asked.

"Certainly."

Nolan thought a crystal-encrusted likeness of a cupcake was a strange little piece of art to carry around, and she wondered what kind of a person would. Someone with a sense of humor? Or maybe it was just something you had to have because it was collectible? She opened it and found a single tube of lipstick, a compact, and Tylenol. No bloody tissues or signed letter from Seth Lehman explaining how he was going to kill his client. "Thank you. I hope you find the owner."

"I'm sure I will." She returned it to the box and excavated a Louis Vuitton logo tote. "This hasn't been claimed. I doubt it ever will be."

Essie Baum was clearly finding some comfort in the distraction of sharing her collection, which struck Nolan as a little odd. But she couldn't begrudge her that, and didn't mind the stalling. "That's an expensive bag not to miss."

"I thought so initially, until I took a closer look. It's an obvious fake. None of my guests would carry a knockoff, so she must have been a plus-one."

The woman had a deep snobby streak, which didn't really surprise her. LA was a material world. Unfortunately, the time for show-and-tell was over, and Crawford, bless his heart, took the lead. This could go one of two ways: bad or worse.

"Ms. Baum, we have something we need to tell you."

"Oh. This doesn't sound good."

"I'm very sorry, but it's not. Your brother was found dead in his apartment this morning."

Her brows furrowed in confusion. "Seth? That's impossible. He sent me the nicest text early this morning, and he's coming here later to help me with David's funeral arrangements."

There was a desperate prayer in her eyes, and Nolan felt it deep in her gut. She glanced quickly at Al, and he was feeling it, too. "We just left the crime scene, Ms. Baum. He was murdered."

She shook her head angrily. "Why would you say such a terrible thing? Nobody killed him, he'll be here soon."

Nolan stood. "Let me get you something to drink."

"I don't want anything to drink, I want my phone. Where's my phone? I'll call him, you'll see." Tears started running down her face.

Nolan sat down next to her. "Are you alone here?"

"Yes," she whispered.

"Is there anybody we can call?"

"The only person I want to call is Seth. He's all I have left." She bolted off the sofa, teetered on her heels, then collapsed on the coffee table. The box toppled, spilling a random collection of treasures across the glass.

Chapter Fifty-Two

NOLAN AND CRAWFORD STOOD OUTSIDE SAINT John's in Santa Monica, sipping coffees in the sun and taking a pause to just breathe. The doctor assured them Essie Baum would be fine physically; it was the mental part that had Nolan concerned. On the way to the hospital, she'd become erratically hysterical as she waffled between denial and acceptance, and even under further sedation, her world was splintered—possibly a protective mechanism, possibly a break from reality. At least her therapist was on the way.

"Really sad," Crawford said, draining his cup. "I hope her shrink offers to join us at the morgue. That's not going to be good."

"I think it might be. She needs to see him before she can start to grieve."

He scuffed his toe on the concrete dispiritedly. "Let's get out of here. We've got a shitload of work to do, and we have to talk to Love. She was with Lehman at the party and after the party, and that's as good as it gets right now."

His phone burped—literally—and he checked his alerts.

"That's so frat boy, Al."

"Maybe, but you can't ignore it." He frowned at the screen. "Jenny Wyler called."

As he listened to his voice mail, a frantic woman rushed toward the entrance. When she noticed them, she stopped dead and glared with blood in her eyes.

"Nice of you to visit your friend, Ms. Wodehouse," Crawford said genially as he pocketed his phone. "She's in shock, but she's going to be okay."

She clenched her fists at her sides. "What are you two doing here?"

"What do you think? We brought her in," Crawford sniped back. "Or maybe you didn't know her brother is dead—murdered—and she's having a really hard time with that."

Her violet eyes narrowed to slits. "Of course I know, why do you think I'm here? Incidentally, I called my lawyer and told him you're harassing me, so stay away from me!"

"Harassing? Hey, you came to us. We were just leaving."

"I assure you, this isn't funny, Detective Crawford, it's deadly serious."

"Not the adverb I would have used."

Nolan had to bite her lip so she didn't smirk. Rebecca Wodehouse was trembling with fury.

"First, you accuse me of killing Evan Hobbes, now you think I killed my best friend's husband!"

"We don't have anything to do with Santa Barbara. They figured it out all on their own because your earring was at the crime scene."

"Those earrings were stolen months ago and I reported it!" she screeched, drawing the attention of the few people in the parking lot. "And I was nowhere near Santa Barbara on Friday night. My lawyer and I made that perfectly clear to the detective."

That was news, but Nolan kept her expression dispassionate. "Nothing to worry about, then."

Wodehouse refocused her murderous stare. "No, there isn't. All of you detectives are incompetent, wasting precious time focusing on me instead of trying to find the real killer."

"As long as we have you, where were you this morning before you arrived at the office?"

Rebecca let out a frustrated shriek. "Now you think I killed Seth? Are you *serious*?"

"*Deadly* serious," Crawford mocked her.

"If you want to speak with me ever again in this life, call Guy Johns. In the meantime, go fuck yourselves." She stalked away, trailing poison in her wake.

"We'll definitely be in touch, Ms. Wodehouse," Crawford called after her. "God, I'm going to miss her when she goes to prison."

"She won't be going anywhere if she's clear for Lehman."

"The notification is over, Mags. You can stop being negative now."

"What did Wyler have to say?"

"She was going through Tanner's Instagram and found a post about Evan Hobbes getting bounced out of Pearl Club last winter after a fight."

"With who?"

"Don't know. But it's irrelevant now, because we know who killed him."

Nolan still wasn't 100 percent positive about that, even though she'd seen the evidence with her own eyes. "It might fill in some blanks. If the fight was with Lehman, that could be motive, which we don't have right now. See if there's a police report."

Chapter Fifty-Three

WHILE NOLAN NAVIGATED THE TRAFFIC SNARL on Wilshire, Crawford worked the computer. Like all technological advances, good came with bad—online banking and easy access to the police database from your car versus a myriad of cybercrime. The scales of justice were always teetering because criminals were so damned adaptable.

"No police report, Mags," Crawford informed her. "No press, either. Guess they solved it like men."

"You'd think Evan Hobbes fighting in a restaurant would get coverage."

"The paparazzi can't be everywhere."

"Did you check Tanner's Instagram for a walk of shame photo?"

He glanced over at her with a sour expression. "Of course I did. It was blurry and didn't show faces. But Sam or Melody might remember it."

"I was just thinking that." Nolan pulled up to the curb in front of Daphna Love's house. It was a very nice Spanish revival off Doheny, and modest by Beverly Hills standards. She appreciated the subtlety. There were no loitering media vans, which meant Shannon Birchard had done a good job absconding with the princess. Her squad wasn't on the street or in the driveway, so she'd obviously moved on with her day.

Love's face was scrubbed clean of makeup, revealing the effects of prolonged crying, but even puffy eyes and a red nose looked good on her. She'd shed her suit in favor of a Los Angeles Rams hoodie and leggings, and she looked like a college freshman, ready to bum around campus on a lazy weekend. Her feet were clad in worn, beaded moccasins, and Nolan noticed how very small those moccasins were. When she turned to lead them into the house, Crawford nudged her in the arm. He'd noticed, too.

She led them into a sunny, lived-in room with a view of the pool and gardens. "Please have a seat anywhere. I have Pellegrino or herbal tea if you'd like."

"We're fine, thank you."

She slumped into a leather sofa and curled her feet under her. "Is Amber Harrison in jail?"

"From the photos and posts on her social media, it looks like she flew to Hawaii yesterday with some girlfriends."

"She could have faked them."

"We don't think so, but we're checking flight manifests to be sure." Love looked absolutely crestfallen, and Nolan understood. She believed with devout conviction that Amber Harrison was the woman who'd screwed up her life in a big way.

"What about Rebecca Wodehouse?"

"We'll be looking at her, too, but this all takes time, Ms. Love. We're sorry we don't have answers for you yet."

She nodded and looked down at her hands. "It just seemed so obvious."

"It did to us, too. And we also have to anticipate neither of them killed Mr. Lehman. Did he mention any difficulties he was having with people other than Ms. Harrison or Ms. Wodehouse?"

"I assume you mean enemies. No."

Crawford pulled out his notebook. "Telling us about your time with him might help us. There may be things he said or did that seemed unimportant at the time, but might be important now."

"Okay. Where would you like me to start?"

"Was Mr. Hobbes with Mr. Lehman for the entire party?"

She shook her head. "He wasn't his shadow, if that's what you mean. He was mingling and enjoying himself when he wasn't doing damage control."

"So, you two had some time to catch up alone."

"Not enough, but yes, we did."

"What happened after you left the party?" Nolan asked.

She breathed out an anxiety-ridden sigh. "This is hard. So sad."

"We know. Take your time."

Love reached for the Pellegrino on her side table and took a long sip. "I got home a little after midnight I think and took a long bath to warm up. I was completely chilled to the bone."

"Not to sound like a nagging parent, but you should have worn a coat," Crawford said with a kind smile, although the purpose of the comment was less than pure.

She lifted her head and tried to smile back, but the weight of her misery held it down. "I was wearing a coat, but it wasn't long enough for the weather."

There was no smooth way to ask outright if the coat had been fur, so Nolan took the baton and moved on. "And after your bath?"

"I didn't want to go to sleep because I was waiting to hear from Seth when he got home. And frankly, I was too giddy to sleep anyhow."

"And did you hear from him?"

"Yes, he called around one. He asked me to come over and I did. I spent the night." Her lower lip trembled. "For the last time."

"Did he seem upset?"

Love finally managed a smile as tears slipped from her eyes. "He was as giddy as I was. We were so happy to be together again. Everything seemed perfect. Meant to be."

Crawford leaned back in his seat and wrote down a few notes. "Was he angry with Mr. Hobbes at the party? Or mention a fight to you later that night?"

She frowned at the question. "Oh, no. Evan was a handful, but he and Seth were like brothers. You probably know this, but David supported him from early in his career and made him a star. They were all family."

"But he must have been annoyed with him. I know I would have been."

"Well, I'm sure he was. We all were. But we understood why he was having a difficult time."

"Tell us about the next morning."

"We got up and Seth went to Petrossian to get us caviar for breakfast. We wanted to celebrate. It was a perfect morning until Amber showed up."

Nolan looked at her own notebook. "From Officer Birchard's reports, Ms. Harrison said some pretty awful things. That was quick thinking to record it."

"She was in a rage, and I didn't want it to be her word against ours." Love's face darkened. "She's a horrible person. I'm not sure Seth was being fully truthful about the status of their relationship, but I didn't care. I didn't even ask, because it didn't matter. Then Essie called with the news about David. I didn't see him again until last night. That's when we decided to get married."

She covered her face with her hands and started crying in earnest. "Seth was so exhausted, and I had my early meeting, so I left around midnight. God, I wish I hadn't."

They let Love take a few moments to gather herself and she finally looked up with impossible pain in her eyes. "Is that all?"

Crawford smiled sympathetically. "Almost finished, Ms. Love. This may seem like an odd question, but do you remember what Seth was wearing at the party?"

"A gray-checked sport jacket. Black sweater and slacks."

"When you saw him in it, was it soiled in any way?"

"Soiled? No, of course not. He wouldn't wear it if it had been."

"Thank you, Ms. Love. We'll be in touch soon."

Chapter Fifty-Four

SAM MIXED A PITCHER OF MARGARITAS—some hair of the dog was in order. In a small part of his mind he largely ignored, he felt guilty about alleviating a headache with the same toxin that had generated it. Most people took aspirin, drank gallons of water, and didn't imbibe again until the next party. But he wasn't most people. They needed an occasion to drink, he just needed an excuse. Dr. Frolich called it an unhealthy relationship with alcohol, but he thought of it as a survival skill: do whatever it takes to get through a day, week, month. In his case, it had been two years, but who was counting?

Melody was working on his laptop, searching through the genetic vault that was Ancestry.com. Her enthusiasm over his pursuit of Peter Easton's story vindicated his gut feeling. On the drive home, he'd started to doubt his motivation; feared that it might just be subliminal avoidance of the larger and more complicated issue of deciding on a career path. He thought the term "vision quest" was a little over the top in this instance, but it was a new approach to confronting his PTSD.

He salted the rims of the green margarita glasses he'd picked up in Tijuana during a lost weekend, sampled his efforts, and approved. Melody approved, too.

"Delicious. Triple sec?"

He scoffed. "Grand Marnier, of course. Only the best for LA's most accomplished and prettiest mixologist."

"You don't have to flatter me just because you slept with me."

Sam laughed; a full, hearty laugh. It felt good. "Not flattery, just the truth. Getting anywhere?"

"Just starting. This takes time and elbow grease. It's not like you plug in a name and find everything all at once. I'm setting up an account for you so you can do your own research whenever you want. I'll show you how it works and get you started. Not that you couldn't figure it out yourself." She smiled up at him. "It will be a fun project. You'll have to channel your inner detective."

"Did you do the whole saliva test thing, too?"

"Yes, but you don't have to."

Sam hesitated for a moment. Family was a sensitive subject for Melody. Her mother had left her extraordinary toddler in the care of her sister and never looked back. She hadn't even resurfaced when that sister had died and left Melody with her abusive, swamp-dwelling father. "What did your spit test and research tell you about your family?" he finally asked.

"I'm mostly French and German. I didn't bother looking up my asshole father, but on my mom's side, I found distant relatives in Germany. Might explain why she ran away to Europe, even if she didn't know where she came from. Maybe genetics call some people."

That comment slammed into Sam's chest like a slug. People were crazy for genealogy now that you could do it from your own home, with a few clicks of a mouse. It was an interesting pastime, and how cool if you found out your grandmother twenty times removed worked in an Italian bordello or fought in some great war dressed as a boy. Or an uncle conspired against the monarchy in the back of his London blacksmith shop with Guy Fawkes. But Melody certainly had a deeper purpose that had nothing to do with amusement. "You would have told me if you'd found your mother."

"Obviously. But I wasn't looking for her, I was looking for a connection to something bigger. She's long gone and I have no interest in finding her. Even if she is still alive. Which I doubt."

She turned the computer toward him, closing the subject. "This is where you enter all your information."

"Looks pretty straightforward."

"It is. That letter was so sad, Sam. I'm glad you're doing this. Peter deserves to be remembered."

"He does. But like you said, I can do this on my own clock. Let's drink margaritas."

They sat in companionable silence, listening to Miles Davis while they sipped. Melody had withdrawn to introspection again—no doubt consumed by thoughts of her mother's desertion and Hobbes's murder, a double whammy. Sam tried to think of some amusing anecdote that might lighten the mood, then decided a private funk was sometimes exactly the right thing.

His phone interrupted their private musings, and he couldn't imagine any circumstances that would prompt Maggie to call him now, when they were swamped with a big case. "Maggie, hi."

Melody reanimated. Her eyes were bright and she was leaning forward, hoping to eavesdrop.

"No, I wasn't working at Pearl then. But Melody was, and she's right here, I'll put you on speaker." Melody finished her drink in a gulp and rattled the ice in her glass absently, but Sam took the gesture as an order. He needed a refill himself. He retrieved the pitcher and topped off their glasses.

"Hi, Detective Nolan."

"Hi, Melody. Do you remember a fight at Pearl Club involving Evan Hobbes? About a year ago?"

Sam watched her brow knit together, creating cute, tiny wrinkles, then those bright green eyes widened. "Oh my gosh, yes! I was working that night. I'd totally forgotten about it."

"Do you know who he was fighting with?"

"No, it was some guy none of us recognized. But we all knew who his date was—he came in with Daphna Love."

Sam lifted a brow at the prolonged silence before Maggie spoke again.

"Was it a fight-fight, or just a pissing match?"

"I was behind the bar, so I couldn't see much, but Ashley—she's the manager—said some punches were thrown, and when Evan's agent tried to break it up, he got an upper cut to the jaw. Security escorted them out. I don't know what happened after that. But I never heard anything about it. The paparazzi weren't hanging around that night."

More silence. Sam was really intrigued now.

"You know Evan's agent?"

"No, but Ashley is totally Hollywood-obsessed, she's knows who everybody is."

"Do you think Ashley would know who the other man was?"

Melody was beaming, her cheeks flushed. "I bet she would. I'll call her and let you know right away."

"We appreciate your help, Melody."

She hung up and gave Sam a swaggering smile. "Detective Traeger at your service."

Chapter Fifty-Five

NOLAN AND CRAWFORD WERE SITTING IN the parking lot of a McDonald's, inhaling Big Macs and fries. She only indulged a few times a year as a guilty pleasure, but today it was merely sustenance. There were better choices, but none as convenient or soul soothing. A McDonald's hamburger tasted nothing like a real one, but it was a mouthful of memories.

Crawford shoved a cluster of fries in his mouth and chewed thoughtfully. "Daphna Love's date goes caveman on Hobbes and punches Lehman. Now that's really interesting."

"I thought so. It's also interesting that half the people involved in the dustup are dead."

"Who knew Hollywood was so dangerous?" He crumpled his empty bag and tossed it on the floor. "Love was a cool customer. Everything she told us seemed on the up-and-up. Never flinched or broke stride. Not even when I asked her about the jacket."

"She's an actress."

"Yeah, but she didn't have the script."

"An actress with small feet."

He puffed out a breath redolent with onion. "I'm not so sure about the accomplice thing anymore. Those prints could belong to somebody else who was just out for a glimpse of paradise. Like you said, no woman would walk in heels on that mushy lawn."

"You're going back on your own pet theory?"

"No, but I'm not feeling it."

"If we confirm Lehman killed Hobbes and hit her with that, we'll see how she reacts then. Don't let your crush affect your judgment."

He scowled. "I take umbrage at that. And I want an accomplice. It would make life so much easier."

"Essie Baum?"

"Still a no. Aside from her attachment to Hobbes, I can't see her carving away a little time from her titanic hosting duties to help her brother dispose of a body."

"Me, either. What I don't get is how Lehman could be so blasé after he just murdered a guy that was supposedly like a brother to him. I mean, he wouldn't be, right? That's the one thing I pulled out of the conversation that could have been a lie."

Crawford shrugged. "I'd forget I killed somebody if Daphna Love was suddenly my girlfriend. And if Seth was a borderline psychopath, like at least two of the women in his life, it would be easy for him to compartmentalize. Are psychopaths attracted to other psychopaths?"

"I don't know. They thrive on lies and manipulation. You'd think it would be hard to do that with one of your tribe." Nolan wiped the grease off her fingers and pulled out of the parking lot. It was full-on rush hour now, and she considered routes back to the office that wouldn't involve sitting on the 405 for two hours. She pondered Sunset, Wilshire, and Santa Monica Boulevards, but they would probably be worse than the freeway. At the last minute, she decided to take a chance on Olympic. Apparently, everybody else had the same idea. She thought about using the magnetic cherry to clear the way, but she was finding the gridlock oddly restful.

Melody's prompt callback surprised them both.

"She's really dialed into the grapevine." Crawford chuckled. "Great ally when you need the inside scoop."

Nolan put her through Bluetooth, and her exuberant voice filled the car's cabin. "Ashley pulled through. I knew she would. Daphna Love's mystery date was a big-time stunt coordinator named Derek Lohr. I hope that helps."

Her heart sped up. "It helps a lot. Thank you, Melody. You and Sam have a good night."

Crawford gave her a puzzled look. "Ring a bell?"

"The Goliath I spoke to at Lehman's building. His downstairs neighbor. And maybe his killer."

Chapter Fifty-Six

LOHR WAS WAITING FOR THEM IN the lobby. His blue polo shirt was stretched tight over his enormous biceps and muscular torso, making it look five sizes too small. Nolan was reminded of an overstuffed Weisswurst she'd had in Munich.

A body by steroids, with the rage that went along with it? A jealous ex-lover who couldn't stand to see the woman of his wildest fantasies in the arms of his upstairs neighbor? Possibly. He had strength, motive, and he certainly had opportunity—a quick elevator ride or a jog up the stairs, no witnesses.

Lohr led them to a seating area with a view of a fountain. He was nervous and beads of sweat clung to his upper lip. "What can I do for you?"

"Tell us about the incident at Pearl Club with Evan Hobbes, and what precipitated it."

He gave them a sheepish look. "How did you find out about that?"

"We're detectives," Nolan said crisply.

"I admit, it wasn't my finest moment, but Evan Hobbes was being a drunk asshole. Daphna Love and I were together then, and she knew Seth from way back, so he came over to say hi. Hobbes came along, and once that happened, he wouldn't leave her alone."

"What do you mean?"

"Seth was like a mother hen, trying to keep him in check, but Hobbes kept hitting on her. Understandable, but then he started saying sexually inappropriate things. It was disgusting, and my fuse was getting short. When he started getting handsy, she slapped him. It had to hurt like hell—she may be petite, but I worked on three of her films and trained with her—she's strong and she can fight. But he kept going at it, so I stepped in and straightened him out."

Crawford leaned forward and placed his elbows on the table casually. "But you hit Seth, too. Messed up his jaw."

"I feel bad about that, but he just got in the way. It wasn't intentional. And he didn't press charges. Hobbes didn't, either."

"You said you were friendly with Mr. Lehman," Nolan said. "I find it hard to believe he didn't recognize you."

"Oh, he recognized me the first day we met in the gym, but I apologized to him. He understood, and we were fine after that."

"When did you and Ms. Love end your relationship?"

"She ended it that night, and the next day, I got pulled from the film we were doing together. Daphna didn't want anything to do with me anymore." He sighed morosely. "I really screwed up. Heat of the moment, you know?"

Crawford nodded sympathetically. "I get it. I would have done the same thing. When did you find out Mr. Lehman was seeing Ms. Love?"

"Yesterday. The fight with that other woman was so loud, I could hear every word, and I recognized Daphna's voice. Later, when I saw her leaving the building, I put two and two together."

"Must have been hard to take, knowing Mr. Lehman was with your ex-girlfriend."

"No, I'm the one who blew it. My fault, not his." His eyes expanded. "You don't think I killed him, do you?"

"Where were you this morning, say between five and seven?"

Lohr blinked rapidly. "In bed. I got up at eight and went to straight to the gym."

"Were you home alone?"

"Yes. Dear sweet Jesus, I didn't kill him. Why would I?"

"Jealousy is unpredictable."

"Daphna and I broke up a year ago. I'm not jealous, just bummed. She's an incredible woman, and not just because she's a star." He looked down at his meaty hands. "Yeah, I really blew it."

*　*　*

"I believe him, Mags."

"I do, too."

"God, Hobbes was a drunk and a total sleaze. And Lehman knew it, too. He saw him in action, probably a million other times. He was wasted at the party, maybe he was harassing Love again and Lehman lost his head. Like Lohr did."

"It's definitely motive we didn't have before. But it doesn't help us with Lehman's killer."

He sighed. "All we've got is Wodehouse. And I'm starting to think her bark is worse than her bite. I looked it up, and she did report those earrings stolen months ago. From her house."

"Was there a robbery?"

"No. Inside job. Household staff was interviewed, but it never went anywhere."

"Which means they were lifted by somebody who knew her and Baum. That narrows it down."

"To about a hundred people who ran in the same circles. Or more."

"Kira Tanner was a young, struggling actress, and a client. Maybe she was at a party at her house, saw the earrings, and couldn't resist. It could be wrong thinking to assume the earring belonged to the killer."

"I hear you. But Sembello is a great cop who just happens to be the sheriff now, she thinks the world of Jenny Wyler, and they're on it. No offense, but micromanaging is a waste of time. Don't mess up your head worrying about somebody else's case."

Nolan was wondering how her head could get any more messed up when her phone buzzed in her pocket with a new text from Remy. She was vastly relieved to see a photo of him a couple thousand miles away with his sister and niece, smiles all around. They were standing in front of an antebellum mansion.

Made it to NOLA. We all wish you were here. Call us when you can.

She showed Al the photo, which made him smile.

"They all look great. Happy. Holy shit, is that his parents' house, or are they visiting a plantation?"

"I think it's the humble family homestead."

He whistled low and slow. "I guess you're off the hook for now, but if I were in your shoes, I'd dump this case and get my ass on a plane."

Chapter Fifty-Seven

NOLAN SETTLED IN AT HER DESK and thought about calling Remy back, but it was wrong to deplete what remaining brain cells she had left on personal business. It troubled her that she was even considering it. She sent a brief, almost terse text instead, with a few bullet points on the case, along with warm greetings to Charlotte and Serena. Good enough for now.

The homicide pen was busy with an evening rush, and Al was mysteriously missing. Probably on a coffee run, or updating Captain Mendoza, if he was still in the building. She called Ike to see how the postmortem on Lehman's computer and phone were progressing, but his outgoing informed her he was away from his desk; hopefully not in a bar somewhere, getting bombed. He was a genius, but he had his demons—any amateur detective could surmise that from the bottle of Jack Daniel's he kept on his desk. Yes, computer people had long leashes.

She thought about bothering Ross, but reined in her impatience and decided to look at the surveillance footage from in and around Lehman's building. It was the best shot they had at the moment.

After fifteen minutes of sheer boredom, she sped up the replay. She'd seen more activity in the morgue. As Archie had warned them, the parking garage wasn't covered, either in or out. The traffic cams and shops across the street did a good job of capturing the trees and lush foliage on the property, but not much else—the landscaping almost entirely obscured the garage entrance itself. A few cars entered and exited, visible only because of their lights, but little to no chance of seeing the killer if he entered on foot. But she had to try.

Al finally returned, brandishing fresh coffees and a sagging paper plate with two large squares of marble cake that wept black and orange frosting.

"Leftovers from Justin in Gang-Narc. He threw an early Halloween kid party yesterday, but he over-ordered on the cake."

Nolan tried to reconcile the scary, towering man with more ink than unadulterated flesh with a dad who hosted children's parties. She didn't know him, but she knew he did undercover work, which was as dark as it got. And she thought her life was complicated. "Justin has kids?"

"Three. Number four on the way." He looked over her shoulder. "Anything?"

"Not so far. You can barely see the garage entrance, and that's the only way in unless you have a master key for the service doors. I suppose we could have a homicidal maintenance worker on our hands, but that's really scraping the bottom."

"I'll go through security's guest and valet log and start calling people, see if one of them saw anything unusual. Hell, maybe one of them rode up the elevator with the killer."

"Wouldn't that be lovely?" Nolan restarted the playback while she sampled the cake. It tasted better than it looked. Maybe the sugar would counteract the fat from the Big Mac. After fifteen minutes of more mind-numbing boredom watching jacaranda trees waving their graceful arms in the breeze, Ross gave them a welcome reprieve. Word from the lab was always good.

"Hi, Maggie. Is Al there?"

"Right here, Ross. What do you know?"

"I know the blood on that tragically wrecked Tom Ford definitely belongs to Hobbes. We also found a pair of Lehman's shoes that match the casts we took from the cliffside."

"I thought you said they matched Hobbes's."

"They wore the same size and both shoes have smooth leather soles, but the depth of the prints is consistent, indicating the prints were from one male. I'd say a heavier person, but neither one of them were big guys."

Crawford's brow perked up. "We were thinking body dump."

"An extra hundred and ninety pounds on soggy ground—that works."

"Are the woman's prints deep for a size six?" Nolan asked.

"No, they were much shallower. I think the toe marks showed up because she was gripping with them, trying to avoid slipping on the wet grass."

"I assume Lehman cleaned up the shoes."

"They were very clean and recently polished, but he forgot about the laces. There was a small amount of blood on them, too, also belonging to Hobbes. So, there you go—one killer down, one to go."

"Nice work. Now tell us who killed Lehman."

Ross enjoyed a good guffaw. "Let me know when you figure it out. There were no fingerprints on the cat statue, it was wiped. We found a lot of auburn hair all over the apartment, and on his clothes and bedding. Girlfriend, I'm guessing."

"Daphna Love."

Ross make a choking sound. "Are you kidding me? Was that moron stepping out on the babe of a century with a blonde? We found more than just the hank you showed me."

"Ex-girlfriend."

"Busy guy."

"Other prints?"

"The doorknob had a mess of them, but it's a doorknob. Inside, there were only Lehman's and a single woman's. So far, it looks like your killer was in and out without a trace."

Nolan sat back in her chair. "What about the fur?"

"Ah, this is interesting, you'll like it. It was chinchilla, and you don't see that every day. We didn't find any in his apartment, though. A couple on the driver's seat of his car, but that was likely a transfer from him."

"Find the coat, find the accomplice," Crawford mumbled.

Ross's brows lifted. "You're still thinking accomplice?"

"Yeah."

"So, my femme fatale theory is still alive and well, just with a different animal. Damn, I'm good."

Chapter Fifty-Eight

DARCY MOORE WAS DOUSING HER EYES with Visine, but most of it ran down her cheeks. How could Anong look so perky and clear-eyed? She was younger, but not by much. Did five years really make such a difference? Her own father was ten years older than her mother, but nobody would guess. She'd certainly never noticed a difference in their energy levels. Hell, they ran marathons together. Maybe that had something to do with it. She gave the Visine another try, with the same irritating results.

"That's an inefficient way of showering, *teerak*."

"Hey, I took a real shower this morning. I even brushed my teeth. Minty fresh. Any action over there?"

"Nothing. I've gone over everything a million times, hoping for some back door, some mistake, but no joy. I even did a broad search for other contacts with the money guy, but that didn't go anywhere."

"Same here. I'm starting to think he isn't active anymore. If Hobbes was his only target and this was a one and done, he would cash out, close his crypto account, and cut off the trail."

"Then let's hope it wasn't a one and done." She stood and pressed her hands to the small of her back. "I've got to move my body and stretch my legs. Good for the brain. Want anything?"

"Twenty hours of sleep, but that has to wait. I'll hold down the fort."

Darcy watched her leave with a bouncy, purposeful gait. It was slightly depressing, but not as depressing as so many hours of dead ends and flagging hopes. She closed her eyes and felt herself instantly dozing off. It seemed like an eternity since she'd slept in her bed.

Thinking Anong and her parents had the right idea—an object in motion stays in motion—she got up and did some yoga warm-ups. The stretches weren't a miracle cure for her stiff, knotted muscles, but at least it got her sluggish blood flowing and she felt a little better. It was a long way from a marathon, but you had to start somewhere.

As she was transitioning from table pose to downward dog, her computer chimed an alert. A very special alert—the one she'd been waiting for; the one that let her know the monitoring software had detected a possible vulnerability in their target's account. The burst of adrenaline flooding her body *was* a miracle cure, obliterating her exhaustion. Screw exercise endorphins, she was a born adrenaline junkie, and she liked her addiction.

She jumped up off the floor and toggled to the notification screen. The dumbass had downloaded the poison pill updates she'd sent, and the VPN was now disabled. She could track this bastard down now. She pinged Anong and got to work.

Chapter Fifty-Nine

SEMBELLO WAS PACKING HER COMPUTER BAG for the night when Jenny Wyler rapped on her door. "Come in, Jenny. I wasn't expecting you'd be back from LA already."

She looked drained and dejected. "It was a dead end. Wodehouse reported those earrings stolen from her home months ago, and her alibi for Friday covers her for Baum's murder. She worked all day, then went to a movie premiere and post-party. I have multiple witnesses who confirm she was drinking and dancing at the Beverly Hills Hotel until two a.m. And there are photos all over the media outlets."

Sembello leaned back in her chair and sighed in frustration. "The earring is still a lead. Somebody stole them from her house, and that person knew Baum. Or at least where he lived."

"It wasn't any of her household staff. She fired them all after the incident, but we tracked them down. Not exactly candidates for blackmail, revenge killing, or anything else, except for maybe flying below the radar. They were terrified."

"Be prepared for a slog. We're not dealing with a typical idiot criminal."

Jenny gave a gloomy nod. "I'm figuring that out."

"What are your next steps?"

"I'm heading back to LA tomorrow to check out more pawnshops. If somebody stole the earrings for cash, they would dump them quick, and the killer could have picked them up there. Those earrings are memorable, so an employee would probably have the transaction burned into their brain.

"Good thought, Jenny." She looked so sad, but this was her quickening, and Sembello knew she'd come out of this a better detective. She'd done a little babysitting this time, but wouldn't have to the next.

"By the way, Detectives Nolan and Crawford were being kind if they said Wodehouse was a lunatic. She's a psychopath."

Sembello hemmed in a smile. "They did mention that term. And a couple others. I'm sure they'd be happy to send you what they've got on their cases, if you think it might help. They've done a deep dive into the Baum family and there could be something there for you."

"Thanks, Sheriff, I'll keep that in mind. Meantime, I'll keep digging and hitting the evidence again hard. What little there is of it. I don't think there are perfect murders, or that any case is unsolvable, so I'll run this into the ground."

Sembello couldn't bear to cast a pall on the enthusiasm of youth, so she kept her opinion on the matter to herself. Her big plans for the night—a bottle of viognier, a carne asada torta from Manny's, and quality couch time in front of the TV with her two love-slug lap cats—were making her feel guilty. "Don't work all night, Jenny. Your brain can't run on empty forever, and that's a lesson that's hard to learn. Get some sleep and keep your head up."

"I will, but I'll finish my report before I go home." She turned to leave, then paused with her hand on the doorjamb. "Have you talked to Will yet?"

"I'm meeting with him tomorrow morning."

"I hope he stays."

Sembello did, too, although she didn't know what that would look like yet.

Chapter Sixty

"CHINCHILLA'S BOUND TO TURN HEADS, EVEN in that crowd," Crawford said, pulling Essie Baum's guest list out of his pocket. "If Ross is right about Lehman's contact with it happening after Hobbes was over the cliff, then they know something. Or did something."

"Give me a page." Nolan dragged her pen down a dazzling list of Hollywood heavyweights. Would Steven Spielberg remember who was wearing a chinchilla coat? No, better chance a woman would notice and know exactly what she was looking at.

Ike surprised them, wandering into the homicide pen looking more drawn and disheveled than usual. But he didn't smell like booze, and his eyes were clear.

"Hey, you two. Sorry I've been AWOL, but I had to take my dog to the vet."

Crawford put down his phone. "I didn't know you had a dog. What kind?"

"A pound mutt."

"You know people look like their dogs, right?"

"Chance is incredibly handsome."

"Uh-huh. Hey, you look a little ruffled, buddy. Actually, you look like shit. I hope it's not serious."

"He had a seizure this morning. It's never happened before. I was scared as hell."

Nolan occasionally wondered what Ike Bondi's home life was like, but a cherished pet had certainly never figured into her speculations. "I'm so sorry. Is he going to be okay?"

He sighed anxiously. "I hope so. The vet said seizures aren't uncommon in dogs. What does that mean, they 'aren't uncommon'? If it was no big deal, he'd say they were common, right?"

"I wouldn't read too much into your vet's syntax. What's the prognosis?"

"They're running some tests now, and they gave me phenobarb to give him. Poor guy is on the road to addiction, but I'll do whatever it takes. Chance got me through some shit. He's still getting me through some shit."

"Think positive and keep us posted."

"Thanks, I will. Just wanted to swing by and let you know I'll get on Lehman's electronics right away."

Nolan gave him a fond, supportive smile. "You're my man."

He grinned. "That's not what I heard."

"You're also an ass."

Crawford snorted. "Yeah, Ike, you're an ass, but thanks for checking in. And good luck with Chance."

He nodded and moped away.

"Hope he doesn't have to euthanize his dog. That might put him over the edge."

"I don't believe he's as close as you think." Nolan returned her attention to the guest list when her phone rang again. When it rained, it poured. But she didn't mind this distraction. "Nolan and Crawford both here, Dr. Weil. You can't be finished with Seth Lehman's autopsy already."

"With dead bodies accumulating in your case, I felt prompt answers would be helpful."

"You have our gratitude. Give us the highlights."

"Just the blood and guts, eh?" Weil chuckled to himself.

Crawford rolled his eyes at the coroner humor, but he was smiling. "Please."

"The most noteworthy conclusion is that the blow to the head didn't kill Seth Lehman. In fact, it was extremely tentative. Not forceful enough to cause a concussion, just enough to break the skin."

"All for show?" Crawford thought aloud.

"It's impossible to tell if the blow occurred before or immediately after he was dead, but he appeared quite placid in situ, so that is certainly a valid assumption. The cause of death was a choke hold, just as with Evan Hobbes. It was reasonable for me to assume they were both murdered by the same person, but then I spoke with Ross and he told me Mr. Lehman was responsible for Mr. Hobbes's untimely passing."

Crawford gaped at her, and Nolan felt her own jaw sag in response. If Lehman killed Hobbes with a choke hold, who killed him with one? Rebecca Wodehouse slithered into her mind again like a malevolent eel.

"Did his body show *any* signs of a struggle prior to death?"

"No. Aside from his brain and larynx, his body and organs were in perfect condition. No bruising except on the neck, which leads me to believe he wasn't in distress, and his body wasn't moved, either ante- or postmortem."

"Then he was killed in bed in the prone position?"

"The autopsy suggests that he was relaxed in death, yes. As do the tranquilizers you found, but toxicology will take some time."

Nolan stared at a far wall and focused hard on the multitude of implications. The whole case was starting to feel like a Rube Goldberg machine gone horribly awry.

"Detectives?"

"Sorry, Doctor, you threw us. Any other bombshells?"

"You asked for highlights, and these things are by far the most important bits of news I have for you, but I'll send you my full report by the end of the day. In case you're in the mood for a little light reading." He chuckled again.

Weil was really on a roll, maybe preparing for a graveyard comedy tour. Except nothing about this was funny. "Thank you, Doctor. We really appreciate your prompt attention."

Crawford chucked his pen across his desk. "Wow. I didn't see that coming."

Chapter Sixty-One

NOLAN WAS SQUEEZING HER TEMPLES, TRYING to compress all her cantankerous thoughts into a single, cogent one. "Take your pick, Al: Lehman and an unsub both used choke holds, or we're looking at a single killer. The only thing we know for sure is Lehman didn't strangle himself."

"If it's two different killers, we're on the right track. Lehman murders Hobbes, maybe accidentally, because he's had enough of his bullshit and he was messing with his girl. Wodehouse killed Lehman because she hated his guts and she couldn't afford the big lawsuit that was brewing."

"That all tracks."

"The problem with that scenario is she wouldn't be able to get into his place unless he let her in, which seems highly unlikely. They were mortal enemies."

"They could have also been estranged lovers. Say she still had the garage code and played kiss and make up to get in."

"There's a lot wrong with that, like he'd have to be a masochistic idiot, for starters. And even if they were lovers, he would have fought her like hell when she tried to kill him, ninja moves or not. Benzos don't render you absolutely brain-dead."

Nolan sighed down at her hands, tangled together cat's cradle-style. "Wodehouse is our number one. Again."

"We'll bring her in tomorrow. With Guy Johns. God, I hate that prick."

"I suppose you have a single killer theory."

He gnawed his lower lip. "Yeah, but you're not going to like it. I don't even like it."

Nolan rolled her hands impatiently.

"Okay. We were thinking Lehman had an accomplice, but maybe he *was* the accomplice. That's why he got killed. It's the only sure way to keep somebody's mouth shut."

She choked on her coffee. "Accomplice to who?"

"We both agree Essie Baum is out. Short of a video of her shoving Hobbes off a cliff, I won't believe it. And she sure as hell didn't commit fratricide. That leaves Daphna Love. She isn't just a dream girl; Lehman was going to make a shit-ton of money representing her. Which wouldn't happen if she was in prison."

Nolan's jaw dropped with incredulity. "That's crazy train."

"Is it? Think about it. He was killed in bed with zero struggle. The blow to the head was an afterthought to give the impression of violence, something Harrison or Wodehouse would do. She's an action star with fight training. She has small feet. She and Lehman were planning to elope after a couple hours at a party together. True love? Or the fact that you can't testify against your spouse?"

"You know that sounds outrageous, right? Killing a colleague, then her long-lost soul mate?"

"Maybe he wasn't. She's a great actress."

"Why kill him if they were planning to get married?"

"One word: divorce."

"You thought I was nuts when I suggested Wodehouse might be good for the Baum murders and Hobbes, and she's batshit crazy."

"We don't know anything about Daphna Love except she's at the top of her game. People in that position don't want to lose it all, and they'll do anything to stay there, like getting rid of anybody who can take them down. Whether she knew about the jacket or not, it's the perfect frame. If she did know about it, that's some brilliant subterfuge right there. Poor Seth Lehman, tragically murdered, and wow, what a shock, turns out he killed his client. Case closed."

Nolan fussed at her tangled hair in frustration. "So you're saying that Love killed Hobbes, Lehman helped her dispose of the body, and then she killed him to shut him up."

"I told you you wouldn't like my single killer theory."

"Daphna Love's success is exactly why she wouldn't risk killing Hobbes, even if she had a motive. They weren't friends or lovers. It sounds like she barely knew him."

He took a bite of Justin's kiddy Halloween cake and wiped a blob of orange frosting from his upper lip. "Crime of passion. Hobbes won't leave her alone and she snaps like Derek Lohr did. Maybe Hobbes dogging her at Pearl Club wasn't a one-off. They could have a past we don't know about. And her success? That's a big fat reason for her to kill Lehman. Maybe he really was her long-lost soul mate, but letting him live was just too much of a risk."

Nolan's stomach burned as the unthinkable began a slow, invasive creep into her chaotic thoughts, reconstituting them into something grotesque. "God. It makes a sick sort of sense."

Crawford looked extremely unhappy. "Yeah. It does." He started pecking at his computer with purpose.

"What are you doing?"

"Checking out the font of all knowledge: the Internet Movie Database."

Chapter Sixty-Two

NOLAN SAT IN STUNNED SILENCE, TEMPORARILY par-
alyzed, while Crawford's hammy fingers chattered on his keyboard.
Conjecture was part of the process and a valuable tool: stream of
consciousness that unfettered your rational brain and allowed you to
freely explore instinct, and often, the absurd. Sometimes you threw
the whole theory out, but occasionally, it pointed you in the right
direction. She didn't like this direction one bit—it was potentially
filled with disillusionment and more hazards than a video game.

There was no hard evidence against Daphna Love; not really even
any circumstantial evidence. She had every reason to be in Lehman's
apartment, leaving bits and pieces of herself. But accomplice, killer,
or neither, the next step was talking to her again, divining for incon-
sistencies that might set paving stones to building a case, or open the
path to a search warrant. *Nice chinchilla, too bad about the blood, do
you think your furrier can get that out?*

Delicate work that required a carefully considered strategy. They
had to control the narrative without arousing her suspicion or losing
her trust. And if she was innocent, they had to make sure their
actions didn't lead to a lawsuit that would drive LAPD's budget into
a black hole and cost them their jobs.

Crawford let out a suffering sigh and turned his monitor toward her. "Love did a film with Hobbes when she was eleven. *The Trouble with Tori*. David Baum was executive producer." He clicked on another tab. "This is a picture of the three of them together at the premiere."

Nolan's blood congealed as she stared at two leering predators with their arms around a stunning, young Daphna Love. She didn't even have breasts yet. "She was a victim."

"It would explain a lot. Hell, maybe she killed Baum, too. We know Wodehouse didn't."

"The earrings are a spoiler. How would Love be in possession of them when she's never even met Wodehouse?"

He lifted his shoulders. "Don't know, but this is all too incestuous."

"Was *The Trouble with Tori* the only film she did with them?"

"Checking."

"God, I hope we're wrong about this."

"I do, too. If we're not, this will be the first time I ever sympathized with a murderer. Or murderers. Baum and Hobbes got exactly what they deserved."

Nolan's mind rewound to the conversation with Love in the entry foyer while they waited for Shannon Birchard to arrive. *I had a meeting with my agent this morning. I had to part ways with him so Seth could represent me.*

"Who's listed as her current agent?"

"Hang on . . . Noah Myers, CAA. Why?"

"She was going to fire him this morning to clear the way for Lehman. I wonder if she did. Time-wise, she would have had to kill Seth before her meeting. In which case, she wouldn't have fired Myers."

He looked up. "It's not a noose, but still a good call. Brick by brick."

Or paving stone by paving stone.

Cop creds were priceless—Nolan had no trouble getting through to Noah Myers, who probably never answered his phone or returned calls unless they came from clients like Daphna Love. The back-

ground was loud and lively—drinks at the Peninsula? An early dinner at the Palm or the Ivy? Someone's cocktail party? Wherever he
was, he was clearly annoyed by the interruption.

"Yes, Daphna came in this morning for an eight o'clock."

"What did you discuss?"

"Come on, Detective . . . Nolan, is it?"

Dismissive little prick. Worse than dickhead. "Yes. *Homicide* detective Nolan."

"I'm not at liberty to discuss private conversations I have with my—"

"What part of homicide don't you understand, Mr. Myers?"

"Are you talking about Hobbes? Neither one of us has anything
to do with him or—"

"Obstruction of justice."

"Oh, please, I'm not obstructing anything."

"You're not in a position to know that, are you?" Nolan felt her
cheeks flame with disproportionate anger. It wasn't just Myers and
his supercilious attitude—what he had to say wouldn't be an earth-
shattering game-changer either way—it was the cumulative effect of
this whole damn case, breaking down her self-control. "I will find
you and drag you in for questioning if you want to go that route."

The connection became muffled—he'd put his hand over his
phone's mic, but she could still hear him snapping at somebody.

"That won't be necessary. Homicide detective Nolan."

She envisioned him sneering; envisioned herself pinning him with
a choke hold of her own, which was so inappropriate, her temper fizzled away in shame, tail between its legs. "Thank you for your cooperation, Mr. Myers. A brief summary of your conversation will do."

"Daphna and I discussed details of a new offer from Paramount.
That's it. Satisfied?"

Not quite. "She didn't fire you?"

His scoff seethed disbelief. "*Fire* me? Detective, I have twenty million on the table for her right now, and I can go up another ten for a—"

"Have a pleasant evening, Mr. Myers. Again, I appreciate your help."

Crawford was looking at her curiously. "Nice impulse control. I thought you were going to throttle him through the phone for a minute."

"I thought about it. Love didn't fire him, Al. They were talking about a new deal this morning."

"She told a pointless lie. Stupid. One step on the road to perdition for my Corinne-sanctioned crush."

"One small step. Did you find anything else?"

He pushed away from his desk and raked his hands through his thinning hair. "Yeah. Love did two more films with Hobbes and Baum, then dropped off the radar for a while. 'For personal reflection' was the official statement, which is Hollywood shorthand for a nervous breakdown or rehab, and most people never recover from that. But she beat the odds and came out swinging—so to speak— with *The Devil's Ward,* the first installment of the Devil series. It's one of the biggest-grossing action franchises that's not in the Marvel universe."

"Nothing to do with Hobbes or Baum?"

"Nothing. She flew that coop." He grabbed his abandoned tie from the back of a chair. "We should, too. Time to go see Love."

Chapter Sixty-Three

NOLAN AND CRAWFORD ROUGHED OUT A game plan on the way back to Love's home in Beverly Hills, but there was no way to anticipate how things would roll out—there were too many variables, including the possibility that their current hypothesis was the deranged result of sleep deprivation.

Daphna Love had opened the gate for them. Landscape lights illuminated the Mediterranean gardens and flagstone path; a warm, light breeze carried the sweet scent of flowers and damp earth. It was peaceful and idyllic and surely not the environs of a double murderer. The heavy front door opened and she gestured them inside.

"Hello, Detectives. Come in."

She had discarded the hoodie, leggings, and moccasins in favor of a demure black dress, low heels, and a single strand of pearls, all suitable for mourning. Her hair was styled in glossy, caramel-colored waves, and her makeup was subtle—also suitable for mourning. If you knew she'd been crying all day, you might recognize the slight puffiness around her intensely green eyes, but in Nolan's opinion, she was camera ready. A candle burned on the foyer table, next to it a handbag and a set of car keys.

"I hope we're not interrupting your evening, Ms. Love."

"I'm picking up Essie at the hospital and bringing her home. I'm so glad she called."

"We won't keep you long, then. How is she?" Nolan asked.

"Destroyed, as you can imagine. And she's just had a falling out with Rebecca Wodehouse."

"About what?"

"She accused her of killing Seth."

Were her eyes sparkling or was it a trick of the candlelight? "Did she say what led her to that conclusion?"

"If it wasn't Amber Harrison, who else could it be? She's violent and evil and she and Seth were in a vicious fight about him quitting. And there's probably more to their relationship none of us knew about. It certainly wasn't healthy. Let's sit."

She led them to the same room they'd been in hours earlier. A gas fire glowed on river stones, and lamplight cast warm shadows on the tiled floor. Nolan noticed two things that hadn't been here on their last visit: a silver-framed photograph of teenaged Lehman and Love, beaming for the camera on Santa Monica Beach, the pier in the background. And a glass of white wine on the side table instead of a Pellegrino.

"It will be good for Essie and me to spend time together. We've both lost the most important people in our lives."

Nolan ignored the sudden vibration of her phone on her hip and gestured at the photo. "You both look very happy. When was this taken?"

"We were sixteen. Such good memories," she murmured, touching the frame tenderly. "That was before I was doing my schooling on set; before Seth and I lost touch. I'll always regret that."

"We understand you did a few movies for Disney at a very young age before you moved on," Crawford said.

"Yes. Three. With Evan, as a matter of fact."

"You said you didn't know him well."

"I didn't. Sometimes colleagues become family, but it wasn't that way with him. We just never connected."

"Is that why you severed ties with Disney?"

She shook her head. "I was starting to get pigeonholed as a child star. A tween star. I wanted to be more than that, so I quit acting for a while to take more lessons and reconsider my career. It engendered some bad feelings, but it was the right choice."

She and Al had decided on the bloody jacket for a big opening salvo, but the conversation was taking a different turn, so Nolan went with it. "Was the incident at Pearl Club last year a result of bad feelings?"

A dark penumbra passed across her face. "That? No, it was a result of Evan's rude behavior. Seth told me one of his demons was alcohol and he was always struggling with it. It was obvious that night. And the night of Essie's party."

Nolan knew what the other demons were. Did Love? "Was he rude to you at the Baums' party?"

She took a sip of wine. "He was too incoherent to be rude."

Nolan squirmed when her phone started vibrating again. "Ms. Love, we've recently become aware that Mr. Hobbes was sexually abusive to young women. I hope you didn't experience that when you worked with him."

Her jaw slipped open. "My God. Are you sure?"

"Yes."

"That's horrible. Shocking."

"Did you experience any abuse, Ms. Love?"

Anger simmered on her face. "No. And I'm so sorry for the ones who did. And repulsed. None of us could have ever imagined he was a predator. Certainly not Seth." Her eyes implored them. "Detectives, please tell me you're making progress with his murder investigation. I need to know how and why he was taken from me."

Crawford glanced at Nolan and jumped in. "We don't know why

yet, Ms. Love, but we know how," he said. "A choke hold. The same way Mr. Hobbes was killed."

Her green eyes widened. "The same murderer?"

"That's a good possibility."

"Then it is Rebecca Wodehouse," she spat. "She's a Krav Maga brown belt, and Seth said she was dangerous."

Crawford redirected to the original plan. "Ms. Love, we're here because we discovered the jacket Mr. Lehman was wearing at the party hidden in a bag in a closet. It had blood on it. Evan Hobbes's blood."

She looked at them blankly. "What does that mean?"

"It's evidence that Mr. Lehman killed his client, unless you know anything different. If you do, I encourage you to tell us."

"That's ridiculous!"

Nolan was exasperated because she was having trouble reading Love, which put them at a huge disadvantage. She was consistently polished and genuine, but she was also a skilled actress. The potential for deception was staggering. "There was indication of an earlier fight, Ms. Love. In one of the sitting areas in the hedges. We found Mr. Hobbes's blood there, too. You said Mr. Lehman wasn't upset when you saw him later that evening—"

"He wasn't upset at all! Seth was obviously helping Evan after he fought with somebody else and that's where the blood came from."

A sound explanation, and one Nolan had mulled over herself briefly. "We don't believe that's what happened."

She blinked at them in disbelief, then shook her head adamantly. "He wouldn't kill Evan. Why would he? And why are you talking to me instead of finding out who killed Seth?"

Nolan's phone was incessant, and it was really pissing her off. "Ms. Love, I spoke with Noah Myers. You told me your intention was to fire him this morning so Mr. Lehman could represent you, but he didn't mention that."

Her expression settled on befuddlement. "I don't know what that has to do with anything. But no, I didn't fire him. On the drive to the meeting, I realized I was being too impulsive and needed to speak with my lawyer first. A breach of contract is a very serious matter. Seth was already dealing with it."

"Passion makes us do impulsive things," Crawford remarked.

She cast a sharp glance in his direction. "Perhaps I should be calling my lawyer for a different reason?"

"That's up to you, Ms. Love." He stood. "Thank you for your time. We'll leave you to your night. Please give our best to Ms. Baum."

* * *

"That wasn't a flat-out bust, but I'm still disappointed," Crawford said morosely as they got back into the car.

"You weren't expecting her to confess, were you?"

"No, but I wanted to get an inkling of whether or not we're heading in the right direction. Still don't know. And next time, she will lawyer up. Who was blowing up your phone in there?"

She checked the screen and felt a small surge of hope. "Darcy Moore."

Chapter Sixty-Four

"YOU'RE ON SPEAKER, AGENT—"

"Darcy. Who's your partner?"

"Al Crawford."

"Hi, Detective Crawford. We have a name for you. The guy who paid for the deepfake."

"Fantastic."

"That's not how I would describe it, because the implication is depressing. And confusing."

Nolan was bursting with impatient energy, but she kept her voice even. "Who is he?"

"I guess we've been a little bit sexist. He's a she. Daphna Love."

"Son of a bitch," Crawford blurted.

"You're absolutely certain?"

"Positive. And I'll tell you why I'm confused. How the hell would a big film star get the kind of skills to navigate the dark web with such proficiency? Not to impugn her intelligence, but that takes knowledge you don't acquire by reading a couple DIY articles on the internet while you're on a movie set."

"*The Devil's Ward*," Crawford said. "She played a hacker trying to catch a killer through the dark web."

Moore was silent for a moment. "So, she did her research for the role. Maybe even had help with this. We'll bring her in tomorrow morning and find out."

"Then she belongs to you for the time being?" Nolan asked.

"Hey, I told you I'd share, Maggie. You have interest in her?"

"Yes, for aiding and abetting a murder, at the very least. Maybe more than that."

"My partner Anong thinks she was one of Hobbes's victims. Is that what you think?"

Nolan was suddenly overwhelmed by a foul despair. God, this was bad. "We do. What are you looking at as far as charges? Hypothetically."

"Don't know, but she didn't produce or distribute that deepfake, she just paid for it. Cornish is in more trouble than she is, at least at the moment. And with her high profile, the funds for a crack legal team, and possible mitigating factors, like Hobbes molested her? It's hard to say until the agents speak with her. And her lawyers, obviously. She won't be coming in alone." She sighed. "Shit, this really sucks. Do you want to observe? I can clear you and Detective Crawford if you do."

"Thanks, Darcy. And we really appreciate you staying in touch."

"Communication is something I've been told to work on. Speak soon."

Crawford dragged his hands down his face, transforming his visage into a Munch scream. "She's right, this sucks." He looked out the window dolefully. "Love hasn't left yet."

"You want to follow her?"

"No, I want to get to Saint John's before she does and talk to Essie Baum."

* * *

Essie Baum was sitting up in bed, staring at a television, which she muted when they entered her room. Several enormous flower arrangements crowded a shelf by a window and battled gallantly against the sharp, antiseptic smell of the hospital room.

Her gown had a pattern of tiny ducklings, and it made Nolan want to cry for some reason; she supposed it was because cute things were in such stark contrast to this ugly world, and a place where people were sick and dying. Maybe it made some patients feel better. Younger. Healthier. She hoped so.

Essie Baum's eyes were glazed, her movements torpid, but she seemed somewhat alert, and oddly, happy to see them.

"Detectives, what a nice surprise. All these people in and out, yet it's lonely here. Sad."

"How are you, Ms. Baum?"

"Horrible. But I'm getting excellent care. And medication." She gave them a lopsided smile. "Thank you both for looking in on me."

It was the least they could do—their bad news had catalyzed her current, unfortunate situation. "We're glad to see you're doing better. We saw Rebecca Wodehouse on our way out earlier. Did you have a nice visit with her?"

She scowled. "Absolutely not. I think she killed Seth." A tear escaped her eye and writhed down her cheek.

"Why do you believe that?"

"She's a bad person, not at all who I thought she was. And she hated Seth. I never knew that. Can you tell me she didn't kill my brother?"

"Not at this point, I'm afraid, unless you know where she was early this morning."

Essie Baum's shoulders slumped and more tears fell. "She and some girlfriends spent the night at my house. She got ready for work and left for the office at seven."

Nolan tried to conceal her disappointment. "Then she's not a candidate, but we'll keep looking at everything."

"I know you will. Thank you."

Crawford poured her a glass of water from the pitcher on her bedside table and handed her the box of tissues sitting next to it. "Did you know your brother and Ms. Love were planning to marry?"

"Seth told me. I was so happy for them."

"It wasn't a surprise?"

"Not really. They've always loved each other, but the timing was never right. And now it's all ruined. Everything is ruined. And Santa Barbara still can't tell me anything about David. I'm so frustrated."

"They're working very hard on it."

"I'm sure they are, but I don't know if they're up to the task. You have to help me, Detectives. Please."

Nolan pitied her. Everything really was ruined for Essie Baum. "I promise we will."

"Ms. Baum, did you notice if anyone was wearing a fur coat at your party?"

She blinked at Crawford with incomprehension, then looked down at the bruise in the crook of her arm where an IV was taped. "This hurts."

"Would you like us to call a nurse?"

"No. I can't imagine they could make having a needle shoved in your vein for an extended period of time any less uncomfortable. You were asking about . . . ?"

"Fur coats. If any of your guests was wearing one."

"Oh. Yes. There were several fur coats. Not very popular these days, but it was a safe space."

Nolan had to concentrate to keep her mouth closed. A safe space for furs. What had happened to the world when she wasn't looking? "Was anyone wearing chinchilla?"

Her brows dipped with a mystified frown. "Daphna had a magnificent chinchilla stroller she'd just purchased in Geneva. She's coming to take me home tonight. We need to be together. That's such an odd question, Detective Nolan."

"Just part of the process of elimination, Ms. Baum. We're sorry to bother you."

"Your investigation is the most important thing to me, so it's no bother." She bit down on her trembling lip. "When will I be able to see Seth?"

"Whenever you feel ready. Just call us."

She closed her eyes. "It still doesn't seem real."

"It won't for a while. We'll let you rest now."

Chapter Sixty-Five

AFTER A VOLUPTUOUSLY WARM OCTOBER DAY, the marine layer had settled over Santa Monica like a sodden, chilled quilt. It blurred the parking lot lights and bedazzled the windshield of their sedan with silvery pearls of moisture almost too pretty to disturb. Nolan flicked on the wipers anyhow, and turned on the heat.

"Harrison and Wodehouse are out for Lehman. And we can't get within a hundred miles of a warrant for Love's place. The DA would have us committed if we tried."

"I wouldn't blame him. We have to dig into what we've got that's concrete and hope something pops."

"All we've got is bad surveillance footage and interviews with party guests and staff we haven't conducted yet. And the fed case isn't going to help us. The deepfake is their problem, but our murders aren't." Crawford clipped his seat belt and directed a vent toward his face. "I get the deepfake. I just don't get why Love would murder the guy she'd just ruined with it."

Nolan thought about that as she pulled onto Santa Monica Boulevard. "She may not have. Prima facie evidence still supports Lehman as our doer. But either way, it doesn't feel premeditated. One of them snapped. God knows there was reason, and there are too many instances when a choke hold killed somebody without intent."

"But then Lehman's murder was premeditated. Dammit, I wish the Pacific Dining Car on Wilshire was still open. We could grab a prime rib and some scotch and all would be revealed to us in a beautiful, lime-green Naugahyde booth."

"Another sorry casualty of COVID."

"Another fallen icon."

"Are you referencing the Pacific Dining Car or Daphna Love?"

Crawford gave her a look of profound melancholy. "Both, I guess."

Rush hour was over and traffic had thinned out, so Nolan picked up the freeway and indulged her need for speed after the long day's battle with gridlock. Making excellent time, they were halfway to the office when Ike called in a spectacular and unprecedented fit of pique. "Wherever you are, get to my office ASAP."

"We're heading your way. What's up?"

"I hope you can tell me." He hung up abruptly.

Crawford clapped his hands together. "This has to be something good. Ike never gets a bee up his ass, no matter what's going on in his personal life."

She nudged the accelerator closer to the floorboard. "Maybe he quit drinking and he's going through DTs."

Or not. They found him pacing his office, swilling Jack Daniel's straight from the bottle.

"Sit down and brace yourselves."

"No foreplay?" Crawford quipped.

"Too freaked out for foreplay."

"Settle down, lose the bottle, and first, tell us how Chance is doing," Nolan said in a calm voice, hoping to mollify him.

He sank to his chair, chastened, and put the bottle in a desk drawer. "Thanks for asking. He's good. My sister is watching him for the night."

"Any news from the vet?"

"Epilepsy. But he says it's manageable."

"That's great news."

Crawford was in bulldozer mode. "Super. Glad to hear it. Now tell us what the hell has you screaming fire in a crowded theater?"

He focused on his monitor as if it had just stolen his lunch money. "I started going through Lehman's phone and computer. First look, it was all pretty benign, so I decided to dig into the external drive you found. That's usually where people keep the most important stuff. It was locked, so it took me a while, but I finally maneuvered my way in. Seth Lehman recorded everything. And I mean *every-thing*."

"Recording things seems de rigueur with the Hollywood set these days," Nolan remarked, thinking of Daphna Love's recording of Amber Harrison's foul tirade. "At least if you're paranoid."

"Lehman was *super* paranoid, and for good reason. All but one of the audio files were marked as Rebecca Wodehouse—does that name mean something?"

"Yes, it does."

"Then you'll probably want to go through the whole sorry, sor-did compilation, but what's really harrowing is this one—the only one—marked 'Daphna Love,' uploaded at six-oh-five this morning." He grimaced, clicked his mouse, and the sound of a woman sobbing filled the office before Lehman's voice overlaid it.

"Shh, Daph, take a deep breath. Tell me what happened tonight."

Sniffle. "*I told you it was an accident, Seth. I didn't mean to kill him, he was just . . . when he shoved his hand up my dress . . . and said 'for old time's sake' . . . I just saw red. I didn't even know what I was doing—*"

Lehman's voice interrupting: "*What do you mean? For old time's sake?*"

P. J. TRACY

"You never wondered why I went off the grid and got so messed up?"

"You were young, making a lot of money—"

"No, Seth. Evan Hobbes started molesting me when I was eleven. It didn't stop until I quit."

Dead silence before a choking, tearful: "Oh, God, Daph. Oh God. That sick, sick fucker. If I'd know that, I would have killed him myself."

Her sobbing increased a few decibels.

"Come here, Daph. I'm so sorry. I'm so fucking sorry. Listen, it's going to be okay. We're going to be okay. No one saw us. He was wasted. Everybody will think he fell off the cliff."

"I can't live with this."

"Yes, you can, Daph. You have to. I have to. Evan was evil. He almost ruined your life. He deserved to die."

"But I didn't have a right to kill him, even if it was an accident . . ."

"You did have a right to kill him. We'll get through this. I'm going to take care of you. I'll take care of everything."

"You saved me, Seth. I owe you my life."

Ike clicked off the audio. "The recording stops there. What the hell, you guys didn't want to give me a heads-up that the queen of my dreams is a murderess?"

It was so much worse to hear confirmation of something tragic and hideous you'd just been projecting in your own thoughts. "We had no clue when we spoke to you," Nolan mumbled. "We just found out she was behind the deepfake, too."

Ike scraped his fingers through his hair like he was trying to rip it out. "That poor woman. God help me, but I'm glad she killed him. How many more victims?"

"A lot more, we think."

"Jesus, I think I'm going to be sick."

"Don't, or I'll get sick, too," Crawford warned. "Fuck, Lehman got a murder confession to cover his bases. He didn't trust her, and she didn't trust him. She killed him, Mags. The irony is, if she'd known about the recording, she wouldn't have, because he implicated himself, too."

"He would have edited out those parts if it came to that."

"Cold. This is all so cold. And so sad."

Ike looked up in replete horror. "Wait. She killed Lehman *too*?"

"Dead men don't talk, but it's going to be a bitch to prove, unless you found snuff audio somewhere in that sorry collection of recordings."

Nolan was suddenly more exhausted than she'd ever been in her life. There would be no happy endings in this whole disaster, whatever happened, but it would revive an issue that never should have dropped out of the public conversation. It wasn't even a part of the conversation when Daphna Love was suffering.

Ike recovered his bottle of Jack from the drawer, poured some into a coffee mug, then offered it up. Crawford took a swig, and Nolan did, too. As he gulped down a heavy dose of his liquid solace, the anguish on his face smoothed, and his eyes sharpened with sudden focus.

"What, Ike?"

"You said 'snuff audio.' Lehman was paranoid, so his phone might not be the only thing he used to record conversations. He could have his whole place wired up."

"Where would the data get sent?"

"Everything goes to the Cloud these days, but if I was obsessed enough to bug my own house, I'd also send it directly to a hard drive as backup."

"But you didn't find anything on his computer. Wouldn't the suffixes be different on files coming from dedicated recording software versus his phone?"

"Good question, Maggie, and yes, they would be, but I wasn't looking for it. And if he converted the files, they wouldn't jump out as anything unusual. Or, he could have a unit somewhere on site just for that. I'll get on it from here, you call Crime Scene and go tear his place apart. If you find any bugs, call me and don't touch anything."

Chapter Sixty-Six

IT DIDN'T TAKE NOLAN AND CRAWFORD long to find bugs in Lehman's penthouse once they knew what they were looking for. They were in clocks, in electrical outlets, in vents. In a closet in the spare bedroom, they also found another computer.

Ike arrived on site shortly after they called him, complaining about working all night when he had an epileptic dog missing him, but his spirits were markedly lifted. He'd had a revelation that could be game-changing, never mind that it might damn the queen of his dreams. Real-life success superseded fantasy every time, and Ike was nothing if not a devoted crime fighter.

Nolan watched him steal away with his electronic prize. They knew who killed Hobbes, and hopefully, Ike would find something that would confirm Lehman had been killed by his lover. If he did, it would make a strong case for paranoia. Baum and Tanner were still wild cards. Had Daphna Love killed them, too? Her heart didn't think so—the spontaneous, accidental death of Hobbes was a far cry from a premeditated trip to Santa Barbara with a gun. If you went somewhere with a firearm, you meant to kill. Love hadn't killed Hobbes for revenge, so why kill Baum? Lehman's death *had* been premeditated, but it wasn't the same kind of violence. It wasn't the same mindset. It was a matter of self-preservation, as warped as it was.

Her head was filled with numbing, hissing static when she finally crawled into her bed at 3 a.m. She knew sleep wouldn't come easily, if at all. How did you shut off all the manic, black thoughts in your mind once they started circulating into a vortex that gained suction with every oscillation? How had Max? How did Sam?

Nolan suddenly recalled something Sam had mentioned about coping with PTSD. How he was learning to redirect the negative thoughts that dragged him down by focusing on positive events that had occurred within the same time frame. "It shunts the badness and makes way for the good. There's balance in everything, Maggie, you just have to find it."

If the technique was successful for him, after all he'd been through, surely it could work for her, confronting a darkness far lesser than combat. It was certainly worth a shot. She thought about her earlier conversation with Melody, and to her amazement, a smile found her lips. She had been so eager to help, and as it turned out, she had. Looking back, the conversation with Lohr about the Pearl Club fight had nudged her and Al in the right direction. When this was all over, she would call Melody and thank her. Then she thought about Remy, a restless soul hoping to resolve family strife in New Orleans without her. She wouldn't be getting on a plane anytime soon, and was surprised by the disappointment she felt.

Her thoughts continued to ricochet, but apparently, her body had finally succumbed to exhaustion, because the next time she woke up, her phone was buzzing insistently and it was almost six o'clock. A few hours were better than none.

"Al. Don't tell me you're at the office already."

"Couldn't sleep, so I've been hanging out with Ike."

Nolan sat up and rubbed her eyes. "Did he find anything?"

"Oh, yeah, he found everything. At least Lehman died happy. His fiancée was giving him a massage before she choked him to death. And she was crying when she did it. Kept saying she was sorry, but knew he'd understand."

She shivered and pulled the comforter up to her neck, which did nothing to alleviate her chills, which originated in a far deeper place. "That's it, then."

"In our eyes. But recordings without consent? It's going to be a long, ugly haul."

"There's supporting evidence out there, and now we have direction. And enough for a search warrant on Love's house for sure."

"Already working on the affidavit, Mags. The captain is in the house, too, he came in when I called him at four. He's not so bad."

"I never said he was."

"But I probably did, a few hundred times. I retract my previous statements. I talked to Darcy Moore, too, gave her the scoop. Love is due at fedquarters at ten. She cleared us if we want to observe."

"I'll be in after I shower."

"Meet me at the Pantry. I need fat and carbs. So do you."

"See you soon, Al." She hung up and stared at her phone's screen. Was New Orleans two or three hours ahead? It didn't really matter— Remy would be up, and she wanted to hear his voice. Actually, she needed to hear it. It was a stunning realization; one that would have distressed her just a day ago, but if this case had taught her anything, there were things much worse than needing another person.

Chapter Sixty-Seven

DAPHNA LOVE SAT AT THE EDGE of her pool, staring at her submerged feet. They were turning blue. If she dove in, how long would it take for hypothermia to claim her? A macabre thought she wouldn't act on, but somehow, it made her feel better.

Evan Hobbes was still ruining her life, even though he was gone. She'd never been able to free herself. Once a victim, always a victim. It wasn't fair. But the emptiness that had defined her life felt different; like it was dispersing and re-forming, losing substance as it did. The truth would finally, irrefutably come out, and people would know. If something good came from all this bad, then maybe she was fulfilling a truer and greater destiny meant for her life.

She thought again of her lost child, and how different things would be now if she'd told Seth. Poor Seth. He was right—Evan really had deserved to die, but *he* hadn't. He'd saved her. But what choice did she have? The guilt would have been too great a burden for him to bear eventually because he was good and undamaged, and when he'd asked her to dispose of his jacket, the rarest of opportunities had presented itself.

She was sorry to betray him; sorry he would posthumously assume the disgrace of her crime, but she liked to think of it as his parting gift to her. He was a hero who had sacrificed everything for her. And she would give the most magnificent, heartfelt eulogy at his funeral.

There would never be justice for Seth's murder, and she was sorry for that, too. It would weigh heavily on her conscience for the rest of her life, but wherever he was now, she knew the love he'd had for her would confer forgiveness.

Daphna stood and tried to stamp away the painful, icy needles shooting from her feet up her legs. She remembered suffering the same feeling in St. Petersburg, after too long on an outdoor shoot without proper clothing. Why the screenwriter had decided the scene required her character to wear sandals and an evening gown in the middle of winter was beyond her comprehension. He was clearly a misogynist.

She stopped to clip a fragrant, red rose from the hedge by the door—for Seth—then went inside to shower and dress. Guy Johns would be here soon.

Chapter Sixty-Eight

SAM SIPPED A SECOND MUG OF coffee while he narrowed down flight options to Pennsylvania. In the background, he heard Melody singing a show tune in the shower, which brought a goofy smile to his face. He'd forgotten how fantastic it was to wake up to a person you cared about and worry about your breath, to share a morning of simple routines that would prepare you for the day ahead. A shower serenade was new to him, but it felt like icing on a very sweet cake.

PTSD carved a desolate hollow in your soul that repelled joy and peace, and he'd believed it would be with him always. But miraculously, he felt that hollow filling a little, and it gave him strength and resolve. It was time to move on.

He eventually pulled the trigger on two tickets to Philadelphia. He and Melody could spend a couple days there, doing some sightseeing and sampling genuine Philly cheesesteaks before making the hour drive to Lancaster. No matter how delicious, they would never supplant a Pink's dog, but junk food lunches were kind of their thing, and you had to sample every regional delicacy.

He closed his laptop and retrieved Henry Harold Easton's letter from the file and read it again, for at least the hundredth time. The impact of those words that shared Peter's story were as powerful now as they had been on the first reading, maybe even more so. This spontaneous trip might not yield anything substantive, but it wasn't about results, it was about the journey that had nothing to do with miles traveled or places visited. Whatever happened, he knew it would change the trajectory of his life, just like Melody had.

Sam refilled his coffee and poured a second mug for her, dosing it with too much sugar, the way she liked it. Then he reached for his phone and made a call that would also change the trajectory of his life. It went straight to voice mail, so he left a message.

"Hi, Maggie, Sam here. Sorry to bother you during your case, I hope you and Al are making progress. That was a stupid thing to say, I know you are. Just calling to let you know I'm going out of town for a while, but when I get back, I'd like to talk about that SWAT job if it's still available. Good luck with everything, and I'll be in touch when I'm home."

Feeling a buoyancy he hadn't experienced in years, he signed off and delivered the sugary coffee to the bathroom. Melody took the longest showers, so he decided to join her to save water.

Epilogue

ESSIE BAUM STOOD ON THE PEACEFUL, deserted Santa Barbara beach, watching the bald orange sun take a swift plunge below the horizon, as it always did the farther south you were. It was so very different from the languorous sunsets of her youth in up-state New York, where she and Seth had enjoyed a marvelous, idyllic childhood together. That life was as distant as a dream, and a part of her wanted to return to that simpler existence.

But she knew she would never return. Couldn't return. There was nobody and nothing there for her anymore, and it would be even more suffocating now than it had been then. LA was her home now. It was where she belonged. Where Seth belonged, too. His ashes were resting now in David's plot, and with the press of a toilet lever, David's were somewhere in the vast sewer system of Los Angeles. It was better than he deserved.

She listened to the gulls cry as they kited above the churning surf, squinted and made out the profiles of two large ships on the distant horizon. What was the crew doing now, so far from land, in such cramped quarters? Playing cards and drinking, she decided, even though that was probably a farcical imagining of life at sea, gleaned from the old pirate novels her father had loved to read.

She opened her fist to take one last, longing look at Becca's diamond earring, orphaned by her carelessness. Why on earth had she worn them that day? She should have anticipated a struggle. And now, the precious pair would be separated forever—one would languish in an evidence locker indefinitely; this one had to be relinquished to the sea. A masterwork of Cartier lost to the world forever. It was beyond tragic, and she had no one to blame but herself.

Essie waded out into the water with her paddleboard, then mounted it. It was far too cold for her, even though she was wearing a dry suit, but a little discomfort was a small price to pay. The high tide tugged her out to sea, which is exactly what she'd been waiting for.

With tears of longing and regret, she released the beautiful earring and watched it sink to watery anonymity before retrieving the mutilated remains of a computer motherboard from the fake Louis Vuitton tote slung over her shoulder. It had been risky to show the bag to the detectives, but so exhilarating to flaunt her dark secret in front of them.

She threw the pieces of the motherboard with violent force, because they were the remaining poisonous, evil things David had left behind. All that was left was the tote and the dismantled gun. She threw those, too. It was unlikely that anything would wash up on this beach with the strong tide, but if anything did, it would make perfect sense that the unknown killer would have dumped it in the ocean. There was nothing that could ever connect her to these things.

She watched the ruffled surface of the water as it consumed her secrets, then paddled back to shore, anxious to sit by a fire with a bottle of wine in the home that had always been hers on paper, but never in reality until now. She was glad Detective Nolan had cautioned her about selling her property too quickly. Santa Barbara was lovely, and she truly had wonderful memories here. Well, she had one—putting two bullets in the back of her husband's head.

Acknowledgments

AUTHORS ALWAYS DRAW FROM THEIR EXPERIENCES and histories, whether it's done with intention or impulse of subconscious. Memory synthesizes imagination and truth, and imbues fiction with soul.

In *The Sixth Idea*, I reconstituted PJ's childhood and my grandfather's clandestine work on the hydrogen bomb during the Cold War. In this novel, I go much farther back in the family history to a distant cousin who fought at Gettysburg and came home badly damaged in body and spirit. The letter in chapter two is a faithful rewording of the one she and I discovered at my grandparents' house when I was a teenager.

That letter has always haunted me. Like "Peter" in this book, my cousin was tethered in an attic to keep him from harming himself and others. His suffering was compounded by the ignorance of the age. He not only relived the horrors of battle alone, but was trapped in new ones that his well-meaning bondage created. Sam Easton's character probably wouldn't exist if I hadn't read it those many years ago.

The understanding and treatment of PTSD is far more advanced now, but war remains a persistent tragedy of the human race. I once believed that it would eventually become a dark footnote in history, but now I'm not so sure. However, I refuse to give up hope that we can be better and do better. Whereas war is a tragedy of humanity, hope is our enduring triumph. There is always good with bad.

Thanks to the incredible team at Minotaur/St. Martin's: Kelley Ragland, editor extraordinaire, whose insights are a scribe's blessing; Hector DeJean, who keeps me out there and busy; Danielle Prielipp, who patiently answers all my stupid questions about social media; and Madeline Houpt, the most helpful and organized person on the planet. To the art department for conjuring the best book covers ever; to Macmillan Audio for sussing out such great voice talent; and to the many others who have my back. I couldn't bring my stories to life without you all.

To Ellen Geiger at Frances Goldin Literary Agency, my agent of many years and a BFF. I cherish your friendship, and PJ did, too. Love you to the moon and back. And to Matt McGowan, Sulamita Garbuz, and Jade Wong-Baxter—thanks for all you do.

To my readers, old and new—you are my inspiration to keep making stuff up. And to family and friends—thanks for always being there in every way.

It wouldn't be a proper acknowledgment without mentioning PJ—my best friend, soul mate, partner, and mother. We were telling stories to each other before I could write my name, and the gifts she gave me are immeasurable. You are still in every word I write. You always will be.